PROFESSORS AND OTHER MISFITS

Tales from Academia

Jack Eugene Fernandez

authorHOUSE®

AuthorHouse™
1663 Liberty Drive, Suite 200
Bloomington, IN 47403
www.authorhouse.com
Phone: 1-800-839-8640

First published by AuthorHouse   2/10/2009

ISBN: 978-1-4389-2899-9 (sc)

Library of Congress Control Number: 2008911927

Printed in the United States of America
Bloomington, Indiana

This book is printed on acid-free paper.

WARNINGS TO THE READER

These stories are set in a university that bears a strong resemblance to the University of South Florida, where I taught for thirty-five years. However, I assure you, dear reader, in the strongest possible language that none of these stories is based on actual persons or events. They have sprung from a brain tortured by thirty-five years of regular faculty meetings and their political intrigues. I believe it was Henry Kissinger who said that academic politics is so vicious because the stakes are so low. That ultimate truth, in part, inspired some of these stories.

I grapple here with some ideas that fascinate me—truth, knowledge, education, and the meaning of scientific theory. However, understanding these stories does not require you to understand even elementary chemistry. They are about people, not about science. At this point in my life, people seem even more fascinating than science.

Also, dear reader, I caution you that some of these tales teeter on the edge of credibility; some might even be called impossible or inconceivable. But that is not to say that they do not contain kernels of truth. I beg you to keep this in mind in the event that a irrepressible desire to curse me should ignite spontaneously as you read.

Finally, while each story can stand alone, I respectfully urge you to read them in the order presented, for there is a tenuous continuity among them.

Thank you.

Jack E. Fernandez
Autumn 2008

CONTENTS

THE COLOR OF WHITE

Sam Iglesias

In spite of the young architect's obvious brilliance and Anna's considerable art experience, Sam insisted on one design correction—a central hallway he had sketched into the architect's drawings.

The architect bristled at the suggestion, "It'll be dark, Professor Iglesias. My design brings the outdoors into every room. You'll enjoy the beauty of the grove inside as well as outside."

"And I love it, but without that hall, we'll have to go in circles to get from one room to the other," Sam said.

"I'd have to rework the design. Your hall won't work."

"But I love your design. Don't change anything except that small detail. Trust me."

Standing, eyes bulging, the architect seemed ready to throw down his pencil. Anna put her arm on Sam's shoulder and said, "Let's sleep on it, Sam, and discuss it next time."

"OK, but I really don't see anything wrong with it."

As Sam walked out of the architect's office, Anna remained a moment longer and whispered, "Sam has strong opinions, but I can bring him around."

She never did; the final plan included Sam's hall.

Seven months later, the white stucco house glistened in the Florida sun. Cubes protruded from different levels in a degree of asymmetry that led the eye from one dramatic space to the next. Even inside, the eye followed, as if drawn by a magnet, from one room to another along angular walls of brick, glass, and plaster. The white house rose out of the orange grove like a neatly-balanced stack of salt crystals.

"White is the color of clarity and reason," Sam insisted. As one might expect in a professor's home, books bound in all the colors of the spectrum graced most rooms and pressed the whiteness into the background. The house's brilliance revealed Professor Iglesia's fascination with detail and reflected his ambition and prominence in academia.

Anna, an art historian, offered stylistic suggestions gently, from a distance—impressionistic strokes of color to add strength and warmth to her family canvas. For her, white reflected purity and tranquility, if not sterility. Though she loved primary colors, Sam insisted on pastels for the public spaces. Preempting the role of family artist, he insisted that color be used only logically, discretely. Anna won her arguments, if at all, through patience and subtle persuasion.

The son of Cuban immigrants, Sam had decided on a scientific career in high school. That choice both mystified and thrilled his doting parents, who sensed he would write a new page in their family history. With a scholarship to MIT, he earned his Ph.D. degree in physical chemistry barely six years after entering as a freshman.

Sam could not resist Anna's regal, Aryan bearing. Her long, blonde hair and brilliant hazel eyes beguiled him the moment they met at a faculty tea in Oxford University, where they were both research fellows. The tall, thin Dane, more stately than beautiful, had been drawn to his intelligence, energy, and tall good looks, blue eyes, and auburn hair.

After two years at Oxford, Sam left with a deepened scientific background, good connections, and a new wife. At the end of their first year of marriage Anna gave birth to a baby girl, who would grow into a tall young woman crowned with swaying auburn hair and longing, green eyes. Moving through her childhood with the grace of a dancer, Sally Anne was a clean slate on which Sam could compose his family legacy.

He had already composed his academic legacy in bold type. With the most productive research program in the university, he was now gliding into the realm of university politics. As one of the administration's most effective spokesmen, he assumed a role his colleagues envied, though they had to admire his commanding presence.

The conference room was long with a door at each end. The only windows were a small one in each door. One long wall had metal bookcases filled with books and journals donated by the faculty and students, the most important of which was a set of Chemical Abstracts dating from 1932 to the present. The opposite wall was bare except for a large portrait of Dr. Allen Johns, the founding university president. The long conference table seated seventeen. A row of student desks lined the blank wall.

Sam Iglesias had come prepared to present his latest success to his colleagues—squeezing a new faculty position from the administration for a promising young African-American. He sold the idea easily because it was a position they would not otherwise have. His argument ended with, "But we'll have to beat out our competitors. I mean a top salary and hefty start-up funding. This man's in great demand."

The entire chemistry faculty was present: Edgar Margin, handsome, blond, crew-cut, wearing a tailored blazer; Donald Quinone, long dark hair mussed and hanging over his eyes, shirt tail puffing out of his trousers, necktie pulled to one side, leaning over his scribbles; Joe Adams, the last remaining charter faculty member, short, thin with bushy gray hair that looked like a mop on a stick, isolated in one of the student desks against the long wall; Brucine Justice, the voluptuous brunette who liked to wink seductively at the younger male faculty members to their consternation; and the Chair, George Buchner, a tall, freckle-faced red-head with bright eyes and a perpetual smile. The remaining twelve chemistry faculty members were all present, a rare event.

"Just last week there were neither positions nor start up money," Edgar Margin said.

"President Taggart has promised a start-up package of $300,000," Sam said.

Donald Quinone slammed his hand on the conference table. "Incredible! With that we could get God Himself."

"I had something like that in mind," Sam said smiling.

"Too bad he can't conjure up that kind of money for us majority faculty," Donald Quinone said.

Edgar Margin was still not satisfied. "That's enough for three new hires."

"It's important for our minority students to see someone like them in the classroom, a role model," Sam said. "But that's not all this man offers. He has the best publication record I've seen in years."

"Right! We'll be killing two birds with one stone," George Buchner said.

"I agree he's exceptional, Sam, but I don't like bringing in a new man so far above his peers," Joe Adams said. "It's bound to arouse animosity." Most eyes turned toward Joe Adams in his student desk against the wall.

"That worries me too, Joe," George Buchner said, "but excellence isn't cheap, and his higher salary will help us argue for raising his peers to his level; in the long run everyone will benefit."

No other objections surfaced. Perhaps no one wanted to bring down suspicions of racism. The vote to hire Harold Pitt passed unanimously.

After the meeting, groups formed in the hall. "I don't like using race to select faculty," Joe Adams said. "How will he feel having had special treatment?"

"Believe me, gentlemen, we'll come out of this smelling like a rose," George Buchner said.

"I hope it's a rose," Donald mumbled.

Harold Pitt joined the Chemistry Department that autumn. The tall, erect, muscular Negro, starkly offset against his white guayabera shirt, walked into the Chairman's office. George Buchner took him through all the initial formalities—paperwork, a tour of the research and teaching labs introducing faculty members along the way, helping find housing. Through it all, Harold Pitt stood or sat erect as if at attention. His aloof demeanor left George breathlessly trying to find words to fill the space between them. Finally he led Harold to his office and lab and told him where his equipment had been stored for him, shook his hand, and left.

Harold did not impress his new colleagues at first, except that he seemed unfriendly. Sam liked him and talked with him almost every day about their research. Noting his diffidence, however, most of his colleagues left him alone. It would be several months, when his lab was running and he had attracted several graduate students to work with him, before his colleagues would begin to take notice.

By early December his lab was in full operation with four research students. By the beginning of spring term Harold Pitt had submitted two grant proposals and two papers for publication. His colleagues began to warm up to him, though his drive and seriousness intimidated some.

For Sam, Harold Pitt was a bright star that would rise to prominence in the chemistry department he was recreating in his image.

At her father's suggestion, Sally Anne enrolled in Dr. Pitt's organic chemistry course that fall. The tall, robust young woman wore her reddish-brown hair in a ponytail tied with a rubber band. Her soft, brown eyes and full lips, like her mother's, gave her face a sad expression even when she smiled. But unlike her mother, Sally Anne had grown gangly with large legs and meaty arms. Her figure was shapely, but tended to thick, unlike her trim mother. Perhaps Sally Anne's most prominent feature was her head, a large, nearly perfect oval with a high hairline and a small nub of a chin. Pulling her hair back added intensity to her countenance. At seventeen she was not beautiful, but knowing her mother, one could imagine that she would soon shed her youthful chubbiness and blossom into a full-blown beauty. But even now, in T-shirt and jeans, she exuded sensuality.

Sally Anne did everything with enthusiasm, as if each time was the first time. Her father saw in her the inquisitiveness and curiosity of a scientist and nurtured her in that direction. With obvious aptitude she received all A's in her first semester's work.

After the first session of second semester organic chemistry, Harold Pitt asked Sally Anne if she would like to work in his lab as a research assistant. Thrilled, she accepted with an enthusiasm that made Harold smile. "Come by whenever you get a free hour."

"Right after my next class. Thanks, Dr. Pitt."

Sally Anne began by helping one of Harold Pitt's graduate students, but by the middle of the semester she had her own project. It was a simple synthesis of a compound that Harold needed for one of his grant projects. She was so excited about having her own project that she worked every evening. When her last class ended, usually by mid-afternoon, she would dash to the lab. Never having seen such passion for research, Harold was reluctant to interrupt her. Normally he left around five o'clock, when the graduate students left for dinner. Sally Anne always wanted to stay on. Not wanting to discourage her or leave her working alone, he stayed.

"Don't you ever get hungry, Sally Anne?" he asked one evening a little after seven.

"I'm having too much fun," she said, plugging a heating element in under a flask half full of liquid ready to distill.

"You can finish the distillation tomorrow."

"If I finish it now, I can start the next step tomorrow. I'm just dying to see how it turns out."

"Well, it's dangerous to work alone … All right."

He sat at his desk and opened a journal he had been reading earlier. He couldn't concentrate for watching Sally Anne move around the lab bench, so agile and efficient. He jumped when she called out, "Can you please hold this flask while I move the heater out from under it? I don't want to drop it."

"Sure." He held the flask and the attached glassware as she gently unclamped the heater and slid it out. Holding the flask and equipment with both hands, Harold could barely move. As Sally Anne worked furiously, stooped over, their arms intertwined, Harold saw that she was wearing nothing under her blouse. He looked away, but then turned back to see ample white breasts moving side to side.

"Thanks. I've got it now."

"Well I'm hungry," Harold said as he backed away. "How about a cafeteria burger?"

"Neat."

The sky's red was dying as they walked across the wide quadrangle. It was warm for April, but neither noticed the heat or the humidity. Sally Anne's mind raced with thoughts of discovery and fame. She walked with a spring in her step and talked energetically, her ponytail bobbing as she moved.

Harold Pitt had his own fantasies, but his were more concrete and far more perilous. She fascinated him; her innocence, her energy, her nubile virility, her athletic body.

At the end of the cafeteria line, Harold paid the bill and led her to a table in a corner. Few students ate there in the evening, so the place was nearly empty. It was a little after eight.

"Daddy said you'd be a great teacher, Dr. Pitt. He was right."

"You're Sam Iglesias's daughter?"

"Didn't you know?"

He shook his head.

"Do you mind?"

"I should have made the connection. You favor him."

"People say I look more like my mother. Have you met her?"

"Not yet, but I'm looking forward to it."

Sally Anne's revelation inserted a new complication. Luckily, she was a good student. He would not be put in the position of having to fail a colleague's child. The word, child, made him stop. He spoke little as she rambled on. When they were finished, he walked her to her car and returned to the lab.

Next morning Sally Anne arrived early. "I have two hours before my first class, Dr. Pitt. I can finish that reaction by then. At least I can start it."

"That's fine, Sally Anne. I'll be busy all morning. If you need help, Charlie will be here in about an hour."

Having set up her equipment the night before, Sally Anne had the reaction mixture boiling in minutes. She pulled over a lab stool and sat down to study while the mixture boiled in front of her. It was a simple reaction to carry out, though she was not sure how to explain it. During boiling, the atoms in the molecules of starting compound rearrange themselves into a new configuration—the product molecule. Because the boiling point of the product was forty degrees higher than that of the starting compound, she could follow the progress of the reaction by watching the temperature of the boiling liquid. When it had inched up to the higher boiling point, the reaction was finished.

Harold's office adjacent to his lab had a large window through which he could watch over the lab. He sat at his desk, mesmerized by Sally Anne. She opened her book and sat down to study, and he returned to his work, but his mind did not stop whirring. He got up and walked out to check his mail. He returned and she was still perched on the stool, reading. Every few minutes she would raise her eyes to the thermometer that stuck out of the flask and then look down again, at the same time stretching and moving. After an hour, she closed her book and turned off the heater under the flask. Then she removed the flask, stoppered it, and set it aside for later. She picked up her books and walked to Doctor Pitt's office.

"All finished! Boiling point's perfect."

"Fine, Sally Anne. See you later."

That evening, Harold stayed with her as usual. As she worked, he sat at his desk watching her. Knowing she was Sam's daughter frightened him, but it somehow added spice to the brew. Each day he waited for her. Each evening she had come and he had watched her work. She was so young and innocent, he thought, so intelligent, so anxious to please. He was sure she had no idea of his fantasies and would probably be horrified to know. At least he could enjoy the vicarious thrill of imagining lifting her T-shirt and grabbing her, then chasing her nude through the lab. *Just an innocent game; they all play it. I'm no different. Everybody has these thoughts; it's natural, inevitable when you're dealing with young women in their prime, free, loose and unhampered by responsibilities.* When Sally Anne called him, he jumped out of his chair. "What is it?"

"I've got it, Dr. Pitt, the pure isomer. I just finished distilling it. The properties check exactly," she said, holding up the flask of clear liquid.

"That's terrific, Sally Anne. Let's see your notebook." Reading her description of the process, he said, "I couldn't have done better."

"I'm so happy I could kiss you, Dr. Pitt," she said, jumping up and down.

Harold looked into her eyes; she stood on her toes and kissed him on the lips. "I'm so happy."

Harold grabbed her and pulled her toward him. Eyes wide, as if in shock, she did not pull away. Without speaking, he kissed her again, this time deeply, passionately; she felt his hardness. When their lips parted, she said, "Gee, Dr. Pitt. I didn't realize …"

"I'm sorry. I didn't know what I was doing."

"I didn't know you felt that way," she said, and moved toward him again and pressed herself against him. "Me too."

Before he could say anything, she kissed him again and again. He took her hand and led her into his office, pulled down the Venetian blinds on the lab window and punched the lock on the door. When he turned to face her she had pulled off her jeans and was lifting her T-shirt over her head, exposing heaving breasts. Within seconds she had wrapped around him as he sat her on the desk and struggled to find comfort on its cold surface. He was blinded. She moved under him crazily, kissing him and running her hands up and down his back. As he entered, he began to panic, but she held onto him, her arms tight around him. They kept moving. Finally they stopped; he lifted his head and looked down at her. "I shouldn't have, Sally Anne … I don't know what to say."

"I love you, Dr. Pitt. Since the moment you walked into our class."

"This is crazy. We can't. It's impossible. You can't work here anymore." He dumbly recited inanities through syrupy feelings of desire.

Sally Anne dressed and sat on his desk. "I know you must feel kinda, like, weird," she said, "but I'm not sorry."

"Don't you understand? I can get fired."

"I won't tell."

Please, Sally Anne, you'd better go. I've got to think."

Harold Pitt awoke from a dream that night: The wind is moving a tree near the light post; light and shadow hover over his bed. He is sitting in a bomb crater in the rain waiting for the Viet Cong to cross the narrow river just a few yards away. Looking out over the rim, he sees them coming, one by one, with rifles in their hands. One takes a grenade off his belt, pulls the pin, and swings his arm. Harold sees the grenade falling toward him, tumbling end over end, until he can see the Russian letters on the side. He can't make them out, but he knows they say something that will save him if only he can make out the words. He looks, knowing he will die if he fails to read the words. Harold's eyes fly open; he is perspiring. *Nothing can save me now. But it's not like being in that crater. It was stupid and avoidable, and I plunged in anyway, endangering my career and dishonoring my family by violating a child. A child! Oh, God! He'll have me lynched.* At four in the morning the most terrible possibilities are the most certain.

Next morning Harold entered the chemistry building determined to dismiss Sally Anne from the lab and keep her at a safe distance in class. She would understand. Perhaps later, when she graduated and was old enough, they could be married if they wanted to. But that would have to wait. There was too much at stake now.

Sally Anne did not show up that morning. Though he was glad not to face her, he felt a tinge of disappointment. In class the first face he saw was hers. In her usual seat, she smiled and love poured from her wide, brown eyes. Love and trust, he thought, the love and trust he had violated.

As he expected, she was waiting for him after the lecture. When the last student left the lecture hall, she approached him with her books under her arm. Wearing a dress instead of her usual jeans and tee shirt, she looked demure, feminine, almost beautiful. "Good morning, Dr. Pitt."

"Sally Anne, I'm putting someone else on your project."

"I know how you feel, but please let me stay. I promise I won't bother you again."

"For heaven's sake, Sally Anne. It was me, not you."

"Can I, please? I promise. If I quit, I'd have to explain it to Daddy. I'll just work. Promise."

Harold Pitt had not thought of that. "Let's talk next class period."

"OK. Dr. Pitt, and thanks." She left ahead of him.

Watching her until she moved out of sight, so graceful, so feminine, he felt he would sink into the earth.

Brucine Justice had been waiting to begin her class. With a wink she said, "I hear the Iglesias girl's working in your lab."

"That's right."

"Sam takes care of his boys."

Turning and walking away he said, "I'm not his boy, Brucine."

"No offense intended," she said, smiling.

Harold trembled all the way to his office, wondering if she knew. But how could she? Harold determined to calm down and simply avoid a repetition of the previous night. But he could not convince himself that Sally Anne was not attractive. In fact, he had noticed her the first time he saw her funny face looking at him in class. But his predicament was weighed down with a leaden ache.

"What are you doing home so early?" Anna said.

"Got to study, Mom. No time for lab work these days." On her way to her room, Sally Anne stopped in the kitchen, opened the refrigerator and took out an apple. Except for dinner, Sally Anne stayed in her room all evening. After she finished studying, she went out through the back door into the grove. Her parents were in the living room and did not hear her leave. Sally Anne found her way with the help of a benevolent full moon, her mind full of photographic details: Harold's shaved head, sensuous and smooth, and his strong arms. His masculine sexuality was driving her crazy. Looking back at their brief contact, she thought it might have been a dream, vivid yet ethereal. But it was no dream, and she wondered what it meant and how it would play itself out. At that moment she knew Harold Pitt was the man she wanted. *He thinks I'm a child, but I gave him what a woman can give.*

It was a crisp March morning when Sally Anne dragged her body into the kitchen and dropped it into a chair at the table, her legs spread at an odd angle as if disconnected from the rest of her. Scurrying around the kitchen, Anna saw Sally Anne with her cheeks in her fists.

"Don't just sit there, Sally Anne; help me set the table."

It took all Sally Anne's strength to pull her legs together and lift herself out of the chair.

"What's wrong, Dear?"

"Nothing."

Sam came in wearing his favorite gray pinstripe three-piece suit and a bright blue bow tie. The colors complemented his blue eyes and tan complexion. "Good morning ladies. Sally Anne, that lipstick's almost black; makes your face look like a mask."

Sally Anne smiled heartlessly.

"What's the matter, Honey?"

"I was up late."

"I know the feeling. How's the work coming with Dr. Pitt?"

"He's wonderful. The lab work is more fun than I thought it would be. I'm sure I'll get an A."

"That won't hurt your chances for medical school."

"Actually, Daddy, I'm not so sure about med school."

"Honey, that's been your dream since you were a little girl."

"I'm not sure whose dream it was, Daddy."

"We'll talk another time. By the way, Anna, I won't be home for dinner. President Taggart is having some senior professors to his home. I think he wants us to tell him how to run the university."

"I don't mind a quiet dinner with Sally Anne."

"Sorry, Mom. I'm working in the lab tonight."

"Hold dessert; we'll have it by candlelight," Sam said.

When Sally Anne and Anna finished in the kitchen Anna went into the family room and sat beside the large glass wall overlooking the pool and the orange grove. Long, morning shadows were still rippling across the pool. Sally Anne came in and sat across from her.

"Shouldn't you be getting ready for class, Sally Anne?" Anna had just picked up her embroidery.

"It's early."

Noting Sally Anne's droopy pose, Anna said, "Don't you feel well?"

"I'm nauseated."

Anna looked up from her sewing. "Probably a virus."

"It's no virus, Mom."

Anna looked up.

"I think I'm pregnant."

Anna jammed the needle into the cloth and dropped the hoop into her lap. A dark curtain fell across her morning as she stared at her daughter.

"Please don't be mad, Mom. I couldn't help it. It just happened."

"It doesn't just happen."

"I was scared and mad at first, but it won't be so bad."

"Don't tell me you want to keep it."

"Sure."

"With all the people who want babies?"

"It's mine, and I'm going to keep it. It'll be neat."

"Neat, is it? You have no idea how a baby can change your life."

"I'll handle it."

"But you're still a child with lots of growing up to do before starting a family."

"Oh, Mom!"

"Don't rush into life, Sally Anne. There's time enough for marriage and family when you've finished school."

"I don't plan to leave school."

"I postponed a lot for my career."

"Big deal; then you gave it up to marry Daddy."

"Jobs were scarce."

"Have you ever regretted it?"

"How can you ask?"

"Have you?"

"Of course not. A career just didn't work out."

"So, you do have regrets."

"No, but you will."

"It's my decision, Mom."

Anna always saw her life as happy and rewarding, but staring now into the blinding reflection of her own youth, she saw herself struggling with her passions, always working toward a goal beyond view, winning and losing with each battle.

"Some decisions are doomed from the start, dear. True, my career was stillborn, but I have no complaints. Sculpting a family may be the most sublime art …. Regret? No. I've helped create a warm home and family."

"That's all I want."

"But it's irresponsible at your stage." Trying to return the discussion to Sally Anne's situation, she said, "Who's the father?"

"You don't know him. I met him in one of my classes."

"Have you discussed marriage?"

"No."

"How you can make a baby with a man you don't plan to marry."

"Oh, Mom; you're so out of touch."

"Have you told him?"

"There's no rush."

"You're ready enough to rush into parenthood."

"I've got to get going."

"Sit down a minute more, Sally Anne. Are you sure about the baby?"

"Pretty much."

"Have you seen a doctor?"

"No."

"May I make you an appointment with my gynecologist?"

"I guess so. Tell Daddy, OK?"

"I think you should tell him."

"Better soften him up first. OK?"

The sun had set when Sam walked in the front door. He left his briefcase on a table in the foyer and walked into the family room where Anna sat looking out the window with her sewing on her lap. "You're home early. How did it go?"

"Some good ideas bounced around. It's up to Taggart now. Where's Sally Anne?"

"She's not home yet." Anna resumed her sewing.

Sam loosened his tie. "You'd think she could stay home one evening."

Looking up, Anna said, "Sally Anne gave me some troubling news today."

"President Taggart congratulated me for finding Harold Pitt. Did you know he was born in a Washington slum? Shows what's possible. Oh, I nearly forgot; I'm being considered for the new endowed chair."

"Wonderful."

"Yep. To support my work on superconductor theory. If I can conduct it to a sparkling conclusion, so to speak, I might have a chance for the big one."

"The Nobel?"

"You never know. It would be great even to be nominated. My mother would be ecstatic."

"That's wonderful, Sam, but Sally Anne …"

"Understanding the structure of matter; that's what my life is all about."

"Sam …"

"Could lead to more funding, speaking engagements, books …"

"Sally Anne's pregnant."

Silence. Then, "Oh, no …"

"Sam, I think …"

"Who's the father?"

Anna resumed her embroidery. "We don't know him. She met him at school."

"We'll put it up for adoption."

"I don't think she …"

"I don't give a damn. She's not going to drag our family into the mud."

"For heaven sake, Sam; she's only a child herself. Try to see it her way."

"I'll talk to her." He stood. "I'm going out to the grove to look around. We may need to disk again."

"But it's dark."

"I'll be back soon."

The grove was Sam's retreat, his escape into the green clarity of childhood. He liked to sit in an Adirondack chair in the bosom of the overarching grapefruit tree deep in the grove, peel an orange with his father's knife, and eat it in solitude. But now, even the fragrance of the tiny, white blossoms would not calm his turmoil. The giant grapefruit

15

tree that dominated the orange grove was the only survivor of a long forgotten freeze. Its green canopy fed his longing for strength. He tried not to imagine what his mother would say. Instead he recalled summer days eating his fill of mangos and oranges. It pleased him that these Old World transplants had taken root in Florida.

The moon was bright enough to light his way, though he could find it in the dark.

"I didn't expect you to be up, Daddy."

"Your mother said you have a problem. Why don't you tell me about it?"

"There's not much to tell. I'm pretty sure I'm pregnant."

With Sam's rehearsed restraint frazzling, he said, "You're behaving like a child from the barrio. What were you thinking of?"

"I don't know, Daddy."

"I'll see Father Cisneros tomorrow about adoption."

"No!"

"What about school?"

"I'll only be out a semester."

"Fat chance of coming back with a child. What about the father? You do know who it is, don't you?"

"Oh, Daddy. How could you ask me that?"

"He's got responsibilities too."

"I've got the whole summer to think about that. I'm tired now."

"I won't let you waste your potential …." Sally Anne had walked out.

Sally Anne's announcement cast a shadow on the white house in the grove. Anna's sewing gave way to staring blankly out the window at the orange trees, as if waiting for the fruit to take on color. Her embroidery had become meaningless threads tangled into white linen. Life in Denmark or England would have been no better, she thought; just different.

Sam tried not to think about Sally Anne's problem and acted as though nothing had changed, while a chasm opened inside him. Sally Anne would not consider putting the baby up for adoption, so he eventually stopped demanding it. At the university he walked around as in a stupor.

"I said, hello, Sam," Donald Quinone said.

"Oh, hi, Donald; hi, Harold," Sam said as he continued to his office.

"Sam, I have an idea about making organic superconductors," Harold said.

"I'm pretty busy; maybe next week." Sam closed his office door.

Harold stood outside Sam's office for a moment then turned to Donald. "What's wrong with him?"

Donald shrugged. "I wouldn't worry about it." When Harold had gone, Donald walked into Sam's office. "Everything all right, Sam?"

"What? ... Oh, yes. I've got a presentation in a few days, and I don't have time for small talk."

"I think Harold had more than small talk in mind."

"I appreciate your concern, Donald, but I really am busy."

"Sure."

Sam would have been quite interested in Pitt's ideas. One of the attractions of the young chemist was his synthetic expertise. Organic superconductors would provide a new testing ground for Sam's theory. But Sally Anne's confession had pushed his work into a small eddy of triviality as he struggled, wounded by the lance of her pregnancy. She had clawed into primitive fears Sam did not understand.

After breakfast two weeks later, Sally Anne said, "I saw Doctor Probst yesterday."

"Sit down and tell me about it while I fix another pot of coffee," Anna said.

"She confirmed it. I'm pregnant. Everything's OK."

"That's wonderful, Dear. Any details?"

"No. Tell Daddy. OK?"

"Talk to him, Sally Anne. He'll be happy to know."

"I can't talk to him."

"It's been a jolt, but he'll get over it."

"Daddy's always been bossy, but he's never been so mean."

"Not mean, dear; he just sees you digging yourself into a pit."

Sam entered the kitchen wearing a new gray suit with a red polka-dot bow tie. "I'm having breakfast with the President this morning."

"I know, Sam."

"Hi, Daddy."

Without responding, Sam turned and walked out. Sally Anne stared into her half-empty coffee cup. Like the ache in her throat, it seemed to have no bottom.

Sally Anne stood around the lectern after class, waiting for all the other students who had questions for Dr. Pitt. When they had gone, he said, "You haven't been around lately."

"Can we talk?"

"I have a meeting in a few minutes and then lunch with the dean. I should be back by 1:15."

"That's fine. Thanks."

It was a few minutes past one o'clock when Sally Anne knocked on Harold Pitt's door.

"Come in," the baritone voice said. Harold's shaved head perched on his well-dressed, erect frame with his arms at his sides gave him the look of a soldier sitting at attention. The muscles of his face twitched as he clamped his jaws. "Sally Anne, I think I know why you're here. It should never have happened. We've got to put it behind us and get back to chemistry."

"I thought I meant something to you," she said, looking into his eyes.

"It's all wrong, Sally Anne."

"I don't know how else to tell you, so I won't beat around the bush. I'm pregnant."

"Oh, God." After a few moments staring at her, he said, "Is it mine?"

Sally Anne's eyes overflowed.

"I'm sorry. That was stupid and unkind. You do mean a lot to me." Harold flinched at uttering those words.

"I don't know what to do."

"There's only one thing."

"I hope you don't mean what I think."

"Do you realize what this will do to your family?"

"I won't!"

"Have you told them?"

"Yes, but not about you."

"What did they say?"

"They're mad, like I expected. My mother's accepting it, but Daddy won't even talk to me."

"Look, Sally Anne. I know how you feel, but it's different for me. This will end my career. I came up from the ghetto. My older brother was killed in a riot. After that, my mother made me the focus of her life. Maybe she expected too much, but that's the way it's always been with us, having to show the world. Your father is a good, equal opportunity liberal, but he'll have me tarred and feathered."

"Don't you care about our baby?"

"Can't you understand? This is America. It'll will catch nothing but shit. You couldn't even put it up for adoption."

When Sally Anne buried her face in her hands, Harold moved to put his arm around her, but could not allow himself that intimacy; her white body seemed off limits now. Instead, he sat back, fighting to contain his anger for allowing himself to fall into such a predicament.

"Does your dad suspect…?"

"No."

"We'll have to get married."

"No. Not that I don't want to. I just don't feel adult enough."

"I understand. Don't do anything silly and don't worry."

Before the guests started showing up for the Iglesias's annual Easter party, Sam called Sally Anne aside. "It's best not to wait for people to ask. You're beginning to show, so just admit it freely, but don't volunteer details. It's going to be the usual, boring faculty cocktail party. Don't feel obligated to hang around."

"I won't, Daddy."

Edgar Margin and his wife, Vivian, were the first to arrive. "Where's Anna?" Vivian said.

"She's putting the last touches on the hors d'oeuvres."

"I'll see if I can help."

"Harold is working out well," Edgar said. "He's managed to put together a pretty good research group."

"And he's terrific with students," Sam said.

"I've been looking forward to seeing him tonight in a relaxed atmosphere. He's usually so reserved and standoffish."

"He called earlier to say he couldn't make it. Excuse me, Edgar. Hi, George. Glad you could make it."

"Wild horses couldn't keep me away," George Buchner said as he shook hands with Sam, Sally Anne, and Edgar.

"How's the research going, Sally Anne?" Edgar said.

"It's exciting. Very different from class work."

"You're looking fit as a fiddle, Sally Anne," George said.

"Sally Anne's expecting," Sam said. "You know how kids are these days." He put his arm around his daughter. "Anna and I don't approve, but what can we do?"

"You're doing it," George said.

"You look happy," Edgar said to Sally Anne.

"Oh yes. She's thrilled about the baby."

"Will we be hearing wedding bells soon?" Edgar said.

"Not until she graduates and he gets his career on track."

"Is he a student?" Edgar said.

"What may I bring you to drink?" Sally Anne said.

"Scotch and water, please."

"Make it two," George said.

Monday morning Harold Pitt was waiting. When he saw Sam walk down the hall he stopped him. "Sam, I have to talk with you."

"I have a meeting in an hour, and I need time to prepare. Can we do it later?"

"I'm afraid not."

Sam was surprised at the urgency in Harold's voice. "Come in then. Please sit down."

Sitting erect with his hands on his knees, Harold Pitt began, "I know about Sally Anne's condition."

"What?"

"She told me about her pregnancy."

"She discussed it with you?"

"I'm the father."

The quiver in his voice sent a shock wave through Sam. He sat motionless for a few seconds, his mind whirring like a dynamo building up electric charge. "You black son of a bitch. Get out before I do something I'll regret."

"I'll go, but we've got to talk first."

"I'll have you up on charges." Sam started to rise, but Harold remained seated.

"I'm not through yet."

"Yes you are."

"We didn't plan it. We were attracted to each other from the beginning. I had never met anyone like Sally Anne, so sweet, so open and honest. I don't know what I was thinking. When she told me she was pregnant, the first thing I thought about was my career. I was angry and urged her to have an abortion. But seeing her so defenseless, I realized she was hurting more than I. With both of us pressuring her, she was going through hell all alone."

"Don't try to make me the villain."

"I know I'm through. I have no business in your world, but I do appreciate what you've done."

"Really?"

"Sally Anne wants the baby. She's the most loving human being I've ever known. Race doesn't matter to her the way it does to us."

"Are you calling me a racist?"

"I'm calling myself one. My first thoughts were my career and hurting other African-Americans instead of that wonderful, gentle human being who feels only love."

"Don't talk to me about love. I know what that means to you people."

"I wouldn't blame you if you filed charges. But what will it do to her?"

"You're the one who's hurt her. You've ruined her education, cut her off from society and her family."

"I've hurt her, but I have not cut her off from anyone. Others will do that."

"Do you expect me to forget it?"

"No, but if you could wait a while, maybe we can figure something out. After all, it is our problem."

"You don't belong in an academic institution."

"Hello Sam. How did it go today?" Anna was in a happy mood, and the aroma of apple pie permeated the house. When she tried to put her arms around her husband, he pushed her away.

"Where's Sally Anne?"

"She's in her room, studying. What's wrong?"

Without answering, Sam stormed up the stairs and into Sally Anne's room.

"Well, it seems you left out one small detail."

"What is it, Daddy?" Sally Anne wondered how much he knew and how he had found out.

Seconds smashed into each other in Sam's brain. "A black man? *Puta!*"

"I'm not a whore."

"I'd better not see him around this house. In fact, the same goes for you."

"Daddy ..."

"Don't call me Daddy. You don't live here anymore." The words shot past Sam's numb lips as if he were a neutral observer watching from outside himself.

"Just one minute," Anna said coming up the stairs. "Sally Anne isn't going anywhere."

"You don't know."

"And I don't care. You are not throwing her out of her home." Anna's tone surprised them all.

"It's Harold Pitt. Can't you see what this will do to me? To us?"

"We'll deal with it."

"This baby can't be part of our family. It won't be black or white; it won't belong anywhere."

"It'll belong to me," Sally Anne said, through sobs.

"You're out to ruin us. You've got to have an abortion."

Sally Anne could barely speak, "Kill my ...? Never."

For the first time in his life, Sam felt like hitting her.

"You're a racist."

"That's not fair, Sally Anne," Anna said. "Everyone harbors some prejudice, even you if you dig a little."

"You'll learn about racism if you have this baby," Sam said.

"Please, Daddy. This is a wonderful event in my life. You're making it horrible."

"You don't know what horrible is."

Sally Anne wept.

As summer congealed into autumn Sam tried to dig into his work, but a dark chasm had developed in his mind. Unable to concentrate he looked ashen and rarely smiled. The white house in the grove had lost its brilliance. It resembled more a pale box with particles bouncing off the walls, ceilings, and floor, avoiding each other. Every time Sam came home, the theory of black body radiation would pop into his mind to enrage him. One night, he awoke in a sweat; in a dream, the house had dissolved into the moon's reflection on a cool lake with an alligator lurking in its depth. He could not read in the evenings and resented that Anna had resumed her embroidery. On an otherwise calm evening, he blurted out, "Can't you put down that damn needle so we can talk?"

"I can talk while I sew."

"I want you to look at me."

"What is it, Sam?"

"That unethical bastard."

"Sally Anne has to share the blame. After all, he didn't rape her. She's in love with him."

"That's it! Rape! That would clear Sally Anne."

"It wasn't rape."

"She's too young. It *was* rape." Sam rose and walked around the room. "The president announced today that the endowed chair went to a woman from California. Predictable."

"I'm sorry."

"I've been on the phone with Percy Wilson, my old mentor in Oxford. He wants me to go there for a few weeks as soon as possible; he has a new idea and needs my theoretical expertise. You and I met in England, Anna; it could be a second honeymoon."

"Sally Anne's due in two weeks."

"Damn it, Anna. What about me?"

"You've got to control yourself, Sam."

"Nothing's going right. I can't concentrate. People avoid me." Sobs jerked his words apart: "Sally Anne has stirred up something that scares hell out of me."

"She worries me too, Sam."

"I'm sure this is what killed the endowed chair."

"You can't blame Sally Anne for that."

Sam could not hide his anger and confusion. "Who should I blame?"

"No one. We have to live with our disappointments."

"What would you know? You've never had to face competition or scheming colleagues, or a ..."

"Or a what?"

"Nothing."

"I've been lucky, I suppose, not being able to pursue the career I loved."

"I didn't mean that."

"It's not so terrible. At least she's not involved with drugs or crime."

"That might be better."

"Come now, Sam. So we'll have a mixed race granddaughter. It won't be the first time."

"What do you mean by that?" His face again stiffened.

"Only that mixed race children are no longer rare. People aren't as judgmental as they used to be."

Sam's gaze softened. He was fighting an impulse to leave the subject. "I only knew two grandparents—Dad's parents—and they stayed in Cuba and had little to do with us. I only saw my grandfather once. Luckily, Mom had had a good friend in Tampa, an old Cuban lady named Tina. Tina became like a grandmother to me when I was little. She told me about Cuba and made me feel part of a continuum, a link in a long chain."

"That's what grandparents do."

"I was crushed when she died; I was seventeen. Later, I wished … There was so much I could have asked."

"We all feel that way, dear."

"Every time the conversation turned to Mom's grandmother they always spoke in whispers. I got the feeling somebody back then was the daughter of a slave. I've tried to research my genealogy, but … nothing."

"What difference would it make?"

"Why did they hide it?" Sam was talking through his teeth, his voice a dark whisper.

"Perhaps your mother didn't like that grandmother; who knows? It could be anything."

"Mom loved her."

"Does it matter? It's you I love." Anna reached out for her husband's hand.

"It matters to me. Anyway, after Dad's parents died, I stepped out of my ethnic past. I was born in America; I was an American. I even considered changing my name; you know, to start over with a clean slate."

"You have so much to be proud of. Who you are speaks for itself."

"Easy to say, but you have no idea what it was like as a kid; the ethnic slurs …"

"Coming from a small village I was completely out of my element when I got to Oxford," she said.

"You really think it's the same?"

"Perhaps you punished yourself more than I did."

"Did you know I'm listed as "H" on the faculty roll? That's Hispanic. Heinz, my German friend, is listed as "C" for Caucasian. He's not even a citizen. I'll bet you thought you were married to a Caucasian!"

"That's to satisfy a federal diversity regulation. It's not directed at you personally."

"Really? They list African-Americans, Hispanics, *and other nonwhites*. I'd say that pretty well defines me personally."

"It isn't accurate or fair, but the intent is just."

"I'm tired of institutionalized racial justice. They've just found another way to single us out. Isn't it ironic? My parents bought this grove to get away from their old neighborhood when blacks started moving in."

"Why don't you wait up for Sally Anne? Talk about something pleasant."

Sam buried his face in Anna's bosom. "I can't. She's pushed me into the shadows of her life, and I'm scared."

Next morning Sam entered the kitchen wearing a plaid shirt and khaki pants. He sat at the table without speaking.

"Good morning, Daddy."

"Hello, Sally Anne. Anna, I'll be home for lunch today."

"I'm sorry, Sam, I have a Women's Club luncheon."

"That's OK. I'll eat at the Chemistry snack bar."

"Could I have lunch with you, Daddy? I get out of class at noon." Sam looked up from his coffee.

"They have good pizza," she said.

"We'll see."

Sally Anne was conspicuously large now and looked happy, but he could not share her joy. Sam's thoughts hovered around that distant ancestor and her warm, breezy, island, where life flowed gently, not like the ruthless academic world he had chosen to inhabit. How could Mom's nameless grandmother deserve such oblivion? The possibilities tantalized Sam, but he would not give them shape or voice. Perhaps she died in childbirth. His heart raced.

"Let's sit outside. OK?" Sally Anne said.

"Sure. I hope this pizza's as good as you say."

"I have all <u>A</u>'s again."

"All I want is your success and happiness."

"I know, Daddy."

"But I'm frightened."

"Don't be. I'll be fine."

"I haven't talked with your mother yet, but how would you like to move into our old house on the other side of the grove; after you rest up, of course. It needs fixing, but we can take care of that. I spent some wonderful years there as a child."

She reached across the table and put her hand on his.

"Many children never learn about their parents," he said, wondering if he should continue, not knowing if it was relevant or even if it was true. But he continued and told her about the whisperings and insinuations between his mother and Tina about that ancestor. As he spoke her face relaxed into an understanding smile. She stood and went around the table and put her arms around his neck. "Thanks, Daddy. I'm proud to be her descendant."

The dingy little diner off University Avenue was small and out of the way, and few students ever went there. Some of the regular patrons had noticed the black professor with the white student, but none had expressed any feelings or even hinted that they had noticed.

"I had a talk with Daddy today. I think he'll be fine."

"What happened?"

"I'll tell you about it sometime. Right now the baby's kicking the hell out of me."

"When I was a kid we loved to tell ghost stories," he said. "Now I know why. We all have one or two hiding somewhere."

"It's something like that, Harold. Tell me about your ghosts."

"Some other time, maybe."

"Please," she said, smiling.

Under Sally Anne's melting smile Harold could not resist. "I haven't thought about it for so long, it's hard to remember."

He took a sip of his coffee and said, "It's not much of a story, Sally Anne. It was the night Martin Luther King was shot. A riot broke out in my neighborhood in Washington, and I went out to see it. My brother Marcus was out there and came home. My parents told him I had gone out, so he went after me. I came in soon after, but he stayed out there looking for me. Finally, he ran after a kid he mistook for me.

The kid ran into a store; Marcus followed him in; seconds later the store exploded.

"I didn't know what to do when we heard the news the following morning. After several days of staring at the walls, I told my folks what I wanted to do. I felt it was the only thing left, the only thing I could do: become a Marine like him. Momma cried and yelled and argued with every fiber of strength, while Pop sat mute. Finally, he told her to be quiet and turned to me. 'I understand how you feel, Harold. I don't like it either, but if it's what you want, I'll go with you to the recruiting station.'"

Harold exhaled a giant breath and said, "The rest you know—four years in the Marines, two of them in Viet Nam. It wasn't so bad; I was paying a debt. Got my high school diploma, Howard University, then graduate school at CalTech, two years at Harvard, and here."

"I'm so proud of you, Harold," Sally Anne said, holding his hand.

Before long he was driving Sally Anne back to her car at the university; then he drove home to his duplex.

That evening, Harold sat in his recliner and tried to think. Recounting the death of his brother had loosened a cord in his chest. For the first time since that night in the lab, his destiny was clear: he would marry her

He picked up the telephone and dialed his parents in Washington. "Hello, Momma. How are you and Daddy?"

"Fine, Harold. It's good to hear from you. It's been a few weeks."

"I'm fine. Working hard. Job's going well." What a way to start, he thought, knowing where the conversation would lead.

"That's good, Harold. Here, your father wants to talk."

"Wait, Momma. I want to tell you something first … I met this very nice girl."

"Wonderful. When do we meet her?" He heard her tell his father what he had said.

"We're going to get married. We haven't set a date yet, but I'll keep you posted."

"Hold on, boy. That's pretty fast."

"You'll like her, Momma."

"Where did you meet?"

"She's a student. Very bright."

"Who is she?"

"The daughter of one of the professors, Dr. Iglesias. You know, I've told you about him."

"The man who got you the job?"

"Yes."

After a muffled silence, she said, "Here's your father."

"What's this all about, son?"

"I heard Momma tell you. Don't worry. It'll be all right."

"It doesn't sound all right, Harold. Sounds like there's something else."

Harold heard his mother say, "She's white, Edwin."

"Yes, she's white," Harold said. "Is that a problem?"

"Not necessarily, son, unless there's more you haven't told us."

"What?"

"Well, I'm happy for you, Harold. When?"

"We haven't decided yet; I'll let you know."

"We'd like to come down and meet her."

"Not yet. I mean, it's better to wait a while. Don't worry. Things will be fine."

When he hung up he knew he had botched it. His first thought was to call them back tomorrow and straighten it out, but he decided it would be unmerciful to let it hang overnight. He picked up the phone and redialed the number. "Hello, Momma. I think I've upset you, and I don't want to do that. Sally Anne's a very nice girl and she loves me."

"But do you love her?"

"I wouldn't be marrying her if I didn't."

"That's important, Harold. Marriage ain't easy. Love's the only thing can hold two people together. Even then it ain't easy."

"I know, Momma." Harold felt like a little boy being scolded.

"Is she in trouble? You know …?"

There it was: her motherly radar. "That's a crazy question, Momma. You shouldn't ask that."

"Then she is?"

"Gosh, Momma. I called because I thought I'd upset you all. Now I'm upset."

"You shouldn't marry a girl for that reason. She can put it up for adoption and you can pay the expenses and help her out, but spending your life with somebody you don't love is not only stupid; it's wrong for the both of you."

"Momma, you're only partly right. Yes, she's pregnant and wants to have the baby. She wouldn't even talk about abortion."

"Thank God for that."

"But you're wrong about not being in love."

"From what you say, she loves you, but your words don't match the sound of your voice. You can't fool your Momma, Harold. You should know that by now."

"I've got to go, Momma. I don't know how to convince you, so I won't try. I'll call again soon."

Harold tried to put the conversation out of his mind. He had work to do before morning, work that wouldn't wait. He went into the kitchen and warmed that morning's left over coffee. When he poured it into his Marine Corps coffee mug, he went to his back room, sat at his desk, opened his briefcase, pulled out a stack of reprints and papers and started to write. By midnight he had completed the draft of a research proposal. His research had gone well, and he was ready to ask for a big grant to support it.

After rereading and correcting it, he tucked the papers back into the briefcase and zipped it up. He went to the bathroom, brushed his teeth, undressed, got into bed, pulled the covers up over him, and again reviewed his conversation with his mother.

It was a mild November morning, and Sam was still sipping his coffee over the morning paper when Anna came into the kitchen. "Sally Anne's in labor."

He put down the newspaper. "I'll drive you."

"No, I'm going to stay with her."

"I'll drop you off."

"Won't you wait with me?"

"Too much work. Call me when you're ready to come home."

It was the longest day Sam could remember. At 10:30 that evening Anna called. "Oh Sam, you should see our beautiful granddaughter."

"See you at the main entrance."

Sam raced along the streets to the hospital reciting over and over, *God, please let her be all right.*

Anna got into the car with a broad smile. "She had a long labor, but she's fine."

"And the baby?"

"Eight and a half pounds and powerful lungs."

"How does she look?"

"Healthy and beautiful."

"You know what I mean."

"Park the car and come; I'll take you to her."

"Later."

Sam spent the weekend walking around the grove and watching TV. He could not concentrate on his work and would not visit Sally Anne in the hospital and could not explain why even to himself. Of course he wanted to know she was well, but the thought of a black baby held him in a panic. And what about Harold? How would they fare? Would they marry? All these questions choked him. He slept poorly and awoke each morning smothering in the fear of Sally Anne's homecoming. The grove offered little comfort. Only the television he despised could shove the fear out of his immediate awareness, but never far enough.

"There they are with the baby," Anna said looking out the window.

"I'll be in the grove."

"Please, Sam ..." but he was already out the door.

Sally Anne stepped out of Harold's twelve-year-old Volvo, and Anna immediately reached for the baby. "May I hold her?"

"Isn't she gorgeous, Mom?"

"Divine." Anna held the baby close to her breast. Rocking from side to side, she looked down to see how the baby was reacting. "It's been a long time, but some things you never forget."

Sally Anne smiled.

"The new dress I made her fits perfectly. Come on in. Daddy's in the grove."

"May I go out to see him?" Harold asked.

"Of course." Anna led Harold to the back door and pointed out the path to the large grapefruit tree. "He hasn't been himself. Please be patient."

Returning to the family room Anna said, "Harold is polite and charming. Now let's see how Pearl likes her new accommodations."

"Could I have a minute, Sam?"

Sam turned away.

"It won't take long." Harold jogged to where Sam was looking at heavy clumps of ripe Hamlin oranges hanging near the ground. "I've brought Sally Anne and Pearl home. I didn't want to come, but she insisted."

"Well?"

"I'm glad I couldn't talk her into an abortion."

Sam said nothing.

"We've talked a lot lately. As rude as it may seem to you, we love each other, and want to get married."

"That'll only compound the problem."

"We can be happy, and she can continue her studies, but she wants your approval. And there's something you can do for me." For the first time, Sam looked into his eyes. "I understand your anger at Sally Anne for getting pregnant, and even at her taking up with an African-American. But you've been acting as if I don't exist. Well I *do* exist, Sam, and I want to be acknowledged as a fellow human being. Scientific recognition isn't enough. I'd rather be hated than ignored into oblivion. I want to love Pearl's grandparents, and I want them to love me. I know that's asking a lot, but ..." His hands and voice were trembling.

Until that moment Harold had been an abstraction, a cartoon character in black and white that Sam could draw and erase at will. Now this strong, handsome man of brown flesh and red blood was asking for love, for permission to exist. In that instant Sam perceived, in the abyss of the young man's deep brown eyes, family echoes of an anguish no person should have to feel. A pained smile spread over Sam's face. "It's not asking too much," he said, putting his hand on Harold's shoulder. "Please go in; I'll be along in a minute."

"Sally Anne is seeing Harold off, Sam. She says they want to get married."

"I know."

"What do you think?"

"I don't know."

"Why don't you go see the baby?"

"I'll see it later."

"It's not an 'it,' Sam; it's a 'she,' and her name is Pearl. She's asleep in Sally Anne's room. It's time you two got acquainted."

Like a little boy, Sam walked out of the bright family room into the dark hallway, that detestable darkness he had planted at the core of his airy white house. That imperfection irritated him now more than usual, as he exerted every ounce of energy to push himself up to Sally Anne's room. He stopped at the door and stuck his head in. The baby was asleep. He stood over the plump infant. She reminded him of a ripe orange. Pulling up a chair, he sat beside the crib and examined her through the railing. Her hair and features were unmistakable. He reached in and stroked her velvety, chocolate skin. She shuddered slightly through her slumber.

Anna saw her husband bent over the crib. Standing behind him she put her arms over his shoulders.

"She is beautiful," he said. He reached in and picked up the baby and startled her. When she began to whimper, he held her close, tucked the blanket around her little body, and smiled. "Is it all right if I take her out to the grove?"

"Of course, dear, but don't expose her to the sun too long. The sun's rays can harm a newborn."

33

Sam walked out of the white house and into the green grove drooping under the weight of plump, ripe fruit. Shading the baby from the sun with her blanket, he walked among the oranges to the huge grapefruit tree and sat underneath. He had never noticed how much of the grove's beauty lay in its shade.

CHALKBOARD HERO

Donald Quinone

The used car commercial ejected Donald Quinone out of the noisy battle. "It's past midnight," Hazel yelled down from their bedroom.

Looking at the clock over the TV, Donald thought, *what the hell, only twenty minutes more.* "I'll be up soon."

Lifting his corpulence from the worn, plaid reclining chair, he walked into the kitchen, slippers flapping, bathrobe open over white boxer shorts. The half-empty glass of milk he had left two commercials ago was still sitting on the counter. The stark overhead fluorescent lights created a glow that reminded him of his high school cafeteria. Donald looked at the milk recalling his father's voice: "A can of beer, Donnie Boy." Returning to the TV swirling the milk in his glass, thoughts spilled out: the Battle of The Bulge, his father who, never able to find his way out of that European forest, had become little more than an ornament in his home, drinking beer, smoking cigarettes, growing ashen. Donald Quinone recalled college days when a student deferment kept him out of the Korean War. Though he had not wanted to go, he felt shame for evading it. The draft had ended by the time he graduated, so he was spared what would have been his inevitable military service. That evasion had left a deep flaw in the crystal of his life.

As the movie resumed he felt himself darting across a battlefield, dodging bullets, crawling under barbed wire, focused only on his fallen comrade. Were these imaginings or yearnings? Is there a difference? And why he had chosen the thick swamp of academic science, itself a muddy world of mock perils and collegial battles that were little more than self-indulgent wallowing. Faculty meetings, his major field of combat, were not the bloody *mano-a-mano* struggle that real men, armed with lethal weapons, face on the field of battle. Numb evenings like this served to bring numb days to their inevitable, noisy close, days in which he had dragged himself through classes and committee meetings and laboratory puttering to return home, covered with invisible scars of the academic underbrush he had trudged through. He forced a sardonic smile knowing tomorrow would reveal only more trivia.

The finale music woke him. He lifted himself off the couch, walked to the TV and punched the "off" button. Pausing a moment before the wall mirror, Donald Quinone imagined sliding a cigarette out of his trench coat pocket, tapping it on the box, flipping open his Zippo lighter, taking a long draw and looking over his shoulder to see who was lurking in the shadows. He slipped his feet into his well-worn, tan, furry slippers, forced his shoulders back and walked, slippers flapping, up the stairs.

"How can you stand that noise?" Hazel said as he walked into their bedroom. "All those explosions and gun shots?"

"You should have stayed to see it. It was great," he said, feigning excitement as he slipped off his robe and turned back his side of the bed cover.

"I heard you snoring during the quiet parts," she said.

"I can't stand those silent scenes."

"Go to sleep, Donald."

"It's too loud and exciting in here."

"You're impossible."

"How about a little goodnight kiss?"

She turned to him and smiled. "I guess you're possible after all."

The secretary's hand reached in to hold the conference door open, and with the other hand, struggled to push in the cart. Edgar Margin, the lone faculty member in the room, stood and held the door as the cart squeaked and bumped through the door. A stack of Styrofoam cups toppled off the cart, and Edgar Margin caught them. The smell of freshly brewed coffee temporarily masked the faint lab odors that had clung to the walls since the Chemistry Department moved in twenty years ago.

Mrs. Singleton plugged in the coffee maker, and Edgar Margin drew a cup of coffee and returned to his seat at the conference table. Mrs. Singleton opened a box of doughnuts and laid them out along with a stack of paper napkins. She looked around to be sure it all looked neat and walked out. Having smiled back at Mrs. Singleton as she left, Edgar Margin's face resumed its earlier scowl as he lifted his wrist into view. "Three minutes after eight, and I'm the only one here," he mumbled, sipping his coffee. "Typical."

The tiny windows in the doors admitted the only view out of that long, narrow conference room. Over the next fifteen minutes professors straggled in and took their seats around the conference table. Those who preferred anonymity sat in student desks along the wall. Some took coffee or doughnuts or both, others sat with eyes unfocused on the blank wall, still others chatted with each other. A few browsed the bookcase from their chairs. At 8:16 Donald Quinone walked in, drew a cup of coffee, dropped his note pad on the table next to Edgar Margin, and sat. With his coffee cup steaming beside him, the Chairman, George Buchner, stood, straightened his tie, and looked down at his notes.

Sipping his coffee Donald Quinone mumbled, "I hate to use a plastic straw to stir plastic milk into my Styrofoam coffee cup."

Edgar pretended not to hear.

With his fingers Donald Quinone raked back his long black hair and pulled his tie loose. His shirttail puffed out around his short, rotund body. Waiting for George Buchner to start the meeting, Donald Quinone slouched in his chair and began to doodle formulas on his yellow note pad. With his nose almost touching the paper he muttered, "The only thing I hate more than plastic milk in my coffee is a cell with no windows."

Edgar Margin, wearing a gray, pinstripe suit and red bow tie, looked the other way and forced a smile to no one in particular. His sparse yellow hair stood at attention in a fresh crew cut. Back straight, he sat forward on the edge of his chair with both hands on the conference table. A racquetball player since college days, he took pride in his trim, athletic physique and posture.

A long smile slashed across George Buchner's freckled face. Bushy red hair stuck out randomly on his head as if each hair had a mind of its own. Finally he opened the meeting with announcements strung together like random beads: "Semester enrollment figures are up. In fact, we now have more students enrolled in chemistry than ever. For this we must thank you, the faculty, for your excellent work...remember: more students means more money for our department, and more money means we can refurbish the teaching labs...of course it also means higher faculty salaries...and additional faculty to take up the extra teaching...after all, academic departments, like all businesses, thrive on growth...without growth, not only teaching, but research as well suffers...fewer dollars means less research, and research is of prime importance for a science faculty...research is the milk that nourishes science...that's not to demean teaching...teaching is our life's blood... research is our life's...our, uh...well...research is extremely important.

Few questions punctuated the delivery until Donald Quinone said, "Why don't we sell apples at the front door? You know, to add to our research coffer."

Some of his colleagues smiled; others frowned disapproval. Donald Quinone merely continued doodling.

George Buchner chuckled and looked around at the bored faces. Fifty minutes had passed when he looked at his wristwatch. "Some of you have classes, so we'll adjourn. If anyone has any questions or suggestions, please stay or e-mail me.

As they left the meeting room, Sam Iglesias said, "Faculty meetings were not this boring at Duke. Is this typical?"

"Usually they're worse."

"If you don't mind my asking, your name sounds Spanish. Is it Quiñones?"

"No. Quinone with a long o, just like the chemical."

"Oh..."

"My Czech grandfather's name was Krivanek. He changed it to Quinone. He thought it sounded regal. Obviously he was no chemist.

Sam smiled.

"My first research publication was, *The Reduction of Quinones*, by Donald Quinone. I keep it posted over my desk."

Late the next morning after his class, Harold Pitt stopped in on Donald in his lab. "How's it going?"

"You're the one who just got married."

Erect, head shaved, deeply black, with pink lips and penetrating eyes, Harold Pitt smiled. "Nice having a wife to go home to." Then, after a moment, "I appreciate your friendship, Donald. Sounds silly, but I just feel good."

"Feeling's mutual. How's the work going?"

"Come on down to my lab. I want to show you an interesting compound I want to make."

In the lab two doors down the hall, Harold slid out a partly visible envelope from under the door and then unlocked the door and went in. Barely hearing Donald's commentary about yesterday's boring meeting, Harold opened and read the note, then crumpled it and sat, still holding the crumpled paper in his fist. Donald stopped talking when he saw Harold's rapid breathing. Harold threw the note into the wastebasket.

Donald said, "What's that?"

"Nothing."

"Nothing wouldn't make you that mad."

"I said it was nothing."

Donald reached into the wastebasket, and Harold grabbed his hand. "Leave it."

"I can guess."

With his teeth clenched so tightly his facial muscles rippled, Harold handed Donald the note. It read:

> *Miscegenation is against the law in some states, but more important: it is against God's law.*
>
> *Revolted Student*

"Son of a bitch."

Harold was sitting at attention, hands on his lap, glaring into the bookcase.

"May I borrow it?"

"No."

"I'll track it down."

"No way."

Donald held up the note. "It's department stationery. See, the letterhead's cut off, but there's the watermark."

"Doesn't mean a thing."

"If it's faculty or staff, we'll nail the bastard."

"I don't want to nail anybody, and I don't want anybody to see it or hear about it."

"Don't worry. Only you and I and the bastard will know."

Half an hour later Donald returned. Harold was still sitting at his desk with his fingers interlaced on his lap. He looked up sharply as Donald burst in.

"The secretary hasn't given stationery to any students. Not even grad students. Problem is: every faculty member has it."

"I told you I don't care."

"It's printed by hand in block capitals using a fountain pen. How many people use those anymore?"

Harold ignored him.

"How many states have an anti-miscegenation law?"

"I know you're trying to help, Donald, but if we find out, what then?"

"Alabama," Donald said. "And who do we know from Alabama?"

"Who?"

"Edgar Margin."

"That's impossible. Edgar's stiff and fidgety, but...no."

"It's hard to believe, but..."

"Drop it, Donald."

"Notice the i's are all dotted with little circles? It's a female. And Brucine's the only woman in the department."

"And the secretaries," Harold said. "Drop it!"

"I'll be back."

As Donald rushed out, Harold shook his head, amazed at his friend's tenacity and curiosity. "You're acting like a TV private eye." But Donald was gone.

A few minutes later he was back. "None of the secretaries dot their i's that way, and neither does Brucine. Might be a red herring."

"Could it be a student?" Harold said, "Or is that too simple?"

"I'll be back."

Edgar Margin was at his computer and turned as Donald walked in.

"Didn't get to spend any time with you at Harold's wedding, Edgar. Nice affair."

"I suppose so."

"Harold's a lucky guy."

"I'll say. No stopping him now."

"How's that?"

"As our white, Distinguished Professor's son-in-law?"

"You make it sound dirty."

"How do you see it?"

"I think it's great. You aren't against miscegenation, are you Edgar?" Donald watched Edgar's face for revealing signs.

"It's my upbringing."

"It's not illegal."

"It is in Alabama."

Donald looked squarely into Edgar's eyes. That this man would agree with the note didn't prove he had written it. He wanted to ask Edgar if he thought it was against God's law, but could not appear so intrusive and argumentative without revealing more than he wanted. Finally he stood and walked to the door, stopped, and turned to Edgar, who was still looking at him.

"You don't think much of me, do you?" Edgar said.

"What?"

"You think I wrote it, don't you?"

"Wrote what?"

"I saw the student who slipped it under his door."

"How do you know what it said?"

"Harold was in class. When I asked if I could help, she said no and started to cry. I asked what was wrong and she said, 'I didn't want to; my father made me. Said if I didn't he would do something worse.'

41

When I pressed her she said she couldn't talk about it; that she didn't mean it, but she had to. Then she took off running down the hall."

"You still haven't told me how you knew what was in the note."

"I pulled it out and read it. I wanted to throw it away, but didn't."

"Christ sake, Edgar, it really hurt him."

"I don't like to meddle."

"Good God!"

"It's too much. He comes here on a made-up position, gets all that federal money, then marries a white girl with her father's blessing. It's too much."

Donald walked out leaving Edgar frozen in his chair and fuming that his friend would think he could have written such a note.

Donald returned to Harold's office with trepidation. He had to tell him, but he was not sure how much to tell. He silently sat down by Harold's desk and looked through the window into the lab. Harold immediately realized Donald had learned something.

"All right, Donald. Spill it."

"Edgar saw a girl put it on your door," he said. Recounting the girl's behavior, he did not mention that Edgar had read the note.

"So now we know. Am I supposed to find out who she is and flunk her and become as vicious as her father?"

"You were right, Harold. It's best to forget it if you can."

"If I can? You think this is new? It's all in a day's work."

"I'm sorry, Harold. I should've dropped it."

The following Monday morning, as Donald Quinone walked through the parking lot, the Science Center hid the morning sun from view. Standing hard against the sky like a stony cloud, it had cast a shadow over his life for over two decades.

He walked into his office at 8:20 without having to greet a single student and turned on the fluorescent light in the tiny inside office whose only window was a six-by-eight-inch glass panel in the door. Donald despised that opening. It could not let in the light of the world, only prying eyes. He never knew whether it was sunny or cloudy or raining until he went outside. To him that office confirmed the administration's disdain for human beings. He could have had an outside office, but it would have been on another floor, away from his lab, a sacrifice he would not make. The only color in that small space came from the books stuffed into bookcases on three walls—new books publishers had sent hoping for an adoption, books he referred to often, journals, and older books, some from his student days. A single picture hung on one wall, a photo of him with several other chemists surrounding Linus Pauling at an American Chemical Society meeting taken years earlier. Journals, books and papers covered most of the desk surface. The only neat pile was the stack of exams he would administer at nine o'clock. As he sat cursing the university, he pulled loose his tie, ran his fingers through his hair, and thumbed through the exams. He pulled out a blank exam paper, sharpened his pencil, heard a knock on the door, and read the first question, pencil in hand to check his answers, until he heard the second knock.

"Come in."

When the student politely and quietly closed the door behind her, Donald at once guessed what she wanted.

"Can I ask you a question about today's test?"

"You just did."

"I'd like to know how much it's going to count."

"Thank Heaven! For a moment I thought you were going to ask me to explain something about organic chemistry. Your question is simple: 40 percent, as stated in the syllabus I handed out the first day of class. Didn't you get one?"

"But you've covered two new chapters since the last test, and the exam's supposed to cover the whole course. I guess the exam won't have anything from the last two chapters. Right?"

"Your assumption, though clever, is incorrect. But don't torture yourself for failing to see the flaw in your logic. You see, I find no problem in testing both the last two chapters and the whole course. I do it by including some problems from those chapters along with problems from all the other chapters."

Feeling she could not leave without saying something intelligent, the girl, gripped by fear born of insufficient study and worry over the C average she felt was teetering dangerously, asked, "How about an extra credit project? A report or something?"

"Extra credit implies you've done work for regular credit. I've repeated throughout the semester that if you solve the homework problems, you'll understand the material and won't need extra credit. Since you haven't come to me for help, I surmise you understood the material." Throughout the exchange, Donald wore a patronizing smile.

"Well, if I don't do well in this exam," she said, "could you turn in an I for me? I'm premed, you see, and I can't afford another C on my record."

"I believe you've misunderstood the I grade. It stands for incomplete, not inadequate. Besides, I doubt if you'll get a C."

"Oh." Dazed, the poor girl left the door ajar as she walked out; Donald walked around his desk to close it.

The 200-seat, fan-shaped, rising lecture hall was nearly full when Donald walked in carrying his stack of exam papers. He paused just inside the door to survey the cavernous room and then resumed his slow, deliberate pace to the lecture demonstration bench and dropped the papers on the bench with a loud slam and looked at his watch. It was five minutes before the hour. Donald liked to start his tests early to relieve students' anxiety and to encourage them to arrive early. The pit, as he called it, might have been good for a cockfight, but not for exams. Each seat in the steep auditorium afforded a clear view of the desktops on the row beneath.

"I am the tester; you are the testees," Donald mumbled inaudibly, as he began his ascent up the center aisle. It was part of his test ritual that helped put the exam into perspective. Feeling like a prison guard, he fed a counted stack of exam papers to the first student in each row.

"Take one exam from the top and pass the rest down the aisle. Don't shuffle them on the way."

When he had given out all the papers, he descended to the front of the room and announced in his most intimidating voice, "I've passed out more than one version of the exam. If you feel tempted to copy from a paper near yours, be advised that a correct answer on another paper might be incorrect on yours. Furthermore, if I see anyone who even looks like he's cheating, I'll do everything in my power to have that person expelled from the university forever. Cheating is the worst crime a student can commit, comparable to murder in the real world."

Donald directed his remarks to all, but especially sought the eyes of the young woman who had earlier come to his office.

"When you finish, read over your answers and remember: many correct answers end on the floor during last minute panic erasures. So don't make changes unless you're sure. If you have a question, don't get up; raise your hand and I will come to you."

He sat on a stool behind the lecture demonstration bench and opened the latest issue of the Journal of Organic Chemistry. He looked up often. Actually he could never read with concentration during a test. Within a few minutes Donald thought he saw a student near the back of the room looking at a nearby paper. Without moving his head he peered at the student over the rim of his glasses. The student did it again and looked at Donald. Seeing Donald looking at him, he went through all the telltale gestures: immediately refocusing on his own paper, glancing frequently at the professor, looking up as if thinking, then looking around, smiling nervously.

"Hah! Did it again." Donald put down his journal and began to stare at the student. Every time the student looked up, he saw Donald's eyes focused on him like lasers from a distant mountain. The student began to act like a lion in a circus ring, fidgeting, clearing his throat, looking at the ceiling with his fist pensively on his chin, looking at his watch and back at Donald. Minutes later, Donald was still boring into him. The student, reduced to an old cat hiding from its master's whip, did not know where to lay his eyes. Donald was a soldier on reconnaissance, the enemy in his sights. *Most cheaters fail anyway; don't know enough to cheat from somebody smart. Can't be dumb and smart at the same time, I guess. This guy's dumb and dumb at the same time. How many times has the poor chump looked this way? I'll bet he can see me through his forehead.* By this time, the student's panic had risen into his hair follicles. A raised hand on the other side of the room shattered Donald's laser gaze.

Within three minutes after the bell, most students had turned in their papers. When the cheater handed his to Donald, Donald put down the papers he had collected and circled the student's name in red as the student watched in stunned silence.

Though he was anxious to see how his students had done on the exam, Donald walked down to the basement coffee shop, bought a cup of black coffee and walked out and down the long hall and up the elevator to his third floor office. When he looked at the stack of papers, he momentarily thought of going home and leaving the grading for the next day, but he sat down instead.

A knock on the door interrupted his thoughts.

"I forgot my sign!" He mumbled. At the second knock he said, "Come in."

A young man entered breathlessly and stood before his desk.

"I haven't graded them yet," Donald said.

"My car broke down; I just got here. Could I take it now?"

Donald's head dropped so his chin rested on his chest and assumed his paternalistic pose, sitting motionless, looking over his glasses at the student, his nose neatly bisecting his malicious grin. "I've been giving tests for twenty years, and I have never failed to arrive on time. Of course, I leave home early enough to avert any problem that might arise, such as car dying or grandmother dying. Let's see. You are…?" he drawled as he looked down his grade roll.

"Bisot, Sir, Henry Bisot."

Donald found the name and saw that his grades on the three one-hour tests were all in the high nineties.

"Are you prepared to take the exam now?"

"Yes sir."

"Well it won't be necessary. As I announced in my syllabus, I don't give make-up tests, and that applies to the final."

"Can't I take the same exam? I haven't spoken to anyone in our class."

"No, rather than break my rule, I excuse you from the exam. I'll base your grade on the average of your one-hour tests, which gives you an A for the course. But don't do it again."

"No sir. Thank you, sir."

After the student walked out, Donald Quinone sat for a moment thinking about another student several years earlier, Jimmy Nonell. Jimmy was also quiet and studious, but he had missed the A cut-off by one point, and Donald never bent his curve. A few days after the final exam, Jimmy saw Donald Quinone in the hall and asked if he had the final grades. Bracing himself for the inevitable argument, Donald said, "Yes. You have a B. It was close. Sorry."

"Yes, sir," Jimmy said. "Thanks. Great course."

When Donald was transcribing his final grades to the registrar's sheet, he did something he rarely did. Since there was no one else with Jimmy's final average, he decided to change Jimmy's grade to an A.

After the first class meeting in January, Jimmy waited. Donald saw him standing alone and said, "Merry Christmas."

"Thank you, Dr. Quinone. I was hoping it wasn't a mistake."

"I hope so too. Don't make it so tough for me next time."

"No Sir."

Jimmy earned the highest grade in the class that semester.

Before he did anything else, Donald pulled the old sign from behind his filing cabinet and taped it to his door:

I AIN'T GOT NO GRADES YET!

Donald had barely started grading his papers when he heard a knock on his door. After the second knock, he said, "Come in."

The stocky young man stood well over six feet with a muscular frame and thick, curly, black hair, thick sideburns and heavy eyebrows. His eyelids drooped over bulging, brown eyes.

"Didn't you see my sign?"

"I gotta talk to you."

"I'm not surprised. Let's see, you're..."

"Trampa, Sir. John Trampa. When I handed you my exam paper you circled my name. What's that mean?"

"Well, Trampa, I saw you looking at the paper next to yours, and I wanted to remember which paper was yours."

"I wasn't cheating, Sir. What are you going to do?"

"Nothing," Donald said. "If your paper is as bad as your behavior suggests, you'll get the grade you've earned, and I won't have to do anything."

"I need a <u>B</u> in this course. I'm applying to medical school next year. A <u>C</u> in organic chemistry will kill me."

"I can assure you'll survive. It might keep you out of medical school, but you'll live."

"You don't understand, Sir. It's my father. I'm supposed to join his practice when I graduate."

Donald pulled out his grade book and looked up the boy's semester grades, 61, 69, 57, a low <u>D</u> average. "Your work's been consistently poor all semester. How many courses are you taking?"

"Organic chemistry, English Lit and Sociology."

"Have a job?"

"Oh, no. My father wants me to devote all my time to my studies."

"Why haven't you come to see me?"

"My father hired a tutor, but organic's tough. I work hard, but I just don't get it."

"Why do you want to be a doctor?"

"There's nothing else for me, Sir."

"I'm sorry, but even an <u>A</u> on today's exam wouldn't give you a <u>B</u>."

"How about some extra credit?"

"I can't change your grade just because you're in a panic."

"You don't care about me or nobody. You resent me taking up time from your precious research."

"That's not fair. This is the first time you've come in. How can you expect to get help when the course has ended?"

John Trampa got up slowly, deliberately, looking straight at Donald, breathing heavily. "You'll regret this."

"I don't think so. But I do think it's time for you to leave."

"You'll be sorry."

"Is that a threat?"

"You'll see…" As Trampa walked out the door, Donald heard a guttural, "Son of a bitch."

Donald's hand trembled and his heart pounded as he picked up the phone. He looked at it shaking and returned it to its cradle. The image of this tough youth stalking him or booby-trapping his car or breaking into his home left his brain reeling. How to handle an irrational kid with such malice in his voice? I'll buy a gun, he thought, but could I shoot a human being? This mean, vicious boy's greatest fear may be his father. Poor kid. Being a doctor may be the last thing he wants. Even if he liked medicine he'd have to work with a guy who would dominate him the rest of his life.

Finally Donald picked up the phone and dialed the Associate Dean for Student Affairs. "Mike, I've just received a threat...from a student... I found him cheating. What's the best...I mean, how..."

"You sound shaken," Mike Boswell said.

"Of course! What do you expect?"

"OK, what's the student's name and what was the nature of the threat?"

"John Trampa. He's not happy with his grade and said I would regret it. He's pretty big and sounded serious enough to scare the hell out of me."

"Can you get him to the campus psychiatrist?"

"You don't think he's still sitting here, do you?"

"OK, OK. Calm down. Call campus security and give them the details."

"That's it?"

"They know how to handle these things. I've made a record of the threat."

"Good Heavens," Edgar Margin said. "I've heard of such things, but I've never actually known of one."

"This guy's big. I could meet him down any hall or on my way home or in my car."

"Maybe you should just give him the benefit of the doubt."

"I might if there were a doubt. He has a clear <u>D</u> going into the final. Even a perfect paper wouldn't raise him to a <u>B</u>."

"Have you graded his paper?"

"Not yet."

"If he had threatened me, I'd think about changing the grade. Did you call the police?"

"Sure. They took all the details and said they would patrol the building."

Edgar Margin thought a moment. "Donald, sometimes people take your humor the wrong way. Like at faculty meetings. You're good at helping students understand chemistry, but you sometimes alienate people."

"I tell them the truth. If the truth hurts—tough! Look, I came here for help and comfort, not a sermon."

"I'm just saying you shouldn't give the impression you're out to get students; that's the truth. I'm sorry if it hurts."

"I get it."

Back in his office, Donald tried to continue grading, but couldn't concentrate. He felt as if the whole chemistry building would fall in on him. The ringing telephone made him jump.

"Hello, Dr. Quinone? This is Dean Wunderbar. I'm concerned about the threat you received today. Could you tell me about it?"

When Donald described the episode, the dean said, "I am certainly on your side in any matter of this sort, and I respect your directness, but I must tell you that students have complained about you occasionally, about your sarcasm, I mean."

"I have little patience with stupidity. If I tolerate it, they only repay me with more of the same."

"Can you make a good case for cheating?"

"Of course not. It's impossible to prove he took answers from another paper, even if their answers are the same. I don't plan to press charges if that's what you're driving at."

"In that case I urge you to go easy. You mustn't take threats lightly."

"Are you suggesting I give him a grade he didn't earn?"

"No. Just weigh the possibilities. If I can be of help, please let me know."

Donald walked down to the coffee shop, drew a cup of black coffee, paid for it, put a cover on it and walked out into the long hall. Through the glass doors at the end of the hall a bright sunny morning beckoned, but he ignored it and took the elevator up to his office. He put the coffee cup down, sat at his desk and looked at the stack of papers. He was tempted to lift out Trampa's paper and mark it, but instead he went through the stack in the order received as he always did. When he came to Trampa's paper, he wondered whether he could be objective. His doubts vaporized when he began to read. With maximum generosity, the boy had 59%. That brought his final average to 61%, just barely a D. As he was about to pick up another paper, Edgar Margin came in.

"I didn't mean to upset you, Donald, but I'm worried. This guy may turn out to be a nut."

"He has 59 on the exam. That gives him a low D average; he's nowhere near a C, much less a B."

"What'll you do?"

"Give him the grade he earned."

"Just be careful. Offer to help. Let him know you're on his side and not out to get him."

"Thanks, Edgar."

Donald turned in his grades the following day, a week before the deadline. The next few days were anxious, but he finally managed to put the threat out of his mind. Two weeks after the exam, he was trying to work out a new research idea on his yellow pad when he heard a knock on his door. He answered it on the first knock.

John Trampa walked in and sat down. Instead of his usual well-groomed appearance, he had not shaved and was wearing a black sleeveless tee shirt and jeans and carried a small leather bag. His physique bulging through his clothes testified to the hours he had spent weight training.

"I got my grades today. I wanted to make sure that D wasn't a mistake."

"You scored 59 on the final exam. Here." Donald reached to the pile of papers on his desk, picked up the top one, and handed it to Trampa.

Without looking up from his test paper Trampa said, "And you won't let me do extra work? I'm willing to do a research project in your lab or anything you say."

51

Unlike his last visit, the boy seemed calm and resigned, perhaps too resigned, too calm, Donald thought.

"That wouldn't be fair to the other students, John. And in the long run it wouldn't be fair to you either."

"You've blown medical school for me."

"College rules allow you to remove this grade from your record. If you repeat the course and get a better grade, the new grade will be the official one. All you need is my approval, and I'll gladly give it. And I'll help you as much as you need with the homework"

"That won't mean anything to my father." Trampa rose and turned slowly toward the door. He took a step and turned to face Donald again, now with a small gun in his hand.

"Don't be stupid, John. Put that down."

"You've ruined my life with your stupid little grade. I don't care what happens to me."

"Don't blow this out of proportion. Your father wouldn't want…"

The sharp pain in his chest preceded the sound. Trampa ran out as the room went dark.

"Good to see you awake, Dr. Quinone. I'm Dr. Hackett. I tended you when they brought you in. You're very lucky. Half an inch up or down, and the bullet would have entered the chest cavity where it could have done real damage. It merely fractured the rib and ricocheted out. You'll be fine in a week or two."

Donald was still looking around at the whiteness of the hospital room with the window blinds closed against the blinding sun. He tried to move his head and felt a sharp pain in his side.

"You mean it's not a dream? He really shot me?" Donald tried not to move any more than necessary; it hurt even to talk. "What about the kid?"

"He's in custody. One of your colleagues heard the shot and saw him run out of your office and called the police. They had him within an hour. "An irate premed, I hear."

"Yeah." Donald thought it prudent not to tell the doctor he taught organic chemistry.

Dr. Hackett smiled, "Organic was my favorite subject. I had a great teacher too. But I must admit I thought about knocking off my physics professor once."

"Nice of you to say so, Doc."

Hazel was not as understanding. "I told him to change the boy's grade, but Professor Perfect never compromises."

By that evening Donald felt better, but the pain in his side still restricted his movements. He still could not completely comprehend what had happened, not believing that a student could shoot him over a grade. With all the nurses on the floor dropping in, he felt like a celebrity and surmised that they didn't see many gunshot victims.

The next day Hazel came to drive Donald home. Donald said, "Before you start, Hazel, please don't. I've been through enough."

"Come on, then. I'll help you up."

Two weeks of sunshine and warm gulf water at the beach failed to calm his battered nerves, so he spent the rest of the summer in his lab thinking about Trampa and his trial, which had been scheduled unusually hastily, and dreading his appearance as the state's chief witness. He dreaded most of all facing that deranged boy with the fire and hatred in his eyes. He wondered what defense his lawyer could conjure up. He imagined the judge charging him with one count of poor teaching and one of unfair grading, knowing it would be impossible to prove objectively that any exam could truly evaluate a student's comprehension without bias. He had, after all, ordered Trampa out of his office. That alone would be enough to establish prejudice in his grading. He would produce the exam paper and defy anyone to grade it, he thought, as he grew angrier. But what if other students joined the complaint? Trampa was not the only failure in his class. If this mushroomed into an infamous case of professor against students, his career could be over.

But his worrying was for naught; Trampa's lawyer pled the boy guilty and asked for probation based on the boy's emotional state and his parents' guarantee that he would undergo psychiatric treatment. At the hearing Donald Quinone explained the situation of the boy's grade and his unrealistic fixation on medical school:

"I'm sure he's smart enough if and when he develops a healthy attitude toward school. His parents have put unbearable pressure on him. I think they all might need help in learning to deal with each other."

To this, Trampa's attorney asked Donald if he felt qualified to offer psychiatric advice.

"Of course not, but I know a troubled kid when I see one. Besides, isn't that what you're pleading?"

The judge granted probation under the stated conditions.

Donald could not erase from his memory the look in Trampa's eyes when he fired the gun; he saw it every time he closed his eyes. For the first time in his career, he did not look forward to the fall term. He fervently wished he could retire early, but that was at least five years away.

On his return to the chemistry building after the summer break, Donald Quinone walked directly to Edgar Margin's office.

"You busy?"

"Sure, but I always have time for you, Donald."

"Vivian OK?"

Edgar squinted and said: "Fine."

"Glad to hear it."

"Come to the point, please." Edgar snapped his wristwatch into view and then abruptly brought it down.

"Sorry, Edgar." Then after a moment, "Maybe later would be better, but I need to talk."

"What about?"

"You know, that research proposal I sent in."

"Looked good to me."

"If it comes through, I'll be able to pay my salary for the year. The project could really take off if I give it full time."

"What about your courses?"

"Doing both drags me down."

"I think there's more."

"Like what?"

"Hazel's pretty worried."

"Where'd you hear that?"

"Vivian. It's a small village."

"She thinks I'm in danger. I'll admit it's crossed my mind, but that's not it. I just don't have the stomach to face two hundred bored students."

"We've got lots of good ones."

"They're smart enough, but they're premeds. Once they get into that mode their only objective is medical school. Imagine a doctor trying to heal people after all the pushing, shoving, and cheating he's done to get his diploma."

"I know lots of kind, competent doctors. The one I see was a whiz in chemistry."

"Come on, you know what these kids are like. The medical schools don't care if they know organic chemistry. We just screen their candidates for them. I should give all <u>A's</u>. That would screw them up."

"A fascinating thought, but it'd hurt the good ones."

"I know." Donald rose and walked toward the door.

"You OK?"

"Oh, sure. Thanks."

"What did you want advice about?"

"Not advice; just talk."

Donald returned to his office and sat at his desk under the heavy fluorescent lights wondering if he should really give up teaching. He had loved chemistry as a young man. Chemistry had opened a bright new world, but that world was now crushing him. Research was difficult, but the exhilaration of a discovery, no matter how small, repaid the effort. Now he thought only of peripheral chores: writing proposals and papers, purchasing chemicals and equipment, keeping up with the growing literature and monitoring graduate students' work. It seemed to have grown to mountainous proportions. And he knew that, as time passed and his research became more routine and more goal-oriented in search of funding, his discoveries had become less exciting and more predictable. That little boy was still playing with his chemistry set, but he had become a technician, a salesman for his expertise. He reached to his bookshelf and pulled out a faded blue book, "Reference Book of Inorganic Chemistry," by Latimer and Hildebrand. He had bought it as an undergraduate because of its famous authors. With a 1940 publication date, it was archaic even then, but its loose, well-worn cover felt good in his hands. Flipping the first few pages kindled memories of difficult ideas cracking open to reveal kernels of joy. He had enjoyed piecing them together into a rational picture of nature. He stopped to read Bohr's theory of electron energy levels and the experimental evidence on which he based it: When hydrogen gas burns it emits an orange flame. But when looked at through a simple spectroscope Bohr saw, not orange, but five sharp, distinctly colored lines. Many had seen those lines, but Bohr was able to imagine what no one else had. The lines, he said, meant that hydrogen atoms were emitting light of fixed wavelengths. Bohr explained the lines by proposing that electrons, torn away from the atoms in the flame, return, as the atoms cool, but only to discrete levels within the atoms, thus emitting discrete energies, hence the separate, colored lines and not a smear of all colors. Each color corresponds to an electron falling into a discrete level. From the wavelengths of the colors, Bohr calculated the energies of the electron levels of hydrogen. Donald loved the simplicity and elegance of Bohr's theory and especially the language. It was language of another era, a time when many of today's scientific facts were still unknown. The language seemed overly precise, as if self-consciously distinguishing between hypothesis and fact, between solid ground and quicksand. Donald always emphasized to his students that scientific theories rest on experiment and are therefore always tentative, but, to make them easy to learn, theories become dogmatic and therefore dull. To the young Donald Quinone, these ideas were astounding and thrilling, and the older Donald Quinone could still enjoy them.

Donald was completely wrapped up in the old text when he heard a knock on the door and then the door opened. It was John Trampa's father.

"May I sit down?"

Jerked out of his revelry by the father of his would-be assassin, Donald Quinone said, "Certainly."

"I wanted to thank you for not pressing for conviction. John's in therapy; the doctor says he's coming along." The tall, heavy, erect man with thick brown hair and thick reddish-brown moustache was wearing a three-piece, gray seersucker suit. His bulk made it difficult to squeeze between the arms of the chair. He looked distinguished, not at all like Donald, with his long hair and wrinkled short sleeve shirt. In his presence, Donald felt both threatened and inferior.

"I feel bad for John. I hope it goes well for him."

"You suggested in the hearing that I bore some of the responsibility for John's predicament. I admit I pushed him toward medicine, and I think I was right. He took me too seriously, I guess."

Doubting the man before him would understand, Donald tried anyway: "I believe people do best at work they enjoy. Following another direction can be excruciating and often leads to failure, especially when it's as difficult as medicine."

"I won't pay for my son to spend four years learning to write poems or talk philosophy. Those guys end up selling hamburgers. We all have to earn our way. Best to choose a career that pays. Money talks."

"Pre-med's tough enough, and after those four years, you haven't even begun to study medicine. Most students can't make it through all that unless they're deeply motivated."

"Everything worthwhile takes work."

"When I went to college, the last thing I thought about was money. I knew I would earn a reasonable salary as a chemist. My only goal was to do chemistry. Its fascination got me through. Students now seem to have different goals."

"Are your goals really different? How many hours a week do you spend teaching?"

"Six in the classroom, not counting preparations, grading, and talking with students. Two courses take more time than you think."

"So you spend a third of your time teaching and the rest on research, right? Tell me about your research. How will your research help people?"

"That's not the right question. Most research fills in details of a large picture. Pure research isn't necessarily aimed at practical problems. It accumulates knowledge for future use. That's how we learn about nature."

"Don't tell me about nature. Tell me about something you've accomplished that helps people." His large, droopy eyes stared at

Donald. "Most professors do everything they can to get out of teaching. And when they're forced into it, they make students toe the mark under the highest standards they can get away with. As if they're getting even for having to teach them."

"Certainly you don't favor low standards."

"Standards should be realistic, but I don't want to get into that. John failed and that's that. When I was a student, we all knew publications were the only thing that counted."

Trampa's diatribe unnerved Donald. These thoughts were not new, but he had never heard them expressed by a non-academic in such harsh tones.

"My only point is that to do his best, your son should study what interests him. I believe success comes only by following your heart's desire. It's an article of faith."

"Faith from a scientist? I came to thank you for not making it hard on my son, not to attack you or your profession, but from what I see, professors don't know much about education. You should have to answer to somebody besides your peers."

Trampa rose when he finished talking. Donald stood and offered his hand. Trampa turned and walked out.

Donald's research should have hummed that summer, but with his graduate students preparing for their doctoral comprehensive exams, they accomplished little research and he accomplished less. He spent time at the lab bench, but his heart was not in it. Dr. Trampa's words had shaken his already ragged convictions. *Maybe Trampa was right. Maybe my work means little to humanity or the world or anyone. Who have I touched? Who have I helped? My work has been competent, but it hasn't changed the direction of chemistry. The chemical world recognizes my work as important, but I don't know. With research you rarely know.*

As he was standing at his lab bench distilling a new product, swirling in a sea of self-pity, he heard a knock on the door. A young man in his late twenties came in. He was wearing jeans, a sweatshirt and sneakers and his hair was tied into a ponytail. "Yes?"

"Remember me?"

"Vaguely, but not your name."

"Manny Garcia. I took organic with you five years ago."

"Sure, Manny. I remember." But Donald's gaze revealed his confusion.

"I don't blame you for forgetting. I didn't do too well."

"I get hundreds of students every year. It's hard to remember them all."

"I was a premed then. You did me a big favor, Dr. Quinone. You talked me out of it."

A flicker of memory struck.

"Don't you remember? We talked for a while and you asked what I really enjoyed."

"Ah, yes, the guitar."

"Right! I remember what you said: 'Follow your heart's desire and forget about money'. Well, I did. I was spending most of my time plucking and strumming instead of studying. Well, I've made a few CD's. I love it and the money's starting to trickle in."

"Manny, you've made my day."

"I heard about the shooting and the trial and all. I figured you must be feeling pretty low, so I wanted to let you know some of us thought you were terrific."

"Thanks, Manny. I'm going to look for your CD's."

"I brought you a couple. Hope you like them. If you don't, remember you made me do it."

As Manny started to move toward the door, Donald embraced the boy. "Thanks again, Manny. I'll never forget you."

Donald sat down at his desk smiling. No one knows how things will turn out. Donald had expected to win a Nobel Prize or at least cure some terrible disease or discover an important new kind of matter. None of that had happened, but he had enjoyed trying. His best successes had come when he did what felt right. *Why can't Trampa see that? Why so intent on pushing his son into medicine? We'll never see the world the same way no matter how long we talk. It's a difference in feeling, not rationality. At least I know the difference.*

The following Friday afternoon, after several hours of lab work, Donald sat at his desk to study the nuclear magnetic resonance spectrum of the compound he had been trying to purify for three weeks. The curves showed that the compound was pure enough to use in the next step of the synthesis. As he looked at the spectrum, planning his next step, Edgar Margin walked in.

"How's it going?"

"Fine. Haven't been shot at in over a month. You were right about not getting out of the classroom."

"Glad to hear it."

"Did you want something, Edgar?"

"Cup of coffee?"

"Why not?"

Harold Pitt walked into the lecture hall in late August of the following year thinking the heat would never end. He laid his books on the demonstration table and looked up at the rising rows of students. He had grown fond of teaching and enjoyed influencing young minds, molding them, making them see things differently, changing their outlooks, not only about chemistry, but also about life. He knew they would not all yield to him, but if he could touch a few he would be happy.

"I won't normally call the roll, but I'm required to on the first day," he said to the class. Many of the names were the usual ones, though he'd noticed each year an increasing number of Arabic, Indian, Chinese, and Vietnamese names. He managed with relative ease until he came to a name that made him shudder. He said the name, stopped, and looked up. The nearly two hundred faces also stopped moving, wondering why Harold Pitt had stopped. One student in the room knew—John Trampa. Harold continued his lecture.

At the end of the period Harold gathered his books and notes and molecular models and walked out of the hall. Instead of going to his office he went directly to Donald Quinone's lab. "Look," he said, holding up the class roll with his thumb below Trampa's name.

Donald inhaled deeply and exhaled, then turned to Harold.

"Any advice, Donald?"

"If he looks at you wrong or acts menacing don't mess around. Call the police."

"What a way to start a course. I wanted to think about students and organic chemistry, not survival."

"If he's back in school, he's probably OK. The court wouldn't have released him otherwise."

"I hope."

At his office Harold found the tall, stocky young man waiting in the hall. Harold opened the door knowing who he was, but acted as if he did not. Before Harold could ask what he wanted, the young man said, "I'm John Trampa. I guess you remembered the name when you called the roll. I thought I'd better see you."

"Sure, John. Sit down, please."

Trampa looked through the window into the lab and saw three students working. "I just wanted to let you know I'm OK now. What I did was crazy. I'm lucky they didn't lock me up. I guess I have Dr. Quinone to thank for that."

Harold nodded.

"I've been in therapy almost a year, and I've learned al lot about myself. Please don't worry. Just treat me like any other student. I know it'll be hard, but I'd appreciate it."

Harold smiled. "I'll do my best. And remember: if you need help come see me. That's why I'm here."

"Thanks." Getting up to leave, he said, "I'd like to talk with Dr. Quinone too. Think it's all right?"

"Sure."

Trampa walked down the familiar hallway and knocked. When he heard Donald's voice say, come in, Trampa opened the door. "Please don't worry. I'm unarmed."

Donald stared at the apparition without expression.

"I guess that wasn't very funny. I don't know what to say except, I'm sorry for everything."

"Sit down, John."

John Trampa sat beside Donald Quinone with his books in his lap. "It was pretty awful, but I had to see you. I've spent most of the year realizing how mad I was at my father."

Donald stared into the boy's eyes.

"He came here, didn't he?"

61

Donald nodded.

"I heard he did his number on you."

Not sure how controversial he wanted to get he said, "We see the world differently."

"Besides realizing how mad I was—actually still am—I know you were right. My father won't run my life anymore. Thanks for trying to explain it to him, but I could've saved you the trouble. He doesn't know how to listen. It almost brought them to divorce."

"Sorry."

"Maybe it would've been good for my mother, but she decided to stick it out. He has no clue."

Donald nodded noncommittally.

"The least I could do was stay out of your class, Dr. Quinone. Dr. Pitt's pretty good too. I'm going to like him. Any advice for my second try?"

"What I tell all repeaters: Everything you'll see will look familiar and you'll tell yourself you know it. That's the big mistake. If you'd known it you'd have done well the first time. Assume you know nothing and start from scratch. It's the only way."

"Sounds right."

John Trampa stood and offered his hand. Donald shook it and said, Dr. Pitt's very good, and I'm here too if you want to talk."

"Thanks."

Donald heard Trampa's footsteps disappear down the hall and felt no relief. John's visit could not erase the image or the pain of the shot and waking up in the hospital. Donald could not believe a person could change so drastically. The boy was young and he probably understood a little more, but a whiff of the old arrogance suffocated his apology. Much like his father, Donald thought. It'll take more than an apology and nice talk to convince me.

Donald walked down the hall to Harold's lab. "Guess who just came to see me."

"I know."

"Did he tell you he would?"

"I think he's trying to make amends."

"Uh-huh. Is that what you think?"

"I don't know. It's not easy, but he's getting help."

"Just keep your eyes open."

The weather had cooled when Harold gave his first test. He watched Trampa for signs of problems, but saw none. Stopping as he swept the large auditorium with his eyes, Harold saw Trampa bent over his desk, writing, never raising his head. At half past the hour, the boy walked his paper down to Harold.

"Already?"

"Yes, sir." Without waiting for further comment, Trampa walked out. The rest of the class was still working with no sign of let up; several students watched Trampa leave, then glanced at their wristwatches, and resumed their writing. Harold lifted his red pencil out of his pocket and read over the first page. Every answer was correct and concise. Trampa's answers exuded authority. As Harold turned to the second page he smiled. When he finally read the last answer he flipped back to the first page and wrote 100% by Trampa's name.

Harold could not wait to tell Donald. Walking into his lab with the stack of test papers under his arm he said, "Take a look at this."

Donald nodded his head as he read each answer. "Hard to believe."

"He's finally working."

"Did you watch him?"

"Like a hawk. He never raised his eyes."

"Good, but don't let your guard down."

"If he'd shot me, I might not be so sure, but..."

By the end of the semester, John Trampa's test scores averaged in the mid-nineties, and Harold's confidence grew. After he had graded the final exams and posted the grades, Trampa dropped by Harold's office.

"Congratulations on a solid <u>A</u>, John."

"Thanks, but that's not why I came."

Harold sat back in his chair.

"I've really enjoyed organic this year. It's been an entirely different experience. I've been thinking I might major in chemistry. I guess that sounds pretty screwy after all that's happened, but, well…what do you think?"

"Why don't you talk with other chemists?"

"Could I work in your lab next semester, you know, to see if I like it?"

Harold's enthusiasm was waning. It was one thing to help him through the course, but quite another to have him in his research lab, where getting rid of him could pose problems later if things don't turn out well. "I don't know, John. You haven't had much lab experience. Better to wait until you've finished the course."

"Maybe you're right, Dr. Pitt. I wouldn't want to be a problem."

"It's not that, John. It's just a matter of experience." John Trampa's disappointment was so palpable that Harold could not bear it. "OK, you can help one of my graduate students. She's synthesizing a new compound and could use some help with the purification and analysis."

"Terrific, Dr. Pitt. When do I start?"

"Come, I'll introduce you." Harold led John into the lab where Lucy Alderman was measuring a melting point. When Harold suggested that John Trampa would be helping her, she smiled and extended her hand. In her second year of graduate study, Lucy's research project was just beginning to yield results.

"How much organic have you had, John?"

"Just one semester."

"Know how to take a melting point?"

"Sure."

Rising from her stool she said, "Good, finish this one."

John sat and looked into the scope at the magnified sample. Every few seconds he would look up at the thermometer and then back down at the sample in the capillary tube. Lucy and Harold walked to his office and left John alone.

"He's bright, and he learns fast, but he's had personal problems. Check his work carefully."

"He seems nice, Doctor Pitt."

Harold and Donald were sipping coffee in the coffee shop when Harold mentioned that John Trampa asked to work in his lab. Donald almost dropped his cup. "Not good!"

"He really wants to work. I think he deserves a chance."

Donald shook his head and shrugged. "It's too pat. I don't like it."

"I think you're overreacting, Donald."

"One year he shoots a professor over a grade; the next he's an A student doing research. No, I don't like it at all."

"What should I have done?"

"Put him off. He doesn't know enough."

"He's only helping Lucy. I'm willing to wait and hope. If he works out, it could be the best thing for him."

"I'm not thinking about him, Harold."

"I know."

The next week, after exams were over, John asked Lucy if she was planning to work during Christmas vacation.

"Sure. I'll take off a few days over Christmas, but I'll be back before new years. Dr. Pitt always works during the break."

"I'd rather not hang around the house. I'll come in too if it's OK. Give me your schedule for next semester, and I'll try to be here when you're in class. I'll keep your experiments going when you're out."

"Gee, thanks."

By the time classes started John had made himself useful enough to impress both Lucy and Harold. Lucy found his work reliable and accurate. By that time she and John had had lunch together several times in the university cafeteria, where they talked almost exclusively about their research.

One afternoon in mid-semester, when they were both in the lab, Lucy asked John to watch a distillation while she went to class. Soon after she left, he adjusted the heating element under the flask and went to the men's room. A strong acrid odor hit him when he returned to the lab several minutes later. Running to the lab bench he saw that the still was boiling over and vapor was pouring out of the receiving flask. The flask in the heater was charred and almost dry. Brown smoke had filled the room. He quickly turned off the heater and saw that instead

65

of lowering the setting he had raised it. He didn't know what to do. The compound Lucy was distilling had taken her three weeks to make; she needed it in the final step of her experiment. He flew into a rage and dismantled the apparatus and in so doing, the receiver flask with the little product that had collected slipped through his fingers and shattered on the bench. The crash of breaking glass unnerved him, and he picked up a glass condenser and threw it across the room, hitting another apparatus that Harold had set up earlier.

When Lucy walked in John was sitting at her desk with his face in his hands. "What happened?"

"I screwed up. That's what."

"But the still. Did you take it down?"

"What did you want me to do, for Christ sake?"

"Don't get excited, John. I'm just trying to find out what happened."

"Don't tell me not to get excited, bitch. I've worked hard for you. Show some goddamn appreciation."

His towering size and the tone of his voice shocked her, and she turned and began to walk out of the lab.

"Where you going?"

"To see Dr. Pitt."

Grabbing her arm he yelled, "Don't."

"Don't worry, John. It's OK. Accidents happen all the time in the lab." All the while she tried to loosen his grip.

"They do, huh? It's all right, huh? So now you'll tell Pitt I'm a jerk who screws things up, huh?"

She broke loose and ran out of the lab, not looking back, and into Harold who was at the door.

"What's going on?"

"I had an accident," John said, "and this bitch thinks it was my fault." He was rocking on his legs as if ready to charge.

"Lucy, why don't you go out while John and I talk?"

As she left, John stood akimbo facing Harold. "Now tell me what happened," Harold said with no show of emotion.

"It was an accident and her experiment's ruined. So what? I'm not perfect."

"Calm down, John. Anybody can have an accident. It's not as bad as you think."

"Damn it! I've had enough of people telling me what I think." He was yelling. "Screw you all."

Harold watched him storm out of the lab and slam the door. Thinking of Lucy he raced along the hall looking into every lab hoping John would not find her first. When he passed Donald's lab, Lucy was standing next to Donald crying. "I guess you were right, Donald. He blew his cork. Come on, Lucy. He's gone. I'll take you home."

"He knows where I live."

"My home then, as soon as I call the campus police. Stay right here."

Lucy stood shaking as Harold made his call from Donald's phone. He told the security officer what had happened and that Trampa was very agitated and could be dangerous. "He's the one who shot Professor Quinone last year."

The security officer said they would send some officers right away.

When Harold and Lucy left, Donald sat at his desk still shaking, his heart racing.

By week's end Lucy had begun to feel like a hostage in Harold's home. Harold's wife, Sally Anne, had taken her in with great understanding and love, but Lucy could not shake off the face of the raging young man. That evening the phone rang in Harold Pitt's home.

"I'm John Trampa's father. What's the idea sending the police after my son?"

"I had no choice. He became violent and threatened another student."

"And what did she do to him?"

"Your son got excited about nothing, really, Dr. Trampa. He was running a distillation for my graduate student and had an accident. It could have happened to anybody, but he flew into a rage and started throwing equipment."

"Is this the way you treat unpaid employees?"

"He wasn't an employee. He wanted to do research. I don't know, maybe…anyway I agreed."

"So he's doing your research for no pay?"

"Look, I gave your son an opportunity to learn the only way anyone can learn chemistry—first hand. And I didn't ask him; he asked me."

"And why was that girl bossing him around? She's just another student. Right?"

"She's a graduate student."

"I see; she's doing your research for you."

"What do you want, Dr. Trampa?"

"I don't like people using my son and then punishing him, especially somebody like you and that bitch you have doing whatever she does for you."

"OK, you've told me. Goodbye."

Lucy walked into the living room having heard most of the conversation. When Harold turned around she was sobbing. "I guess you heard; that was John's father."

She continued to sob uncontrollably and lay face down on the couch.

"He's a real bully. I can see what Dr. Quinone had to put up with…Don't worry, Lucy. John dropped out of school."

"Are you sure?"

"I called the registrar's office this afternoon."

At that news Lucy sat up and wiped her face.

Next morning Harold met Donald in the mail room and told him about Trampa's phone call.

Donald was sifting through his mail as he answered, "He did the same to me. Don't worry." At one letter Donald stopped and said, "Oh, no!"

"What is it?" Harold asked, scooping his mail out of his box.

"The return address gave me a chill. Look."

Harold read the name, John Trampa, in the upper left corner of the envelope. As he looked through his mail he found one addressed to him.

Looking over Harold's shoulder Donald said, "Mine seems to be a copy of yours."

They both silently read the letter. "Sounds like he's coming out of it," Harold said.

"I wouldn't be so sure. He sent copies to his father and his therapist."

Donald reread the letter aloud:

Dear Dr. Quinone: I am writing to ease your concern. I have at last found peace. I've been trying too hard to accomplish things that don't matter. Realizing this I feel much better. Over these past months, probably years, I've been in constant turmoil about things that don't matter, but that is all behind me now. I have finally figured out the real cause of my turmoil and I am set on a solution. I assure you things will soon be better.

I want you and Dr. Pitt to know that I appreciate all you have tried to do for me, more than those who should. I thank you for that. John

"Why do you think there's a problem?"

"Damn it, Harold. It's a suicide note. He's found peace; he's settling his debts and soon it'll be over. Don't you see? He's saying goodbye."

"We should call somebody."

Donald picked up the phone book and looked down the T's until he came to Dr. John Trampa. Here it is." Donald picked up the phone and dialed. "I want to speak to Dr. Trampa. This is Dr. Quinone at the University."

"I'm sorry, but Dr. Trampa's gone home for the day."

"Can you give me his home number?"

"Sorry, we can't give that out."

"Damn it, this is important. It concerns his son."

"I'll tell him you called. Please leave a number where he can reach you."

Donald gave it and hung up.

Both Harold and Donald waited in Donald's office for nearly an hour, but no call. Finally Donald said, "That's bad. Either this guy's a real bastard and can't be bothered or John's done it."

The phone rang and Donald did not wait for the second ring. "Hello, Dr. Quinone speaking."

"Dr. Quinone, I'm Detective Rodriguez from Police Headquarters. You may remember me from the Trampa trial."

"Sure. What's wrong?"

"Do you know a Professor Harold Pitt?"

"He's right here."

"Put him on, please." When Harold identified himself, Rodriguez said, "I understand John Trampa was working for you."

"Yes; until about a week ago."

"What happened?"

"He had an accident and spoiled another student's experiment. When she asked him what happened he flew into a rage and became abusive."

"Have you met his father?" Rodriguez asked.

"No, but I've talked with him on the phone. Can you tell me why you're asking these questions?"

"The boy shot himself a while ago. He's in critical condition, not expected to live."

"My God," Harold said. "Donald, John's attempted suicide."

"How is he?"

"Bad." Then to the detective, "Are you sure it was suicide?"

"Yes. He was sitting under a tree in his parents' back yard. His mother heard a shot and went out to see what had happened and saw him on the ground with blood gushing from his head and the gun in his hand."

"What can we do?"

"I'll be in touch."

"What about his father. You asked if I know him."

"He's claiming you and professor Quinone drove him to it."

"Certainly you don't believe that?"

"I don't believe anything yet. Thank you."

When Harold hung up he was perspiring and looking out the window.

"What is it?"

"The father says we drove him to it."

"Bastard!"

"Harold! What are you doing home? It's not even lunchtime."

He told Sally Anne about the letter and the phone call, and she sat up with a look of disbelief. "He can't blame you."

"I think the guy's pathological the way he treated his son and then tried to cover for him."

"Are you in trouble?"

"I don't know. The detective didn't sound like it. He was trying to get the facts, I guess."

"Why don't you go to the police?"

"That's so against everything I've always known, but…I'll think about it. Donald might want to go along."

"Certainly the detective will look into the trial record. It's obvious Donald tried to help the boy."

"Is anything ever obvious?"

The next day was Saturday and Harold came home from work and sat in his overstuffed chair in their sparse living room looking up at the ceiling; Sally Anne sat across from him on the sofa. "You know," he said, "when things begin to look good, watch out."

"Please, dear. Everybody knows you did all you could to help him."

He stood and punched on the TV. "Maybe we'll pick up something on the twelve o'clock news."

The first item on the news was brief: "The young man who was found shot at his parents' home this morning died a few minutes ago. His name was John Trampa. He was a student in the university. His father is a prominent Tampa internist."

Harold froze. "My God!"

"Daddy says you're the kindest professor in the department. Nobody can accuse you of anything."

"Depends on your color."

"Oh, Harold. Don't start that."

"I gotta see Donald. If we don't go to the police they'll come for us."

"I'm fixing fried chicken, grits and green beans for supper. Think about that when you feel bad."

Donald was sitting at his desk staring at the blank wall when Harold walked in. "Did you hear?"

"Yeah. Hazel called. It was on TV."

"Let's go down there before they call us, Donald."

As Donald stood, the phone rang. "This is Lieutenant Rodriguez at Police Headquarters. The Trampa boy died. I'd like you and Dr. Pitt to come down for a statement. I called Dr. Pitt's home, but he wasn't in."

"He's here. We just heard and were about to go see you. It'll take about twenty minutes."

The drive down I-275 was busy, and a tie up delayed them. Forty-five minutes had passed when they walked into Lieutenant Rodriguez's office.

"Thanks for coming, gentlemen. Please sit down."

The Lieutenant's office was painted a battleship gray color and had two windows. Donald envied Rodriguez for them. The lieutenant called in a stenographer and asked Donald to relate what had happened saying: "Since you were named in the letter, I need your statement." Donald told about the shooting and the trial, and Lt. Rodriguez asked Harold to do the same. When Harold had finished, Rodriguez told the stenographer to type it up for the record. Then, pulling a cigarette out of a pack in his shirt pocket he said, "I've read the trial transcript, and I take my hat off to you, Dr. Quinone. Most people wouldn't be so generous. The boy was more deeply troubled than anybody thought. Apparently he sent the same letter to several others." He lit the cigarette with a paper match. "Now we know what it meant. It may not have been obvious to you, but the psychiatrist called his father as soon as he read it."

"We suspected it and tried to call his father, but he'd gone home and didn't return our call," Harold said.

"Well, when the psychiatrist got to Dr. Trampa and told him what he thought the letter meant, Dr. Trampa immediately drove home, but he was too late. His wife, in hysterics, pointed to the tree where the boy was sprawled out, his fingers still gripping the revolver. His father ran to him and started kicking and cursing him. When Mrs. Trampa saw that, she fainted, and Dr. Trampa ran to help her up. When he went back to his son he saw that he was still alive and ran back into the house and called 911.

The ambulance got there in four minutes and all the time they were moving the boy into the ambulance, Trampa yelled obscenities at them."

"Why?" Harold said.

"According to the ambulance people, he told them they took too long to get there, and he didn't like the way they were handling him. His wife hadn't revived consciousness, so one of the medics examined her and said it looked like a heart attack. They took her too. When the emergency room doctors saw that the boy had been shot they called here, and I went to investigate. That was when I met Dr. Trampa. He was yelling at the doctors and nurses and at his wife, who was lying in the hall with a doctor working on her. She died a few minutes later."

"The man's deranged," Donald said.

"When I tried to talk to him," Rodriguez said, "he yelled at me too and said I'd better find out who was responsible or he'd have my job. I've dealt with lots of hysterics, but this was the worst. I kept up my questioning until I had what I needed. If I had my way, he'd be locked up. You're not under suspicion, gentlemen. That's crystal clear. If anybody's to blame it's his father. That's why he tried so hard to blame everybody else."

"What happened to him?" Harold asked.

"According to the hospital administration, he's back at his office, working as usual."

On the way home, Donald said, "I think we should stop for a beer."

"I don't think one's going to be enough."

They stopped at a small tavern near campus and talked for over an hour.

As they stood to leave, Harold said, "I always thought professors led boring lives."

"Me too, but the world is full of crazies."

"Yeah, walking free, posing as normal."

TIME

Edgar Margin

Edgar Margin held the elevator door and glanced at his watch as the young woman waddled toward him, smiling apologetically. His watch showed 7:56. The heavy girl swayed side to side, step by step, as did her short-cropped, limp hair. As the door began to close, she held out her hand to stop it.

Good God! He thought. *Five seconds.*

When she was in, Edgar Margin pressed the close door button and then the fourth floor button. The young student's obesity revolted him, but he forced a smile, thought a moment, and said, "It takes four seconds for the door to close if you punch the floor button. However, if you punch the close button first, the door closes in one second. By that simple act I save thirty seconds each workday; that's approximately two hours a year."

The girl looked at him blankly with her backpack dragging on the floor at the end of her arm.

"Pardon me," Edgar Margin said. "What floor did you want?"

"Actually, I was coming to see you, Professor Margin."

He looked down at his wristwatch. "I have a faculty meeting in three minutes. See me after class. You are—?"

"Sarah Lamb."

Pretending to recall her name he said, "Of course." He remembered her in class, the girl with the fat legs and arms. "You sit in the front row by the window."

Edgar Margin recoiled as she nodded, blushed, and raised a meaty arm to push back her short, brown hair. His eyes became magnets drawn to slacks that bulged almost to bursting. As he tried to avoid her eyes, a pungent perspiration odor found its way into his nostrils, and he stiffened and looked away to avoid it.

Neither spoke as the elevator moved up, the girl fidgeting with her backpack, Edgar Margin at attention, seemingly deep in thought and trying to hold his breath, knowing that when he took the next breath the scent would still be there. He looked at her eyes; she smiled girlishly and looked away.

A red and white striped tie provided striking counterpoint to his gray, three-piece suit. He liked to look fit and hoped to be a model to his students and colleagues. Slim and sturdily built, he was rather handsome with pinkish cheeks. Beneath light eyebrows that almost disappeared into his fair skin, his large, sky-blue eyes bulged slightly, conveying thoughtfulness, intellectuality, and interest. But those eyes could as well become penetrating, dogmatic, even accusing and judgmental. His facial features seemed delicate, overly handsome, one might say effeminate. Having begun to lose his sandy hair in his twenties, he wore what was left of it in a crew cut, as if in retribution. Now nearing forty, he had come to terms with impending baldness by using a cream that kept each hair standing at attention the way he liked to stand—ramrod straight.

The elevator door opened, and Edgar Margin held it open and nodded gallantly.

"No, thanks, Dr. Margin. I'm going back down. See you in class."

Edgar Margin stepped out toward his office, the tapping of his hard heels on the plastic tile floor reverberating in the long corridor. He always counted them: twenty-seven taps, no more, no less. The small window at the end of the hall offered a sense of movement toward a clear objective in those twenty-seven steps, which he had timed as taking thirteen seconds. He was a human metronome ticking out clear, methodical, clean, orderly time in a space clear of artifice, his mission to ferret out scientific truths that would contribute to a more orderly world, a more precise, more rational, more understandable world.

Edgar walked into the conference room as the secretary was hovering over a serving cart. She had just plugged in the coffee urn and was arranging Danish pastries, bagels, cream cheese, and jellies in neat rows. Mrs. Singleton smiled, "Good morning, Dr. Margin."

"Good morning." He looked down. His wristwatch read 8:00. To Edgar Margin, punctual meant neither early nor late. With an impatient smile he looked around at the empty chairs neatly arranged around the long conference table.

"Good morning, Edgar, Mrs. Singleton" George Buchner said as he walked in. Six feet four inches tall, George Buchner slouched seemingly to compensate for his gangly body. He was far from handsome with thick, straight, unruly, red hair, freckles and protruding chin and nose. But his warm, toothy smile and strong handshake softened his otherwise angular visage.

Edgar Margin could not hold back: "This meeting was called for 8:00; it's 8:04."

"One of these days everybody will show up on time, and we'll all faint," George said smiling.

"You're the chairman, George."

"Right, Edgar. Time is money." Then smiling, "But haste makes waste. They'll be here directly."

Edgar lifted his watch into view.

"Edgar, I'd like you to call the tenure committee together."

"For what purpose?"

"Brucine Justice."

"What about Brucine Justice?"

"Tenure, Edgar. Surely you know she's put herself up again."

"Don't make me guess at your meaning, George. Communication depends on clear understanding."

"Well, she's put herself up and we have to act."

"By act I assume you mean we must decide whether to recommend to grant or to deny tenure?"

"Right, Edgar." Slouching in his chair, George began to thumb through his notes.

"May I assume that her tenure has not already been determined elsewhere?"

"Of course not, Edgar. The tenure process begins with us."

"You mean with the department faculty."

"Yes, Edgar. With the faculty."

"I'll call a meeting this afternoon."

Donald Quinone was the last to arrive at 8:16. Overweight, pear-shaped, shirttail ballooning in back, and shoulder-length black hair across his brow, he stood over the coffee urn, drew a full cup, broke open a plastic container of coffee whitener, and poured it in as he let out a loud sigh. Most of the faculty members had finished their coffee and pastries and were chatting, waiting for George to start the meeting. Brucine Justice, the only woman on the chemistry faculty, stirred her coffee as she glanced sphinx-like at each colleague. Conscious of her figure, she passed up the pastries and drank her coffee black. Her colleagues' disdain did not bother her, but only fed her feminist crusader self-image. No one could miss her overt, sexually attractive movements or her perfume, which had announced her entrance as the door opened. Trying not to seem interested, male faculty members remained aloof even as they sneaked glances. Edgar tried never to catch her eye because she would wink, and he would blush. Thirty-two and well proportioned, with shoulder-length wavy auburn hair, large, deep brown eyes, and full, sensuous lips, she enjoyed center stage. In her presence Edgar Margin kept his rigid posture and struggled to ignore her, though his pulse always increased when she entered the room.

I stretch to hold his hand. It's so big mine gets lost in it. They talk and laugh. She giggles and Daddy smiles. "Son, get me a cup of water from the dispenser in the hall." I walk back with the cone-shaped paper cup, staring down, walking carefully trying not to spill it. I look at his secretary and my arm hits the door. Her dress is all wet. Dad picks me up. He shouts: "Be more careful." She's mad. I'm scared.

Donald Quinone took a Danish pastry and a napkin, pulled a chair noisily away from the table, and sat next to Edgar across from Brucine.

"This is an important meeting," Edgar whispered.

In a voice that rippled across the room, Donald Quinone said, "You know me, Edgar; I like to be fashionably late."

"What do you mean by that?"

"Just a joke, Edgar."

"That's insensitive and inconsiderate." Edgar's eyes bulged.

"What is?"

"You know what I mean: your tardiness," Edgar's teeth were clenched.

Donald dunked the Danish into his coffee. Then he looked at Brucine and winked, as if to beat her to the wink.

She smiled and lifted an eyebrow.

After dragging the faculty through a morass of familiar detail about the kind of person they were hoping to hire and how important this hire was to the growth of the department, George Buchner began a summary of each of the three final candidates' qualifications.

"Anyone who has taken the trouble to peruse the files knows all this, Dr. Buchner," Edgar Margin said. "I move we vote."

"Haste makes waste, Dr. Margin," George Buchner said. "I want to be sure we all know who we're voting for."

After hesitating to select the proper wording Edgar said, "In other words we must waste time because a few of our colleagues haven't bothered to examine the files."

"You're right, Edgar. The files have been out for four weeks, but sometimes it's not easy to find the time."

"I'm as busy as anybody, and I found the time," Edgar said, as he looked over the heads of his colleagues.

"Well, then ... any questions or comments on any of the candidates?" George asked, looking around.

Raising his eyebrows and smiling maliciously Donald Quinone said, "How about summarizing each candidate's file for us, Edgar, and give us your recommendation."

Without looking at him Edgar said, "That won't be necessary, Dr. Quinone."

Hearing no other comments, George Buchner passed out slips of paper and asked each to write the name of one candidate. With little hesitation each person scribbled a name on the slip, some hiding the writing with his hand, folded it, and slid it down the table to the chair. Donald slid his unfolded and face up. As George Buchner counted the ballots, his smile broadened. Finally he announced the unanimous result. No one was surprised, except Edgar Margin, who always expected the worst. But even he was smiling when the group began to murmur.

"Just a moment please," George said. "Before we adjourn I have another item. "I've received a directive from the President's office. Beginning next Monday we will no longer have class bells."

"What?" Edgar said, slapping his hand on the table.

"It's part of the President's austerity program."

"But we haven't been consulted. It's preposterous!"

"It's done, Edgar. I don't like it either, and I let him know, but I'm afraid it's water under the bridge."

"Tell you what, Edgar," Donald Quinone said, "I'll go to your classroom and tinkle when it's time to start."

"I've had enough of your facetious joking. This is serious." Edgar stood.

"Easy, Edgar," Donald said. "I didn't turn them off."

"Of all the inept administrations this is the worst," Edgar said, still standing.

A murmur moved around the table like a wave, more in surprise at Edgar's outburst than at the loss of class bells.

"Gentlemen, please," George said. "Let's keep our perspective."

"There is no perspective," Donald said. "Edgar's right. This administration is one-eyed and one-dimensional."

"Does austerity include holding up tenure?" Brucine Justice said.

"Tenure was not mentioned, Brucine."

"It better not be."

Edgar was not ready to drop the issue. "Isn't the world chaotic enough? Are we supposed to smile gratefully as this small vestige of order disappears? And merely to save a few pennies? Well, perhaps I don't give a damn either." With that little speech he rose and walked out before George Buchner could adjourn the meeting.

But Edgar could not turn it off that easily. His head throbbed and his heart pounded as he strode down the hall, heels pounding the floor like primitive drumbeats. Through the flames roaring in his brain, he did not hear Donald Quinone call. He thought only about his well-honed classroom performance that would be demolished: opening the door dramatically with the ringing bell, setting his materials on the lectern, ceremoniously returning to the door to lock out tardy students. No time wasted on chitchat; no sports, no politics. Edgar never pandered. Standing dramatically silent, arms crossed over his chest, he would wait until the inevitable hush had spread across the room. Then, after posing a provocative question, he would carefully weave strands of facts and logic and truth on a loom of intellectual thought to lay strong, clear meaning and clarity over his original question, all the while allowing no queries to interrupt and wrinkle his artfully woven scientific fabric. As the final punctuation to his fifty-minute presentation he would drop his chalk into the chalk tray as the bell's echo reverberated. All that would now disappear with little fanfare or clanging of contrary opinion.

"Hey!" Donald said, catching up with him.

"Not now, Donald."

"Not now what? I haven't said anything yet."

"Can't you see how upset I am?"

"Because of the bells?"

"There's no conscience, no educational foresight, no concern for truth and order. Only money, money, money."

"How about a cup of coffee?"

"Why so calm?"

"I don't like it either, but it's not the end of the world. Come on, Edgar."

"I don't believe it's to save money. How much can it cost to ring bells a dozen times a day? Not even pennies a month. But no one cares. It's eat or be eaten."

"You're eating pretty well, Edgar: early promotion, lots of funding and graduate students. What's the beef?"

Edgar could neither argue nor agree. He had become full professor at thirty-five with a long list of papers and grants, but his fame felt hollow. His work, once fun and exciting, had become drudgery. He felt he had been digging in the same hole for years, and was finding only sand and no gold. All his life he had sought nuggets of truth. It was the way he saw chemistry–the search for abiding, natural truth. That search had excited him and sparked a ruthless drive. And his work had been sound, his results true, but they had hatched few new questions. He had answered the same question over and over. Now he lived in fear that funding might fizzle if people began to wonder where his work was leading. But most of all he was tired of digging. The hole he had dug seemed empty, cavernous, sterile. In his perennial quest for funding and more papers, he was spending most of his time writing grant proposals and prodding his graduate students to keep digging. Where would he find time for new ideas? *If only I had more time.* But that could not be the problem. Somewhere in his mind lurked the suspicion that he was digging in vain, that he had buried real truth in a deep, dark cavern where he would never find it.

"The beef?" Edgar asked. "Oh … You wouldn't understand, Donald."

"I'm too low on the food chain, eh?"

Edgar's face dropped its scowl for the first time. "No offense, Donald, but …"

"But it's more fun to be miserable."

Edgar raised his head, straightened his back, and looked down on Donald.

"Brucine's the one who ought to be worried," Donald said. "There's no way she'll get tenure."

"As committee chairman, I can't comment."

"I'm on the damn committee too, but I've got an opinion, and so have you. One lousy note in a second rate journal in five years? And her students can't stand her."

"This discussion belongs in the committee." Then, looking down at his watch, "Sorry, Donald. I have one minute to get to class." Edgar turned and walked to his office. Seconds later, he slammed his door shut and jogged to the elevator with his briefcase under his arm. Donald watched him fly past.

After standing silent for a few moments in front of the class, Edgar glanced down at his watch and began as the second hand touched twelve. Soon his lecture began to flow as usual: a beautifully woven, rational explanation of the simple truth of acids and bases that, in his opinion, only the dullest student could fail to comprehend. Dropping his chalk into the chalk tray, it hit as the bell sounded. He smiled, gathered his lecture notes, slipped them into his briefcase, slid the textbook in, and turned to the door ignoring the chaos, as the auditorium exploded with slamming books and notebooks, unzipping and re-zipping backpacks, banging of receding arm rests and folding seats, and the rising chorus of chattering.

Just before he reached the door he heard his name. *Oh, no. No questions. Not now.*

"Dr. Margin ... Sarah Lamb ... this morning, remember?"

Edgar stopped and turned to face the huge girl as she lifted her backpack over her shoulder.

"Well?"

"It's about the last chapter."

"After lunch. I've got something now."

"One o'clock?"

"Fine, fine," he said, turning and walking out the door.

In his office he picked up the phone and dialed Donald Quinone's number. "Can you meet now to discuss tenure for Dr. Justice?" he asked brusquely. "In the conference room."

"What's the rush?"

"I'm busy and I'd like to get it over with."

"OK, Edgar. See you in a few minutes."

"I'll call Joe Adams."

Four minutes later Edgar waited in the conference room for the rest of his tenure committee. Joe Adams arrived first. Edgar noted that he was one minute late. Without speaking Joe sat in one of the armchairs near the wall. Joe Adams was the oldest and most senior member of the department. Bushy graying hair atop a thin body made him look like a mop leaned against the chair. He had joined the faculty when the university opened and was approaching retirement age, though he looked older.

Dropping his frail frame into one of the student desks near the wall he said, "Donald's down the hall. He'll be here in a minute."

"I don't understand why he's always late."

Donald Quinone shuffled in holding a cup of black coffee and sat at the conference table. "OK. Let the game begin."

"We have only one tenure case this year. You've read her folder, I trust?"

"Didn't take long," Donald said.

"Shall we vote and get this over with?" Joe Adams said.

"No matter how we feel about this candidate, we should discuss her merits and demerits," Edgar said. "Dr. Adams, would you summarize for us?"

"Come on, Margin," Adams said. "She's the worst tenure candidate I've ever seen."

"I agree," Donald said.

"Donald, would you please comment on her publications?"

"It's singular, Edgar. One short note in five years."

"Did you read it?"

"Sure. She's dotted a few i's and crossed a few t's. Nothing even close to significant."

"Dr. Adams?"

"OK, Margin. We'll go through it: Her one and only paper is half a page long and reports some properties of three well-known compounds. The properties she gives had not been reported before. It narrowly qualifies as original work, but hardly significant."

"Does either of you have anything to say about her teaching?"

Through a broad yawn Donald said, "Her students say she seems unprepared and doesn't like questions during class."

"I don't like to be interrupted either," Edgar said.

"But you can answer their questions, Edgar. It appears she can't."

"Look, Margin," Joe said. "I've got too much to do to spend an hour on this. It's the most clear-cut case I've ever seen. I vote to deny."

"Me too," Donald said.

They both looked at Edgar.

"It's easy for you, but I have to write the report. How shall I word it?"

Joe Adams leaned back and, as if reading from a prepared statement, said, "Her only publication is brief and inconsequential. According to her teaching evaluations and the personal testimony of Joe Adams, who attended several of her classes last term, her teaching is shallow, poorly organized, generally rambling, and well below this department's standard. We therefore recommend that tenure be denied." He took a sip of coffee and said, "I don't think we need to mention that she is combative and uncooperative."

"I also sat in on several of her classes," Donald said, "and I agree."

Edgar was still scribbling. "All right. What you say is true enough. I'll clean it up and get it to Dr. Buchner this afternoon."

"What's your vote, Edgar?" Donald asked.

"The same as yours. Do you want a formal vote?"

"No. Just like to be precise," Donald said, winking. Then, turning to Joe Adams, "Good job, Joe. We through, Edgar?"

"Meeting adjourned."

Edgar remained in the conference room recopying Joe's statement so the secretary could read it. He looked up and saw Brucine's face through the small window in the door. Seeing him alone, she came in.

"Well?"

"Well what?"

"Yes or no?"

"We only recommend. The chairman adds his recommendation. The provost makes the final decision."

"In other words you voted to deny."

Without looking up, Edgar nodded.

"Relax, Edgar. I won't shoot. I just don't want to waste any time with the next step."

"What next step?"

"See you later."

Edgar walked to the department chair's office and handed the secretary the report. Donald was waiting outside the door.

"How did she take it?"

"How did who take what?"

"Come on, Edgar. I saw you talking with Brucine."

"She was calm, as if she expected it."

"Smart girl."

"I think she's up to something."

As a full professor, Edgar occupied one of the larger faculty offices. He kept it spotless and in perfect order with his books smoothly arranged in the bookcase and his desk clear of everything except what he was working on at the moment. His desk stood in the center of the office with his swivel chair backed against the window and facing the bookcase. On a cork bulletin board to his right, thumbtacks held up eight of his most recent research papers. To his left stood a single straight-back chair; there was no room for a second. The window behind him overlooked a quadrangle of crossing walkways cut into a grassy plane from which the administration building rose like a monument a hundred yards away. The palms around the chemistry building had reached his fourth floor window and soon would block his view. The window provided light; his books provided color.

Spread before him on his desk lay an open journal, a pad and pencil, a bag lunch, and a half-pint carton of low fat milk from the basement coffee shop. He reached in and extracted a neatly wrapped ham and cheese sandwich and an apple. Laying a paper napkin on his lap, he began to eat. As he munched he perused the journal, noting down articles related to his research. As he began jotting notes he heard a knock on the door.

"Come in," he said, continuing to scribble.

Sarah Lamb opened the door and peeked in, apparently worried by Edgar's tone and his large, staring eyes.

He looked down at his watch and said, "Well, don't stand there; come in and sit down."

Sarah Lamb removed the backpack from her shoulder, extracted her textbook, laid the backpack on the floor beside her, and began flipping pages.

Daddy's so tall, and handsome in his new suit. "You shouldn't wear your new suit to eat supper at home," she says. "I don't spill food like you do. Maybe you shouldn't eat so damn much," he says. When he talks to her like that my stomach tightens, and I can't eat. Mom and Daddy sit facing each other at the table. She's wearing a housedress. She's so big her bottom hangs over her chair. Why does Daddy smile when he's angry? It scares me. I start to cry. I know I shouldn't. Mom puts her hand on my arm and tells me to finish my mashed potatoes. Daddy says, "Leave him alone."

After a long while, as Edgar tapped his pencil rhythmically on his desk, his mind wandering, she found the page and laid the book on Edgar's desk. "This," she said. "The chart; I don't get it."

Edgar glanced at a chart that showed a plot of the energy of a hydrogen atom as the electron moves away from the nucleus. "What's the question?"

"How did they figure it out? I mean can they actually measure that sort of thing?"

Expecting the usual question about what will be on the test or how to get extra credit, Edgar smiled.

"Very good, Ms. Lamb! You're absolutely right. We can't actually measure the energy of an electron as it moves away from its nucleus. Those figures are calculated from theory. You assume a distance and then calculate the expected energy using quantum mechanics."

"Then it's not really true?"

"Well, truth isn't that simple, Ms. Lamb. Theories are not true in the usual sense of the word. We assume they're true so we can solve problems we couldn't solve otherwise."

"Then we're learning things that aren't really true?"

Slightly flustered at having to explain a metaphysical idea, Edgar said, "Let me put it this way: We use a theory as long as it's useful. When a theory no longer gives us useful or accurate answers, we look for a new theory. Anyway, you shouldn't worry about that. We're teaching current scientific theories so you can go out into the world prepared to solve problems. If you get into science, perhaps someday you'll create a new theory."

"Did you say quanta mechanism?"

"Quantum mechanics. It's very complex, but it helps us comprehend atomic behavior."

"We going to do quantum mechanics?"

"Heavens, no. It's too sophisticated for a beginning course. That comes in senior physical chemistry. Are you a chemistry major, Ms. Lamb?"

"I want to be a nurse. I liked nursing chemistry last year. It was pretty easy, so I thought I'd sign up for your course."

"Commendable, Ms. Lamb. You enjoying it?"

"You get a little far out once in a while. But once I catch on, it's fun."

"Well, Ms. Lamb, come by anytime. And don't worry about an appointment."

"Thanks, Dr. Margin."

She stuffed the book into the backpack, zipped it up, lifted it to her shoulder and stood. "Thanks again."

As she walked out the door, Edgar Margin's brain labored trying to estimate the energy she expended moving that much mass. *Poor girl. Nearly two hundred pounds; ninety-one kilograms.* After a moment he stopped trying to compute the energy in his head. *How could a bright girl let herself go like that?*

He picked up the remains of his sandwich and resumed his lunch. As he recalled the faculty meeting and the class bells the dark curtain of anger descended.

Vivian went directly to the bedroom and laid out her purchases on the bed to show Edgar. Edgar had been anxious lately, so she thought she would model them for him, hoping to bring a smile. Edgar walked in a few minutes later, slammed the door, and sat in the living room sofa. It was a bright room, not large, but well furnished with traditional furniture upholstered in flowery pastels. Sheer, billowy curtains over two large windows let in a soft breeze and lent the room an air of relaxation. But it was all wasted on Edgar Margin. Because of its proximity to campus, Edgar had chosen the contemporary two-storey house on the edge of a new subdivision. Vivian had preferred the older, upscale Hyde Park area, but gave in after a year-long argument

"It's four o'clock. You're early. Didn't Tom make it?"

"It's 4:19. I didn't feel like handball."

"You know what they say about all work and no play, Eddy-Teddy."

"I'm not like you: I don't enjoy wasting time."

"It would be nice if once you could come home with a smile instead of a grump."

Fashion model thin and nearly as tall as Edgar, Vivian did not shy away from high-heels. One would not say she was beautiful, but her bright, open face lifted barriers. In her late thirties, she retained a simple, girlish appearance with bleached hair poofed out like a halo, pale pink complexion, and clear, green eyes containing not a trace of hazel or of artifice. But focused as he was on detail, Edgar could see time's footprints around her eyes and lips. The hollows in her cheeks gave her face a shriveled look. He still thought of her as attractive, but distrusted what he considered unnecessary frivolity in her grooming.

"Why does a woman your age try to look like a teenager?"

"Screw you, Edgar!"

"Must you always resort to profanity?"

"Must you always be so mean? Sometimes ... well, you're just mean."

"Tom was late again. I waited five minutes and left."

"Way to go, Eddy-Teddy! You showed him."

"If I let him get away with it, well ..."

"Either way he controls you."

"Please, Vivian. I've had enough abuse for one day."

"Never any fun for Eddy-Teddy," She said and turned to the kitchen.

"What do you want me to do?"

"For such a brilliant scientist you're pretty dumb, Eddy-Teddy."

"Damn it! I've told you not to call me that."

"Profanity from Eddy-Teddy? Your pressure gauge ready to blow?"

He returned fuming to the living room sofa and sat with his elbows on his knees, his face in his fists.

"Didn't anything good happen today?" she asked standing at the kitchen door. "A good student paper? A pleasant lunch? Anything?"

"The tenure committee met about Brucine Justice."

"And?"

"And what?"

"What did you decide?"

"You know we only recommend; besides, tenure deliberations are confidential."

"For Heaven sake, Eddy-Teddy. I'm your wife. Besides, you brought it up."

"I'll depend on your discretion ... we voted to deny."

"That was the good thing for today? Poor Brucine; and the only woman in the department."

"Tenure isn't based on gender."

"Well, why did you hire her?"

"You may remember I was against it, and so were the majority, but we didn't have any women in the department, and ... well, there was pressure. As usual the administration smothered the facts in hot air."

"So you all didn't want her from the start."

"She had a chance to prove herself."

"What about her students?"

"They don't like her either."

"Poor Brucine."

"She's incompetent, for heaven sake. Why are you so bent on defending an incompetent?"

"I'm just thinking of her future."

"She'll be better off elsewhere."

Vivian returned to the kitchen.

"That's not all."

"Not another crisis."

When he told her about the class bells, anger twisted itself into a smile. "So, all this fuming, all this dumping on me and Brucine because they've stopped the bells?"

"You're no better than Donald Quinone."

"Poor, compulsive Eddy-Teddy. You're an expert in driving yourself nuts."

"Are you suggesting I drive you crazy?"

"Never happen, Eddy-Teddy, but your compulsions aren't much fun."

"I can't be like you, Vivian. Incompetence drives me crazy, and I'm surrounded by it."

"Really?"

"I don't mean you, Vivian."

"Can't you see you're in a straitjacket?"

Sensing an old, unspeakable urge rising in his breast, he stiffened. His brain whirred like an overheated dynamo. *I'd never do that ... never ... never.*

"Look, Vivian, we see the world differently. Maybe I'm a bit compulsive, but I don't hurt anyone. I demand the same order of myself. Can't you indulge me a little? Life's no picnic."

"I try to concentrate on the picnic part. With you it ain't easy."

"What is happiness without duty, character, integrity, responsibility?"

"Or, … never mind …"

"Oh, God! Please, Vivian. Don't start that. It wasn't my fault."

"I can't remember the last time we made love."

"With all the pressure I don't need this. How can you expect …"

"That's one thing you've taught me: don't expect much."

"Is your life that bad?"

"I don't like to complain, but …"

"But you're going to."

"You're impossible, Edgar. Unbending, overbearing … shit, I'm not going through all this again."

"Let's settle down and look at things clearly. It's my career. Nothing I can point to, but I just feel things are too tentative. I can't express it, but …"

"I can. You're so involved in your career that you have nothing left for wife, family, or anything."

"It always comes to that, doesn't it?"

"Without a family and with your obsession with career, Edgar, what can possibly hold us together?"

"Have you forgotten? I wanted one too."

"Sure, after years of pleading. Sometimes a woman's window of opportunity is small."

"I can't take this, Vivian. We tried; it didn't happen; it wasn't my fault. Why can't you accept truth and reality?"

"Truth is easy for you, but what do I have to show for these ten years?" Her lips were trembling.

He rose and started up the stairs.

"You want me to be as miserable as you."

Hearing Donald Quinone's word in Vivian mouth rattled him. When he was half way up she was still looking up, as if waiting for a response.

The violent urge tightened. He shook his head to loosen its grip, swallowed hard and said, "I'm truly sorry, Vivian. Truly. You've got to believe that."

When he reached the top step and looked down, she said, "Go lie down a while. I'll call you when dinner's ready.

Like a little boy he went to his room and fell into bed.

Dinner went down with deadening silence. Each had learned how far to push that issue without an irreversible blow-up. Edgar picked at his plate, ate little, but the roiling would not stop. When Vivian tried to talk about her purchases he smiled dutifully and nodded in a way that told her he was not hearing. Finally, in desperation she said, "I'm sorry, Edgar. I shouldn't have mentioned it. Please try to forget it."

"This steak is excellent, and the mushrooms add a great flavor."

"You haven't touched your wine."

"I don't feel like wine tonight. The supper was good, though. Really."

"We're back to banalities."

"It's better than arguing."

"People argue and fight about things they care about. This is the kind of conversation I have with the grocery check-out clerk."

Edgar stood and said, "I'll help with the dishes."

He picked up his dishes and hers and carried them to the kitchen. "Relax," he said. "I'll clean up."

"Oh, no. The last time it took a week to find everything. I'll help."

He smiled gratefully.

When they had finished in the kitchen Edgar went to his study, and Vivian stayed in the living room to read.

Coming to bed two hours later, Edgar found Vivian's peaceful breathing irritating. He slipped off his robe like a banana peel and slid into bed quietly and began to review the day. When he looked at the clock by his bed, it was 2:46. His heart raced. Anger welling, he rose and went down the hall to his study, opened a journal, and stared at the page, but the words conveyed no meaning. After rereading the same paragraph several times, he slammed the journal closed and stood. His heart felt as if it would hammer through his chest. Then, like an electric bolt, an idea struck him. Time itself was the problem! It felt like the most ingenious idea he had ever conceived: a way to relax and simultaneously diminish his fanatical focus on his watch, a simple plan to unravel tension. He paced around the study as the plan coalesced. Within minutes he had added flesh to his idea and followed its ramifications to their logical conclusions as he would with any scientific hypothesis.

Back in his bedroom he slipped quietly into bed and looked at Vivian. Her jaw was slack; her wrinkles had dissolved in slumber. He turned off the lamp and lay on his back imagining all the ways his plan would ease his life and maybe even bring them closer. Yes, he thought, I'll change … a little … not much … I'll enjoy myself. Feeling calm, almost confident, he fell asleep.

The ringing woke him, and he instantly threw off his covers and went into the bathroom to brush his teeth and shave. Vivian could not believe his energy. He was humming as he ran the electric razor across his face. She dared not break the spell by inquiring or commenting. She accepted the blessing and went downstairs to start the coffee.

After a few minutes he bounced down the stairs in his robe and sat at the table. Normally he dressed for breakfast. Still wondering, Vivian commented on the beautiful morning with no inkling of the reason for the bizarre behavior nor any desire to rile him with questions.

"Sleep well?" she asked.

"I was awake for a while, but not long. I feel terrific. How about you?"

"You've a class this morning?"

"Yes; at ten." When he had finished his egg, toast, and coffee he said, "I'm staying home to read this morning."

"Oh?"

"I won't be interrupted here. My office is like an airport."

He walked up the stairs humming the Beatles song, *Yesterday*. In his study, Edgar opened the journal he had tried to read the night before and sat down with a pad and pencil. He was surprised how many interesting papers that issue contained. They were not related to his research, but he enjoyed reading them. He wondered if he had been missing others by attacking journals with such urgency.

By the time he looked at his watch it was 9:48, and a hot rush flooded his chest. *Calm down. If I'm late, it's all right.*

In his room he put on his shirt, socks, and shoes and then the gray pinstripe suit he had laid out the night before. He glanced down at his shoes and considered shining them, but decided not to overdo it. By this time he was floating on a cloud of fantasy, imagining strolling into class fashionably late! *Why not? Donald Quinone routinely does it. How wonderful! The new Edgar—slow, relaxed—to hell with punctuality!*

He soon found himself nervously pushing his shirttail into his trousers. Catching himself, he slowed down, though the relaxed feeling had vanished. He stood at the mirror and passed his hand lightly over the thin brush of blonde hair, then folded his tie carefully over his hand to make an elegant, symmetrical knot, all the while smiling through a pounding heart. *Students will think I died when the bell rings and I'm not there. Donald will think his watch broke when he gets to the next faculty meeting ahead of me. I'll have the wisecrack this time.*

Still looking in the mirror, he noticed his hands trembling and looked at his watch.

Vivian called up from the living room, "You said ten, right?"

"Right."

"Well, it's almost that."

"I'm coming."

He hopped down the stairs, kissed her, and bounded out the door, across the porch and into the garage.

Edgar's odd behavior drew Vivian to the window. In a moment his car backed out, jerked to a stop in the middle of the street, and screeched off, tires wailing. The elderly neighbor across the street, in her bathrobe, newspaper under her arm, stopped to watch his car lunge down the street and squeal around the corner.

As he drove a strange panic possessed him.

Why couldn't Daddy come? How long will I have to stand here? "How cute, neatly combed, all grown up, staring at his watch," she says and chuckles, lumbering toward me, moving more side-to-side than up-and-down. I hate the way she walks. "Please, Mom. I got us up early so

93

we'd be on time. We're going to be late." Beads of sweat drip across her smile. "Please, Mom; it's graduation. The whole sixth grade class'll razz me." She stretches her hand to open her door and says, "They won't graduate anybody till you get there."

I help her out of the car and jog ahead to hold the auditorium door open. The others are already on stage when I hop up the four steps. Her short-cropped, heavy hair waves side to side and makes her look even bigger waddling down the empty aisle. Why does she have to walk that way? I fall to my knees. I'm anchored down ... can't figure it out ... stepped on the edge of my robe ... still standing on it. I tug and pull and try to stand ... the kids laugh. I want to crawl away.

He raced along the broad avenue to the campus entrance. With his foot on the floorboard he made the turn into the parking lot and hit the speed bump so hard his head hit the ceiling and he swerved into the chemistry lot, jerked his car into a narrow space, making it nearly impossible to open his door, squeezed out, slammed the door, and ran into the building, down the hall to the stairs and, in twos, climbed the three floors to his office, grabbed his textbook and notes, returned downstairs, and reached for the classroom doorknob. Looking down at his watch he saw 10:00! Relief curdled into disappointment as he walked in puffing, beads of perspiration on his brow, his beautiful plan subverted. Laying his books on the lecture table, he looked up at the stunned students without locking the door.

Stammering, he posed his usual initial question and then stopped a moment to clear his mind. Soon his lecture was spinning out comfortably, his thoughts weaving and threading. He looked down at his watch every few seconds and at Sarah Lamb. At times she smiled; at others her brow would wrinkle, and he would pause until she nodded, remembering how he had underestimated her intelligence and interest. He struggled not to let his mind wander off his subject. The obese young woman fascinated him the way her mass seemed to smother her chair and her bosom seemed ready to burst out of a blouse stretched to its limit. All he could feel was panic, pity, and anger.

At the end of his lecture, he announced that beginning next week there would no longer be class bells. "However, I expect everyone to be here on time as usual. I will begin and end on time as always and lock the door punctually at 10:00. So be warned."

Before moving to leave he gathered his materials and stood at the lecture demonstration table for a moment. When he saw Sarah Lamb walk past him heaving her backpack onto her shoulder, he smiled. She smiled back and walked out.

That evening Vivian came to him as he walked in the house. "How did it go today?"

"Fine."

"You weren't yourself this morning."

The last thing he wanted was to discuss his aborted plan, but he said, "I tried to be late on purpose. You know, to see how it felt."

"And?"

"And what?"

"How did it feel?"

"It didn't work."

"Why not?"

"I got there on time anyway ... What's so funny?"

"Nothing. Sorry, Eddy-Teddy. Not a bad idea though."

"Must you ridicule everything I do?"

"I mean it. I'm sorry." She stifled a smile.

"You think I'm a weirdo, don't you?"

"No, Eddy-Teddy. It's just ..."

"Well, I'm sick of it. I am what I am. I'm not like you. I can't be, and I don't want to be."

"All right, all right. Don't start."

"Then drop it."

"Would you like dinner?"

"Of course."

Vivian went to the refrigerator and took out two filets she had bought that day and then, from the bottom drawer, took two potatoes out of a plastic bag. Edgar stood at the kitchen door watching her unwrap the steaks and lay them out on the cutting board. She took the potatoes to the sink and began to peel them.

"What's wrong with the potato peeler?"

"Knife's faster."

He reached into the sink and picked up a thick chunk. "My God!" he said. "Look at what you're throwing out."

"That does it!" She slammed the potato into his hand. "You peel it."

"Just a suggestion," he said, shocked by her sudden anger.

"Go on, Eddy-Perfect."

"Why so huffy?"

"Call me when you're done."

Edgar looked down at the potato with disbelief. "What's happening?"

No answer.

"Come on, Vivian," he said, raising his wrist to look at his watch. "You know eating late is bad for my stomach."

"Then you'd better hurry, Eddy-Perfect."

"I work all day. I shouldn't have to do your work."

"Then hire a maid."

"It's been a miserable day, Vivian." He was pleading now.

"A day like every other. Tough!" She walked out and let the back door slam behind her.

Edgar took his briefcase up to his study, sat at his desk, and tried to hush the noise in his head. The refrain kept repeating: *How could I trap myself like this? So what if the plan failed? ... It was my own fault. Maybe I'll try again tomorrow ... but why did it fail?*

A few minutes later he appeared on the back porch. Vivian was rocking on one of the wicker rockers staring out into the back yard.

"Sorry, Vivian. Let's try again."

"Supper ready?"

"Let's say I just got home and start over."

"OK, go ahead."

"Why so hard?"

"Want me to pretend you're not a pain in the ass?"

"I said I'm sorry."

"For sure!"

"What about supper?"

"Why don't you take me out?"

"I will if you want, but …"

Feeling sorry for him, she said, "All right, Edgar, but stay out of the kitchen."

"I will." He held out his hands to help her up.

After supper Vivian settled into the living room sofa with Proust's *Remembrances of Things Past*. Sitting across from her, Edgar pondered his infernal affliction. *How can she bear to get halfway through a 2265-page book?* The worm had gnawed its way into his deepest self and was munching on his sanity. Rather than living in the clear, orderly world of the rationality and truth he so urgently desired, he felt like a leaden mass pulled through life by a heavy chain ratcheted to a sluggish motor. Dragged inexorably forward across time's minutest demarcations, his insistence on control was sending him out of control. The membrane separating order from chaos had long since dissolved into a syrupy quagmire. Instead of helping manage his life, his fervor for punctuality pulled him by the nose like a lumbering ox.

There was a time when Edgar Margin took pride in his punctuality. But over the years that pride had nurtured a parasite that had grown so gradually he had barely noticed it. Obsession, compulsion, panic had broken through the skin of his carefully honed self-image and threatened to push him into ever-darker caverns of solitude.

What to do? Approach the problem scientifically; the only way I know! Starve that miserable worm! Loosen its devouring grip, so it'll shrivel up and die.

Those thoughts collided with the ticking he felt inside as he walked up the stairs. *That relentless inner pulse, ticking, that diurnal motion and its linearly dependent drive mechanism … must cut them off! … They've forced me through its orifice into a tight cell … insensitive to my deepest needs … only panic and confusion … must deaden dependence on that clicking ratchet that shoves me mercilessly out of one minute and into the next … what a horrible invention, the digital watch of Vivian's … its tormenting, robotic pulses … that magnet that drew my eyes, my soul … staring from one minute to the next, watching, watching, watching the liquid crystal screen beat silent seconds like a crystalline heart pumping electrons … pumping until the minute, tightly poised on one toe, drops into the next liquid crystalline minute ... no longer living in minutes ... but in seconds ... wouldn't blink for fear of missing it ... clung on each second, each minute, each hour ... excruciating ... at least this old watch Mother bought me pours out time continuously, gracefully, with humanity ... the earliest clocks had only hour hands ... before that ... bells to announce church services ... how good to break the manacle to that clicking cyclops with its cynical scowl.*

His brain simmering, he riffled through Vivian's cosmetics pouch: *All this chemical junk ... vanity ... just to stop time ... ah, here it is!*

He walked into his study, sat bent like a question mark over his desk, removed the crystal of his watch, and carefully began his delicate surgery. *Maybe these things can serve a useful purpose for once,* he thought. Afraid to damage the action, he examined the watch carefully under a magnifying glass to see whether the hands screwed or snapped in. Seeing that the minute hand was wedged in, he gingerly worked it back and forth with Vivian's eyebrow tweezers while pulling it directly out from the stem. After placing the minute hand in a small test tube and corking it, he held the watch to his ear. The gentle, grateful ticking calmed him. He replaced the crystal and returned to the living room and picked up his journal.

The next morning, pulsing with anticipation and feeling freed, Edgar told Vivian what he had done.

"Don't you dare mess with my clocks."

"It'll free you too."

"I'm free enough. For God's sake, Eddy-Teddy, I need to know the correct time."

"Why? You're always late."

With cheery logic she said, "I like to know how late I am."

Settling for what he could get, Edgar looked on the bright side—*no more jerking my wrist into view hundreds of times a day—life's bound to improve—and all with a simple, delicate surgery.*

With no class bells to escort him through his day and time now only a scar on his wounded watch, Edgar felt giddy, but slightly lost. With the hour hand pointing slightly to the left of ten o'clock, he walked tentatively into class and looked around. The only student in the room was a bearded, otherwise nondescript young man reading a newspaper. He did not look up. Edgar had calculated that the space the minute hand sweeps in one minute takes twelve minutes for the hour hand to sweep; he would have to guess at smaller intervals. His liberation had hatched a new problem: how to handle stragglers once they realized he didn't know the precise time. He put his materials down and walked to the men's room, forgetting that he had gone a few minutes earlier. He washed his hands and then walked down the hall to the stockroom, where a large wall clock peered down on him.

By the following week, Edgar had devised several ways to get to class on time. From a distance he would watch students enter the classroom, or he would wait for Brucine Justice, who had a class at the same time in the next room. She was always punctual. One afternoon he went to the handball courts and found his friends absent. After waiting a while he left in a fury, knowing that no matter how inaccurate his watch, he would not tolerate their slovenly disrespect of their commitment.

When he got home that evening, still wearing his shorts and tee shirt, Vivian said, "I thought you weren't playing today."

"What?"

"The big faculty meeting ... you cancelled the game. Remember?"

He stood helpless; *she's right. I missed the semi-annual, college-wide faculty meeting!*

Feeling stupid for his anger he said, "I forgot." On his way upstairs to shower he mumbled, *still as bound as ever; the time has me even more entangled, and I'm wasting even more energy.*

In spite of close attention to his hour hand, the next morning he got to his ten o'clock class several minutes early. Seeing only a few students in the room, he dropped his books and materials on the lectern, turned to leave, and nearly walked into the door as a student pushed it open. After apologizing, the student said, "Could I ask about the last lecture?"

"After class."

"It's still early, sir."

99

Edgar could hardly refuse. With eyes sweeping the room he said, "Well?"

"Could you repeat what you said about acids and bases?"

"If you didn't understand it the first time, what good would it do to hear it again?" Edgar said. Several front row students turned to listen.

He watched Sarah Lamb lumber across the room and sit in her usual chair by the window. The first student persisted, "I just don't understand all this stuff about acids and bases."

"You've already said that." He looked at his watch, but its message was impenetrable. "Ask a specific question. For example, what molecular feature renders a substance acidic?"

"Hydrogen ions?"

"And how does a base react with an acid?"

"I guess it neutralizes the hydrogen ions?"

"And which ion of the base neutralizes the hydrogen ions?"

After a long pause, the student said, "Hydroxide?"

"It appears you understand more than you wish to admit." Edgar was enjoying making the student focus on small, answerable questions. Other students inched into the conversation. Soon four students stood around him at the chalkboard. Some of the others were taking notes, including Sarah who had consumed several minutes putting her books away and squeezing into her chair. The rest were staring out the window, reading the school paper, repairing their makeup, or doodling in their notepads.

A lull in the discussion gave Edgar the opportunity to call the class to order. While the students found their seats, Edgar looked at his watch. The hour hand had drifted beyond the one-minute mark. He tried to figure out what time it was, but didn't want to look befuddled. He had forgotten to lock the door.

An uneasy feeling gripped him as he looked into the sea of faces. If they were not clear about acids and bases, how could they understand today's lecture on chemical equilibrium? Instead, he said, "Who can tell me if an acid-base reaction is an example of chemical equilibrium?"

Two students raised their hands. Edgar caught a glimpse of Sarah in a large tee shirt and overalls looking as if she would explode. Seeing her fat arm flap as she waved her hand, he felt embarrassed for her.

"Ms. Lamb."

"I don't think so."

"Why not?"

"Because neutralization is complete. If it were an equilibrium there'd be some acid and base left over in equilibrium with the product salt and water."

"Good reasoning, Ms. Lamb, but let's look at this more closely. Equilibrium doesn't mean that a reaction can't give mostly product. He drew an equation on the board. In the case of strong acids and bases the equilibrium so favors the products that you can't even measure what's left of the original acid and base. However, with weak acids and bases you can. But your thinking was very sound."

Sarah Lamb beamed.

He kept up the questioning and discussion, weaving clarity into the murky ideas of chemical equilibrium, and, with precise questions, wove the complex threads of experimental evidence into a beautiful fabric.

Sarah Lamb raised her hand.

Again focusing on her large, fleshy arm, Edgar nodded, "Yes, Ms. Lamb?"

"It's past eleven o'clock, Sir."

Before Edgar Margin could dismiss the class it disintegrated into the usual cacophony as students started shuffling out. As Edgar erased the board and gathered his books and notes, students surrounded him:

"Good session, Doc."

"That really helped, Dr. Margin."

"It finally makes sense."

Edgar Margin's hour hand stood well past eleven o'clock. Questions and comments continued until only Sarah remained, now struggling to stuff books and jacket into her backpack. From across the room, she said, "Thanks, Professor Margin. That was great." As she approached puffing, Edgar imagined she was a giant marshmallow.

He held the door for her and stared dumbly into his wristwatch. Sarah lumbered out, struggling to move gracefully.

"Don't forget, Ms. Lamb, come by if you need help."

"Thanks, Dr. Margin."

Edgar did not discuss his watch or his classroom experience with any of his colleagues until days later, when Donald Quinone asked him for the time. They were both shuffling through their mail in the hall outside the mailroom. Edgar paused to stare at his watch. After a moment Donald stretched to look.

Donald's hair hung limp over his face. "Say, you've dropped your minute hand."

Edgar's first inclination was to lie, but instead he told Donald what he had done.

Donald smiled. "Why that's terrific, Edgar. Now you can get to class late and miss meetings and your favorite TV shows; there's no limit to the doors you've opened."

"I don't watch TV!" he said, belligerently. Then, "You don't understand, Donald. A wonderful thing happened. I didn't know the exact time and got to class early. Students began to barrage me with questions. I didn't realize how little they understood, so instead of lecturing, I asked the questions. It was marvelous! And they loved it."

"Congratulations, old boy. You've invented the Socratic method."

Pulling back, Edgar stared at Donald. "I beg your pardon?"

"The Socratic method. It puts responsibility for learning on students where it belongs."

"Oh. Yes, I guess that's right."

"But with all due respect, Edgar, I'll keep my minute hand. See you at some indeterminate hour."

After such a personal conversation with a colleague Edgar Margin felt disrobed.

Edgar was opening his mail, grumbling, as he waited for Sarah Lamb. At the knock on the door he said, "Come in."

"Hi, Dr. Margin," she said, trying to catch her breath.

"When you make an appointment with me, Ms. Lamb, I expect you to be on time. I was just leaving."

"I'm really sorry ... elevator's not working ... had to use ... stairs ... three floors ... got to me ... had to stop ... catch my breath."

"All right. Sit down."

Sarah's intelligent questions calmed him. The way her body spilled over the seat reminded Edgar of his mother smothering the dining room chair at dinner.

Daddy looks handsome in his new suit, but he's grumbling ... again. Sure, Mom's big. I wish she'd stay inside when my friends come. Daddy works hard. "You should be ashamed," he tells her. "But, honey, I can't help it." "Stop eating like a pig and you won't look like one." Please, God, don't let Daddy get mad. I'm not hungry, but if I don't eat he'll get mad at me.

In a few minutes Edgar cleared up Sarah's questions.

"Sounds easy."

"Anything else? You've got my attention."

"No, thanks. I've got more studying to do before I bother you again."

"No bother, really, Sarah. Tell me about yourself." Edgar immediately felt he had overstepped.

"Nothing much to tell. I graduated from Hillsborough High three years ago."

"But you started last year."

"Had to work two years ... you know ... to save up. My father died five years ago. He left us enough to live on, but Mom's been sick and can't work ... you know. I didn't want to use up her money ... you know."

"That's doing college the hard way. You have my admiration."

"I'm the first in my family to go to college. I'm going to be a nurse, I hope." She lifted crossed fingers.

"You will, Sarah. Just keep up the good work."

For a moment she looked at him adoringly and then brought her eyes down and began stuffing books and jacket into her backpack.

"Do you have any siblings?"

"A brother."

"What does he do?"

"Graduated from Hillsborough last year."

"Is he at the university?"

"No, sir. He never liked school."

"It's tough finding a good job without a degree."

"That's what I tell him, but he wants to be free."

At the next long silence she said, "Sorry I kept you waiting."

"No problem, Sarah. I'm here all day. Come by any time."

She smiled, slung her backpack over her shoulder, and said, "Thank you, sir.

Edgar walked her to the door and watched her amble down the hall to the stairs. When she was out of sight he moved to the window to watch her exit the building. He waited several minutes knowing she would have to rest along the way. A river of thoughts washed over him: *stopped at each landing ... could be pretty ... impossible to see it through all that blubber ... so insulated from life.*

The green campus spread before him with crisscrossing sidewalks overflowing with students.

College isn't as great as I thought. No free time. How do the others manage it? The library is dusty and dark, but I have to. Sometimes I get tired of reading. Sure miss Mom. Why did she have to die? Thank God for Grandma. Why am I worried? I get all A's ... how can they waste their time on football ... and parties ... no real friends ... There's more to college ... ah, handball!

Sarah Lamb walked out of the building and onto the sidewalk three floors down, heading north toward the cafeteria. He wondered what her life was like. As she moved out of focus among other students he imagined a huge honeydew with legs. Some students turned to look and snicker at her as she passed. He watched until Sarah disappeared into the mass of students. Without realizing it he was enjoying the scene and the beautiful day. *Looks a lot like Mom.* As his mother's image came into focus he suddenly realized he had been dawdling too long. He jerked his wrist up. The one-armed freak yanked him back into the moment and broke the spell of languorous thoughts and warm afternoon sun.

Edgar threw himself with such fury into drafting a research proposal that the next time he looked at his watch the hour hand had moved well past five. He never stayed that late and felt exhilarated at having lost track of time. It was a small victory, but a victory. Putting away his papers, he thought of Sarah Lamb. Somehow she had soothed his anxiety. Perhaps in loosening up and relaxing, he hoped he was beginning to change. Whatever it was, Sarah Lamb's intelligence and curiosity cheered him. She reminded him of his student days.

Edgar could not help frowning as he opened the front door and peeled off Vivian's note:

"Back 5:30, Viv."

Each evening he had come home determined to have a pleasant time, and each time they had bickered. The reasons were varied and numberless and near the surface. Today he promised himself that, whatever she said or did, he would not be drawn in. He felt good, and he would make her feel good too.

He ran up to his study. Holding the lab tweezers he had brought home, he sat at his desk, opened the drawer, and took out the test tube with the minute hand, warming himself in the realization that evading time was stupid: *Don't evade—conquer!* He snapped the tweezers open and shut a few times, took off his watch, leaned over it, removed the crystal, and carefully replaced the minute hand. He went to the television to get the correct time and set his recovered watch to the second.

When Vivian appeared at six-seventeen she saw Edgar reading in the living room and walked past him and up the stairs.

"Hi. I'm home," he said.

"Uh-huh."

"Something wrong?"

"I'm going to mother's for a while ... to think things over."

"Think what over? I want to tell you about my wonderful afternoon."

"One afternoon can't make up for ten lousy years."

"It's not that bad, Vivian."

"It's been awful. And I don't give a damn about your afternoon."

Edgar was stunned. "What happened?"

105

"For starters I'm not happy and haven't been for way too long. I'm sure that's not news to you. I tried to deny it to myself, but these past weeks ..."

"Who filled you with this garbage?"

With her fists on her hips, she looked at him and said, "I thought it up all by myself."

"But ..."

"I've had it, Edgar."

"How long will you be gone?"

"You'll be the first to know."

"Have you talked with your mother?"

"Of course."

"What does she think?"

"I didn't ask for an opinion, and she didn't offer one."

"What about George Buchner's party? The whole department's going. We said we'd go."

"Tell them I'm on vacation from you."

"I can't believe this, Vivian. Please, let's talk it over."

"No."

"I don't get it."

"That's 'cause you're dull, Eddy-Teddy. It doesn't take a genius to see we growl at each other more than we talk."

Edgar stood dumbfounded as she ascended the stairs. "Didn't you notice my packed bags?"

"I didn't look in the bedroom." Then in desperation, "I fixed my watch, Vivian. I can tell the time again."

"I'm thrilled, Eddy-Teddy. Now you can be perfect again."

"I wanted to tell you about it."

"Some other time. I'm booked on the eight o'clock flight."

"I'll drive you."

"I've ordered a limo."

"Come on; give me a chance."

"It's a new day, Eddy-Teddy."

"What about me?"

"Start counting minutes again."

Why can't Dad stop yelling? What can't he take? Mom doesn't understand it either. I'm scared … can't eat … my stomach … I'm going to throw up. Mom touches my brow and my cheeks. Dad's yelling. I try to stand and fall down. Mom can't kneel to help me and says, "See if he's all right." Dad stands over me, fists on his sides, puffing hard. Mom sends me to my room then sits with her face in her hands. I leave crying. It's dark and quiet except for my heart pounding … like somebody pounding on a door. What's that noise? Where's Dad? Why didn't she stop him?

George and Alice Buchner's house stood near a small lake with tall pines in the front yard and cypresses behind, near the lake's edge. Edgar Margin always admired that property and dreamed of owning a house like that one day. One tall pine looked down on him as he knocked on the door.

George Buchner held out his hand and, looking past Edgar, said, "Hi. Where's Vivian?"

"She's out of town."

"Alice was looking forward to seeing her. Visiting relatives?"

"Her mother."

"That's nice."

"I don't know what to do."

"When will she be back?" George said, looking around at the room and the display of snacks.

Edgar shrugged.

"Sorry, Edgar. I didn't know."

"I guess I'm hard to live with. I don't know how to …"

Through the front window George saw Donald and Hazel Quinone approaching.

"We'll chat later, Edgar. Remember: everything happens for the best."

"Sure, George."

"And by the way, thanks for the tenure committee's report. Good job."

"Thanks."

"Excuse me, Edgar. Hello, Donald, Hazel. Glad you could make it."

Brucine Justice entered behind them, looked around, and walked directly to the punch bowl without greeting anyone. In a clinging, white dress with pleated skirt, blood-red stone necklace, and matching shoes, she looked stunning. Her wavy, auburn hair combed up made her look taller and thinner.

Hoping to calm her obvious resentment, George Buchner approached her.

"Haven't been here since I was hired."

"I should have more of these, I guess."

"No need to be friendly with an assistant professor until she's tenured."

"Don't be silly, Brucine. If your tenure doesn't come through, I have lots of industrial connections. I'll be happy to make some phone calls."

"Thanks." She turned to the punch bowl and ladled another cup. Her cold tone and icy smile left George speechless.

"I'm glad the weather's cooperating," he said, excusing himself and wandering toward a small group of colleagues. "Anybody talked with Brucine?" he asked.

Donald Quinone's sardonic smile spread over his face. "I'm afraid to get too close. She may have rabies."

"She knows about the committee's report," Edgar said.

"Funny," George said, "She acted like the cat that swallowed the canary."

"Probably got a job lined up," George said.

"Don't be too sure," Donald said.

"I don't think that's it," Edgar said.

Pretending an interest in her tenure situation, but attracted to her animal sexuality, Edgar walked to the punch bowl in the middle of the long table set with a neatly arranged array of glass cups. A large, doughnut-shaped piece of ice floated languorously over the punch and reminded Edgar of a lifesaver. He imagined himself on a sinking ship trying to force himself into it. As he moved the ladle through the punch, orange and lemon slices rose lazily then drifted to the bottom.

"How are you?" he asked as he poured a glassful.

"Fine." She smiled noncommittally. "This stuff looks harmless, but it's got a good slug of brandy."

"Oh, really?" Edgar looked into his glass.

"I wouldn't have expected such good booze from George."

"It is nice. Wonder what it is."

"Sangria. White wine—chardonnay, I'd say—fruit, and a hefty shot of brandy to make it worth the trouble."

"Have you heard anymore about tenure? The next step, I mean?"

"Not yet."

"It wouldn't hurt to review your folder before it goes up. Some of it could stand editing. And make sure it's complete."

She nodded with a coy smile.

"It's better to do all you can before it gets to the provost. It'll be more difficult after he makes his decision."

"My lawyer and I are meeting with him tomorrow morning."

Brucine's pushiness both annoyed and attracted Edgar. She laced every move and word with suggestions of mystery, perhaps even availability. He could not imagine why she was being so seductive. It wasn't that kind of situation. But every movement, however casual or slight, exuded raw animal heat.

"I hate department parties: everybody trying to make nice."

"Yes," he said.

"I kicked Roger out two weeks ago."

"Oh?"

"Insufferable boor."

"Vivian's visiting her mother. I hope she …"

"Should've done it long ago," she said.

"What?"

"Roger. He wouldn't get a job; spent all day in bed watching TV. And as for sex, well, he was a limp dishrag."

After another glass of punch Edgar said, "You seem OK about tenure."

She took a sip and stared into his eyes. "Don't count me out, Edgar. I've got …" She stopped for another sip.

Watching her sip, Edgar was becoming aroused. "You've got what?"

"If they expect me to crawl silently away, they're full of it."

"The provost can't go against the faculty, the tenure committee, and the chairman."

"Really?"

"Sounds like you have a plan."

"Very astute, Edgar. Buy you a drink?"

"I have one."

"How silly of me. Why don't you just run along now?"

"Have a seat, Dr. Justice," the secretary said. "Dr. Klein is on the phone. Shouldn't be long."

Provost Klein's outer office was large, almost as large as a classroom. On one wall stood a coffee urn with china cups, milk and sugar. Two small sofas faced each other with a coffee table between them. On the table, neatly placed, lay several magazines, the school newspaper, and the Chronicle of Higher Education. The furnishings angered Brucine. They could have been those of a bank president. She and Carl Helms, her attorney, sat facing each other. She picked up a newspaper and began loudly flipping the pages. After nearly fifteen minutes she said aloud to the secretary, "My appointment was for nine o'clock. It's well past that."

"I'm sorry, Dr. Justice. Shouldn't be much longer."

"I hope not." She resumed turning pages.

After several minutes more she turned to her attorney and said, "Come on, Carl. I'm not putting up with this shit."

"Sit down," Carl Helms said. "It's standard practice. He's just letting you cool your heels."

"Well it's not working." She picked up another magazine, imagining the arrogance of a man surrounded with such opulence while faculty worked in tiny offices. At nine thirty-three the secretary ushered them into the provost's office.

Provost Klein's office was even larger and plusher than the waiting room. Floor-to-ceiling windows ran the length of the north wall and faced the quadrangle with the student center building in the distance. The provost's extra large mahogany desk was clear of all papers and books. In the middle lay a large rectangular blotter pad with leather corners, and above that stood a desk set with two silver pens. The Provost stood with his back to the windows; the glare behind him rendered his face almost imperceptible. As they came in he walked around the desk and ushered them to two leather chairs facing a leather sofa.

"This is Carl Helms," Brucine said. "He's representing me."

The two men shook hands cordially. The provost looked dashing in his gray suit. Silver streaks blended into his full head of light brown hair.

"May I offer you coffee or tea?"

"Can we get down to business?" Brucine said.

"Of course. Settling into his chair Dr. Klein looked into her eyes and said, "Dr. Justice, I've reviewed your case. I'm afraid I agree with the faculty's recommendation. I see no case here. I suggest you accept their decision and begin exploring other possibilities."

"Bullshit! This old boy network is going to rip right here. This university has kept women down long enough."

Carl Helms turned to look out the window.

"Please, Dr. Justice. I've seen no evidence of unfair treatment. What justification do you have for such a charge?"

Before Brucine could respond, Carl Helms said, "Sir, could we talk alone?"

Looking at him with gritted teeth Brucine said, "Just a minute, Carl. This is my career."

"You asked me to represent you, Brucine. You must let me do it. I'll come to your office when we're finished."

The provost looked at his watch and said, "That would be all right, Mr. Helms, but I don't see any ..."

"Just a few minutes, sir."

"Well, then I'll ask the university counsel to join us."

"Good idea."

The provost walked to the door and asked his secretary to summon the university attorney, as Brucine walked past him and out the door. She stalked across the quadrangle to her office looking no one in the face.

At her desk she pondered what she would do if the provost turned her down. She could not stand the thought that two men would decide her fate. She took out a sheet of paper and began to scribble. *That's it, a letter to the son of a bitch with copies to the president and the newspapers.* She wrote furiously for several minutes, reread the note, and threw it in the wastebasket. She stood and walked around the small office mumbling curses on the provost and his opulent quarters. Her desk was clear and her office was neatly arranged, except for two pencils, a small clock, and a glass vase of fresh wild flowers.

Too angry to think clearly, she walked to the basement coffee shop. Seeing Edgar Margin sitting alone she bought a cup of coffee and sat with him.

After a few moments of silence Edgar said, "How'd you like the party?"

"Boring! I left early."

"Me too."

"I didn't want them to think I'd shrink away."

"If I could offer a little advice, Brucine, your aggressiveness might make you feel better, but it doesn't help your case."

"You mean don't piss off the boss?"

"Not exactly. I mind my own business, avoid controversy, and keep my nose out of things that don't concern me."

"Where do you like to keep it? Your nose, I mean."

"What?"

She put her hand on his lap. "I've been through it, Edgar. I know how you feel."

Moving his leg he said, "But I want her back. That's the difference between us."

"Want to talk?"

He shook his head.

"Well, if you change your mind, I'm available."

"Sorry, I guess I'm a little jumpy."

"You're going through a rough time. If you need a friend, you know, a little comfort ..." Remembering her lawyer she stood and said, "Got to get back. And don't forget: any time."

Confused and aroused, Edgar Margin watched her strut out of the coffee shop.

A full hour later in his office Edgar had not been able to get Brucine out of his mind. He had stared at his draft research proposal, but had made no headway. His brain was filled with conflicting images: *her hand on my lap ... her perfume ... what would Vivian think ... about another woman ... my career ...*

Dad's trying to let go my hand, but I hold on. I wish they'd stop. I'm scared. Why are they whispering? She puts her hands on his shoulders; he pulls away from me and puts his hands around her waist. I start to cry. "Go out in the hall." I don't want to leave. He said he'd play with me. I don't like her. Mom will have dinner ready. He shoves me into a chair. I'm still crying. He gets mad and takes me by the arm to the hall. I'm still crying. The woman says, "Don't. We'll have another time."

Brucine burst into his office without knocking and, with a broad smile, said, "If you're not doing anything this evening, I'll put some strip steaks on the grill."

"I've got too much work."

"Stopped eating too?" Her eyes flashed.

"Uh ... what time?"

"Seven?"

"What about the Provost?"

"No comment."

Edgar drove into Brucine's driveway drowning in a brew of apprehension, excitement, and guilt. He had never considered having an affair. But now, faced with the reality of a sexy, available woman, he felt driven. *Why me? I opposed her tenure? Maybe she thinks I hold power over her.*

Fighting through panic, reckless desire pushed him to ring the doorbell.

"Martini?" she said, smiling.

"Uh ... I guess so."

Following her through the small living room to the kitchen he said, "Thanks for the invitation, but I'm still wondering why."

"It's simple: I know how you're feeling, and I want to help."

He stood silent in the kitchen as she poured the drinks she had mixed earlier. She filled the two chilled glasses, handed him one, and raised hers. "To freedom."

As they touched glasses and sipped, Edgar was not sure how he felt about that toast.

"Sit down while I do my stuff."

Arousal crept over him as she moved toward the stove in her clinging, loose-fitting dress with obviously little underneath, jiggling as she moved. He was mesmerized as she took two potatoes out of the oven and put them on plates. Then she laid two thick steaks on the broiler. Edgar imagined Vivian working in their kitchen, graceful and sexy too, but somehow different.

"It's worked out for you? The divorce, I mean."

"Nothing beats freedom. I come and go as I please and do what I please with whomever I please. I answer to no one. Divorce was my declaration of independence."

As he listened, Edgar felt loneliness and dread at the thought of returning to his empty house.

"Sounds good."

Brucine came closer and put her arms on his shoulders. "The loneliness won't last long when you start enjoying your freedom."

With wrinkled brow he wondered if he had understood her meaning.

"Relax and enjoy your drink. I'll turn the steaks."

With fear sinking its talons ever deeper, he stood.

"I'm sorry, Brucine. It's really good of you, but I can't …"

"Afraid of being raped?"

"Of course not."

"Life is short; why not step up to the banquet table?"

"I just can't. Not yet."

"OK."

"Thanks. I feel awful about this." He started to turn and said, "I have an important proposal to finish this evening, and it's getting late." He turned to the living room and looked at his watch. The minute hand seemed swollen, like his brain. Though he wanted more than anything else to go back and devour her, he left.

"See you around, Edgar." Brucine turned and flipped one steak, then picked up the other and threw it into the garbage.

Why do I have to sit out here alone? He's with her every day. He said I would spend the day with him. Why can't I go in? I won't tell Mama.

The next morning Edgar arrived a little before eight and stopped at Brucine's office. Finding it locked and dark, he left a note on her door asking her to call him. Barely able to concentrate on his ten o'clock lecture, he fumbled the pages thinking of nothing but her. *I must apologize, but how, and for what?* It was 9:45 when she called.

He picked up the phone on the first ring. "Got your note."

"May I drop by?"

"Sure."

In a few seconds he was standing inside her office not knowing what to do with his hands. He closed the door behind him. The way she reclined in her chair caused her skirt to slide well above her knees. She crossed her legs and rocked her top leg over the other. "Well?"

"Sorry for last night."

"Don't sweat it, Edgar. It was stupid, but I understand. You're just confused."

"You're very understanding, Brucine. Could we try again? I mean when my mind's a little more settled and I'm not under all this pressure."

"I was hoping I could help settle it."

'Yes. Well, maybe soon then."

"Don't wait too long, Edgar. I'm not famous for patience."

"I know a good restaurant in Ybor City. How about this evening?"

She smiled dubiously. "I could manage that, Edgar, but are you sure?"

"Pick you up at seven?"

"Sure."

The Columbia Restaurant was busy, so the headwaiter escorted them into the lounge. "Your table will be ready in a few minutes; you can wait here," he said and walked away.

Edgar had never been in the lounge before. To him the blood red, papered walls, thick red carpet, and dark mahogany bar seemed to drip with depravity. The curved bar looked soft and alive, like an internal organ, a womb perhaps. Though the air was cool, he felt hot. Sitting next to Brucine at a small table by the wall, he imagined the place as a brothel. Small shaded lights against the red walls provided minimal lighting, not enough to reveal patrons' secret desires except to a close companion.

"Nice place," she said. "Very upscale."

Edgar did not respond, except to nod agreement and look at his watch.

"What'll you have?" he asked.

"Martini, up, no olive."

Edgar signaled to the waiter and ordered two. He was having trouble making conversation while trying to remember his first date with Vivian. "I don't come to Ybor City often. This is the only restaurant I've tried."

"Has a bit of the old world and a hint of sin. I like it."

Again he was caught unawares. "Sin?" He immediately regretted uttering the word thinking he would look stupid again.

"Bars and honky-tonks. They're fun and sinfully exciting."

"I guess so."

"For God's sake, Edgar. Loosen up. We're adults. Do you have any idea how many times you've looked at your watch since we sat down?"

"I know. That's … don't worry; I won't walk out this time," he said, trying to sound firm.

"Good. I'd hate to get stuck with the tab."

"Oh, no. This time it's on me."

When the waiter brought the drinks, she lifted hers. "What'll we drink to this time? Freedom didn't go down too well last night."

He forced a smile. "To freedom."

"That's better. And to fun and exciting lives."

When the waiter brought the second round, Edgar was smiling. "I rarely have more than one."

"There's your problem. It'll take at least four to dissolve all the inhibitions out of the pure, crystalline Edgar Margin."

The headwaiter reappeared and led them to their table and picked up their drinks, saying, in a thick accent, "I take them to your table, Señor."

The floorshow was beginning when they sat. While the first flamenco dancers twirled and stomped their heels, the waiter came to take their order.

"We need another drink first."

Brucine smiled, nodded, and finished hers.

The next two hours of dancing and singing poured out calmly, slowly, with another martini, then a bottle of Rioja wine, salad, seafood paella, dessert, and coffee. While they waited for the coffee Edgar lifted the wine bottle to fill their glasses and found it empty.

"How about another?"

"Let's have our coffee and go somewhere else."

"Something I've been wanting to say, Brucine … the tenure committee … I could reconvene them and …"

She shook her head in exaggerated motions.

"Why not?" He was barely able to focus through the blinding alcoholic haze.

"Don't say a word, but my lawyer and I met with the provost, and the old
boy's thinking it over."

"How? I mean, how can he?"

"My lawyer's very good."

"Must be." He was still looking at her, his eyes a little crossed trying to bring the two images together, wondering if he had heard correctly.

"Well, he's the boss. Guess he can do what he pleases … the provost right or wrong, but the provost to the letter. That's from the old movie, *Les Miserables*.

Putting her fingers to her lips she said, "Don't forget, not a word."

The waiter laid the check down. Edgar tried vainly to read it. He opened his wallet, laid his credit card on it, and said to Brucine, "Where to?"

"Don't you think we should wait for your credit card?"

"Oh, yes, of course. How silly of me. Then where?"

"My house for a nightcap?"

"Sounds good."

Edgar awoke confused by the unfamiliar surroundings and the bright sunlight streaming in the window. He did not immediately recognize the room until he saw Brucine next to him. He tried mightily to reconstruct the previous evening. Something about coming to her house and having another drink or two and then she unbuttoning his shirt as he watched her fingers work, scientifically observing them as they moved delicately down his shirt. After that—blank.

He rose quietly and dressed. As he washed his face and looked in the mirror, the curtain over the evening began to inch up like a skirt: dancing to music ... tumbling into bed ... moving ... fast breathing ... then ... blank.

While he was washing his face, Brucine called out, "Edgar?"

"Here," he said, returning to the bedroom.

"You're not leaving?"

"Got to get to work, and so do you."

"My class isn't till eleven. It's only 8:15."

"My God! I hadn't seen the time. I've got to go home and shave."

"Jesus! What jitters. What happened to that other, relaxed, Edgar?"

"That was last night. By the way, I enjoyed it. Thanks."

"Thanks?"

"I'm sorry, I'm being stupid again. This is new to me."

Brucine got out of bed. She was not wearing anything and Edgar stopped to look. He recalled more details of the previous evening: lifting her dress over her head ... kissing her ... sparks in the darkness. When she slipped into her robe he picked up his necktie and threw it over his collar. "Will I see you again?" he said.

"Our offices are twenty feet apart. You should be able to find your way."

Though exciting, that evening left Edgar Margin feeling spent and empty. Deciding not to rush to work, he sat alone in his kitchen that morning with the newspaper, a cup of coffee, and a bowl of dry cereal and milk before him. But he could not bear to look at his food. True, he was hung over, but the adventure should have left him with a feeling of triumph, of conquest, instead of failure and depression. She had been the seducer and not subtly at that. The idea of being seduced titillated him, but also left him vacant. As fascinating and sexy as Brucine Justice was, he did not like her. Perhaps, he thought, the apparent contradiction was the difference between animal lust and human love. Whatever the meanings of those words, he knew he did not want any involvement with her or any other woman. Vivian irritated him, but he loved her, though he was not sure he could explain his feelings analytically. The irrationality of his feelings disturbed his scientific orientation; he thought that irrationality was unforgivable, yet she attracted him. *But marriage means something, even if I can't articulate that either. How could I allow myself to be seduced? Was I hungry for sex, or companionship; were there deeper motives? Was I trying to punish Vivian?*

What is daddy doing in there? Why does he like her? I'm tired of waiting out here. But daddy's good to me; I can't be mad at him.

Amid the confusion and excitement, Edgar realized he did not feel love for Brucine. He avoided her the rest of that week and spoke only when they met face to face. Because she had spent so much time in the administration building, the faculty buzzed with speculations about her imminent departure. Edgar, of course, pretended disinterest. In every group the topic of Brucine inevitably arose—would she leave gracefully and quietly, or put up a loud and obnoxious fight? Most expected a fight; some even hoped for a fight that would entertain from a safe distance.

The following week Brucine met Edgar in the hall. Stammering he said, "Hi."

"What's the matter Edgar? Not still hung over."

"Of course not. How are you, Brucine?"

"Just fine."

"How is it going with the provost?"

"My attorney said not to say anything until I get official word."

"Of course. Well, nice seeing you."

"I'd like to get together again. What do you say?"

"I don't know. My research has come to a boil, and I'm completely inundated. I don't think any time soon."

"Blowing me off?"

"No, just ..."

"Can't take fun and excitement?"

"Please, Brucine. Don't ridicule me. I'm just not ready to make any commitments."

"Who said anything about commitment?"

"I don't think we should see each other again."

"Suits me, little man."

"Well, I'll ..." He did not finish, knowing he had angered her. Perhaps, he thought, it was inevitable and even better to make a sharp break.

"Uh-huh."

Edgar had intended to check his mail, but the encounter unnerved him, and he found himself back his office.

Why doesn't he come out? What are they doing? Mom must have dinner ready by now. I want to go home ... Oh, Mom ... It's getting late. It's dark outside. What's he doing? Why do I have to play dumb all the time?

Remembering the mailroom, he walked out and found Donald Quinone and George Buchner talking. "This is ridiculous!" Donald said. "He can't get away with it."

"No use crying over spilt milk, Donald."

Donald handed Edgar the memo. "Look at this."

Edgar nodded as he read.

"Did you know?" Donald said.

Edgar shook his head and said, "But I'm not surprised."

"Well I'm shocked and furious!" Turning to George, Donald said, "Aren't you going to do something?"

"I did all I could."

"And?"

"He doesn't want a lawsuit. It's cheaper to keep her. I told him she's not doing any useful research, so she's going to teach her head off. He agreed."

"So we give our worst teacher more students. Have we no conscience?"

"I agree, Donald, but she'll have to pull her weight one way or another."

George returned to his office and Donald and Edgar walked into the hall. "This is awful, Edgar."

"She's tough as steel."

"So she gets tenure over our dead bodies."

"As you say, Donald: it's not the end of the world."

"She wields her feminine charms like butcher knives."

Edgar shrugged and excused himself, feeling he was unwittingly playing her henchman. He left Donald, took a few steps, peeked down the hall and, seeing no one, walked to Brucine's office and knocked. When he closed the door behind him she said, "What now?"

"Congratulations. I just saw George's memo."

"I don't care what anybody thinks. I'm a permanent member of this august body now, and the old boys can go screw themselves."

"I mean it. I'm glad for you. Well, I guess that's it."

"That's right."

Returning to his office he found Sarah Lamb waiting in the hall.

"Hello, Sarah. Come in."

She seemed worried sitting on the edge of the chair without removing her backpack from her shoulder.

"What's the matter?"

"I have to drop."

"But you've got an $\underline{A}$ and the term is two-thirds over."

"I know, and I really appreciate your help." She lowered her head, reached into her backpack, pulled out a tissue, and wiped her eyes and nose.

Not knowing what to say he opened a desk drawer, took out a box of tissues, and set it before her.

"My brother's in kind of bad trouble."

"What kind?"

She looked down.

"I'm sorry. It's none of my business."

"He was busted."

"Drugs?"

She nodded. "He's only nineteen. He's a good boy, but the police want to put him away."

Edgar felt too sorry for the girl to say he agreed with the police. "First offense?"

"That's the problem."

"Was he supporting your mother?"

"Not really."

"I thought you had enough money to finish the school year."

"Lawyers cost a lot."

"The court will appoint one."

She shook her head. "He'll need a really good one this time."

"A little punishment might straighten him out."

"I can't let him go to jail."

"It's not your responsibility. He did it to himself."

"He's really bright, but he had, you know, bad luck, got in with a bad bunch ..."

Edgar could feel himself being drawn into an impossible situation that didn't concern him, but the poor girl's predicament seemed overwhelming. "What would it take to keep you in school?"

"It's no use, Dr. Margin. I just can't."

"May I talk with your mother?"

"No! Please, don't do that."

"It's a shame to let you drop out. You've got a good mind and a good future. I hate to see you waste it."

"Mom can't make it alone."

"Leave it to me, Sarah. Let's see what I can do."

Edgar had no idea in mind, nothing he could do except pay the lawyer's fee himself. He repeated variations of a common academic mantra: *Never get involved personally with a student ... it's her problem ... she is responsible for her future ... university isn't for everybody ... life's tough ... I'm reacting like her, sticking my neck out for a loser like she's doing for her brother.* Before him sat this grotesquely huge girl, talented, but with little hope for success, a teetering home life, and possibly future health problems. But, in spite of everything, something nudged him forward into a possibly irreversibly position. And for what? He argued with himself throughout their discussion, but rationality counted for nothing; she had pierced his heart in a way few human beings had. He did not understand these feelings and did not wish to. All he wanted was to help this girl no matter how limited and uncertain her life was.

"Don't stop studying and don't drop out. Give me a chance first."

"This isn't your problem, Dr. Margin. You don't have to."

"I know that better than you. But I want to."

"Just don't call my mother."

"I understand, and I won't"

Sarah Lamb did not thank him or even smile as she stood and turned to the door. Before she opened the door she stopped and said, "I just don't want you to get hurt, Dr. Margin."

"I won't, Sarah, but give me a couple of days before you do anything."

Listening to her shuffling footsteps her words rattled in his mind, and he wondered, "How could I get hurt?"

I slept late again and almost missed the funeral. I thought I hadn't slept, but I did it again. What's wrong with me? I hate to see them roll her casket over that hole. Too many people in this tent ... scorching ... everything's so quiet, except the rattling memory of the kids' laughter at graduation! Will that preacher ever stop droning? Stop it! I don't understand anything ...still the laughter ... why can't I cry? Feel heavy as mud ... no, stone. Why are all these people here? I don't know most of them. Where's Dad? He should have helped her instead of always getting mad. Why didn't he? Aunt Bea is my only relative here. It can't be Mom in that box. Just matter ... mass ... weight ... not her ...no!

With nothing but a vague plan Edgar called David Swain, director of financial aid, for an appointment. It was unlike Edgar Margin to act without a clear plan, but he felt driven, and his doubts could not stop him. On one point he was clear: he did not want to visit Sarah's mother. He had promised and did not want any entanglement with her family. But a simpler solution had raised his interest: Sarah's intelligence and motivation should qualify her for financial aid. That and the knowledge that scholarship money goes unused every year propelled him toward the administration building.

David Swain was cheerful, handsome, and slightly older than Edgar.

"Hello, Edgar. Haven't seen you since we were on the faculty Senate. What brings you here?"

"I have a bright, motivated student who desperately needs help. She worked for two years to earn enough to come here. Now her family is in financial distress."

"Too late for this year, Edgar, but I'm sure we can get her something for next year."

"That won't do, David. She's planning to drop out today."

"That's a shame. Wish I could help, but the funds are all accounted for."

"There must be something."

"Can't she wait a while? By next fall we'll have our new budget. If she's as good as you say she'll be at the top of my list."

Edgar did not want to reveal any personal involvement, but panic was rising as he shook his head. "That won't do, David."

"Well, if it's that dire, perhaps ..."

"Anything, David. She's the most deserving student I've had in years, and she needs it now."

"I've got an office slush fund. I guess I could scrape up something."

"How much, David?"

"Does she need room and board?"

"I'm not sure."

"I can waive her tuition for the current year. That'll get her a refund on what she already paid. Also perhaps I can arrange some credit in the bookstore if she's that good a risk."

"She is."

"You really moved me with this girl's story. I always thought of you as primarily a researcher. It's good to know you're also involved in helping students. Helping students is what we're about."

"Thanks, David." Though Edgar was glad he did not have to bring up her brother's problem, he worried about having omitted information. *To filter out ugliness from the truth is to lie. But nothing I told him was untrue. She needs help, and that's the clear truth.*

"Got to check one thing." David Swain picked up the phone and punched a number. When he got an answer he said, "Records? Dean Swain here. I need Sarah Lamb's academic record. And could you please tell me her GPA?"

When he got the answer he said, "Please fax her record ASAP … Fine. Thanks," and hung up.

"Your little girl got a perfect 4.0 in her first year. Wish she'd come by last year. Sometimes I feel like I have to beg students to take scholarships."

"Then it's set?"

"Have her come by and fill out an application. We have records to keep too, Edgar."

"Wonderful, David. I'll see her tomorrow in class."

Edgar Margin basked in his victory as he walked back to the chemistry building. The class break had just ended, so he met only a few stragglers. One was a young woman whose perfume felt like spring to Edgar. He nodded as he passed, thinking, how wonderful to be young and facing your whole life, like a chick breaking out of its shell and seeing the world for the first time. Summer had finally dissipated, and a fresh autumn breeze brushed his face. He unbuttoned his jacket as he walked into the breeze to welcome the cool October.

Never one to open up, even to those closest to him, he felt cleansed by waters of redemption. He wanted to tell Vivian. She wouldn't listen, he thought, even if she were here. The memory of her departure curdled his feeling of renewal. Perhaps he should call her, demand that she come home, that he was a new man, more relaxed and alive, more in touch. But he knew she would need assurance, and he had none to give. He had said it all before, and she knew better.

Instead of sitting at his desk he stood at the window thinking about Vivian, as a flock of black birds flew across his vision. They were so close he thought he heard their wings fluttering through the glass. His mother used to say black birds brought bad luck. *Nonsense!* But the memory of his mother sent a shiver through him, and he looked down at his watch. An hour had passed since Sarah Lamb left his office and, though he had helped Sarah, the feeling of emptiness remained. I've helped a student ... that's my job ... but that doesn't bring in research money. So he lifted his proposal file out of his desk drawer, opened it, and, with his head in his hands, reread what he had written.

Edgar arrived in class early the next morning. He knew it would break his routine, but he could not wait to see Sarah. Her desk was unoccupied; he looked around the room hoping she had not already dropped out. Instead of locking the door he looked out the tiny window. In the distance Sarah lumbered toward him as fast as she could. He stood outside so she could see him and know she would not be locked out. Smiling nervously she approached and he said, "Glad to see you; see me after class."

"Yes sir."

As the hour dragged by, Edgar's eyes shifted between Sarah and his watch. Most of the time he lectured from her side of the room, hoping not to attract attention by deviating from his usual style of standing ramrod straight behind the lectern.

When he dismissed the class and the room burst into chaos, he walked to Sarah's desk.

"See Mr. Swain in the administration building. He has financial aid for you."

She looked at him imploringly. "I can't, Dr. Margin. I just can't."

"Don't be silly. And when you're through come to my office. I'll be waiting."

"OK, but ..."

He turned, gathered his books and notes and walked out.

Twenty minutes later she appeared at his door. "I can't, Dr. Margin."

"Don't you understand? You've got tuition and books. You can give your saved cash to your mother and brother."

"I'm going back to my old job."

"Nonsense. The tuition scholarship is retroactive. You'll get a refund for the tuition you've paid."

"You're very nice, Dr. Margin, but my place is with my family."

"You live with your mother?"

"Yes, but ..."

"She'll be glad to keep you in school."

"You don't understand. She was against it from the beginning."

"So your brother is just an excuse to get you home?"

"No, she really needs me."

"How old is she?"

"Forty-two, but she's very sick."

Sarah's lame excuses and her mother's iron grasp on her exasperated Edgar. He turned and looked out the window not knowing what more to say. He looked out the window for the blackbirds, expecting to see them hovering. Repelled by the thought, he turned to Sarah. "It's up to you, Sarah. You've got to decide whether to sacrifice your future for a worthless brother and an insecure mother or make something of yourself."

She looked down and reached for her backpack.

"Am I wrong?"

"I don't know, Dr. Margin. I just don't know. I want to stay more than anything, but ..."

"At least finish the semester. If you leave you'll lose the tuition you already paid."

"I'll talk to Mom. Maybe I can work part-time."

"Good. Tell her what I said. Tell her she can call me here or at home."

Not long after Sarah Lamb left Edgar's office, he heard a tap at his door. Thinking it was a student, he ignored it hoping whoever it was would go away. But instead, the door opened and Brucine appeared.

"I knew you were in. I watched your favorite student leave a moment ago."

"I'm pretty behind right now, Brucine. Could you come back later?"

"Come on; you can't be that busy. I've been thinking about you, Edgar. I have access to a nice beach house for this weekend."

"Now look, Brucine ..." He hesitated as she sat down beside him. "That's not a good idea."

"We're both free; no strings attached."

"I've been thinking too. This relationship is a bad idea. We're colleagues; it could complicate things."

"Life is complicated, Edgar. The only way to avoid complications is too boring for words."

"I don't want to be ... disrespectful, but ... No, Brucine. It won't work."

"It worked all right the other night."

"I wasn't in my right mind ... I wasn't myself ... I was drunk ... that wasn't me."

Suddenly frowning she stood. "To hell with you then. The last thing I need is another pansy around the house."

"No need to be insulting."

"Freedom means I can say anything I damn well please. You live in your straitjacket if you want; I won't."

Brucine left the door ajar as she walked out.

Edgar was livid: *straitjacket ... just what Vivian said ... but pansy ... she had no right ... I'm as good a man as any ... dependable ... efficient ... always on time ... she liked me enough the other night ... deserves to have the hell knocked out of her ... God! No. Don't even think it.*

By the time the phone rang Edgar saw Brucine as a totally unattractive reptile. But the sound made him jump and quickly slap his hand on the telephone. He lifted the receiver and said hello. A shrill voice screamed out of the earpiece.

"You mind your own goddamn business, Dr. Nosey. I don't need no up-itty professor telling me how to bring up my daughter."

"Who is this?" he asked, knowing.

"Mrs. Ruth Lamb, Sarah's mother. She just called me. Said you're trying to force her to stay in school. And even after she told you I need her here."

"Wait a minute. I'm not forcing her to do anything. I got her a scholarship so she could stay in school, and ..."

"Stay out of our lives, or I'll ..."

"Can't we talk calmly, Mrs. Lamb? I just want to help Sarah."

"I know all about helping a poor, defenseless, handicapped girl who can barely help herself."

"She's a very good student, Mrs. Lamb. As a nurse she'll bring in more money than she ever will in a menial job."

"She ain't gonna … She got plenty nursing to do right here with me."

"Are you ill, Mrs. Lamb?"

"Damn right I am. I had to quit working when my husband died. She's all I got now."

"What about your son?"

After a long silence she said, "What did she tell you about him?"

"That he's in trouble and needs her help. I assure you, Mrs. Lamb …"

"Don't assure me nothin'. She should'a never told you nothin' about him. Ain't none of your damn business."

"But she'll get back the tuition money she paid this semester. That ought to help."

"She don't belong in no university. She belongs here with me."

"But …"

Mrs. Lamb had hung up.

By the end of two weeks Edgar knew Sarah had dropped out. He considered telephoning her mother, but recalling her raspy voice made him cringe. *If she won't help herself, I can't do it.* During that time he felt stronger about himself and his ability to be more human, a phrase Vivian used to describe his shortcomings. Twice he called Vivian, and twice she refused to talk to him. Her mother seemed sympathetic and told him not to give up, to give her more time. Happy to have her on his side, he spoke sweetly to his mother-in-law and wished her well.

As he waited for his morning toast to pop up he dialed his mother-in-law's number and sat down. The phone rang four times and he was about to hang up when he heard Vivian's voice, timid and tentative: "Hello."

"Vivian, I've been trying to reach you. Glad you answered."

"Mother refused to take it."

"How are you?"

"Fine."

In the background he heard his mother-in-law say, "No she's not." Then a muffled, "Hush, Mother."

"Edgar, I'm busy right now. Some other time."

Noticing that she did not hang up he said, "Please, Vivian. I'm really sorry. I think I'm beginning to understand myself. You were right. I'm trying very hard to change and I think it's working."

"Uh-huh."

"Really, Vivian. It's quite complicated; I don't completely understand it, but I believe I'm really changing."

"Call me when you're sure. Goodbye, Edgar."

She hung up.

He took the toast out of the toaster and poured another cup of coffee and sat at the table with the newspaper. A headline over a brief article near the bottom of page one read, "College Girl Assaulted." As he read, a chill rattled his bones:

"A young woman was mugged outside a McDonald's Drive-In near the university last evening a few minutes after leaving work. The assailant has not been apprehended. Witnesses said he was a young Caucasian male. Police at the scene could find no witnesses who could describe him further. The girl was taken to a local hospital. She had not regained consciousness at this writing. Two McDonald employees identified her as Sarah Lamb of Sulphur Springs, a recent university drop-out."

Edgar almost spilled his coffee in his lap as he reread the item. He reread it again looking for the name of the hospital. It was not there. He looked up her mother in the telephone directory, but could not find a Ruth Lamb. In desperation he called the university registrar's office and got Sarah's home address. He did not shave, but dressed and drove directly to the Sulphur Springs address.

Sprawling oaks and scraggly, overgrown plants nearly hid the rusting trailer that stood on concrete blocks. An old Chevrolet with the front right fender missing stood next to the door. Edgar heard the creaking sounds a car makes when cooling down. He stepped up onto a concrete block and tapped on the door.

He heard muttering through the door, but could not make out what they were saying.

"Who is it?" said the gravely female voice.

"It's Professor Margin. I came to inquire about Sarah."

Through the closed door she said, "She's nearly dead and can't see nobody."

"Can you tell me the name of the hospital?"

"None of your damn business. If it wasn't for you she wouldn't be there."

"Could you please open the door so we can talk?"

"I got nothin' to say to you. Now get the hell outa here and quit pesterin' us."

After more shuffling sounds he said, "I won't leave until you tell me the name of the hospital."

"University Community, but leave her alone. You've hurt her enough already."

Without responding Edgar jogged back to his car and drove away.

The hospital lobby buzzed with visitors, patients in wheelchairs and on crutches, and doctors and nurses moving in the halls. Edgar approached the information desk nervously.

"Sarah Lamb, please," he said to the receptionist.

Without looking at her computer screen the middle-aged woman said, "She's not having visitors, Sir."

"I'm Doctor Margin."

"Oh, I'm sorry, doctor. Room 419."

Enjoying his little deception he walked toward the elevator hoping to look like a physician making rounds. His heart beat like a drum recalling Mrs. Lamb's vicious accusations. Dull, inarticulate feelings tightened his breast as he walked down the hall. He was far more nervous and shaky than he could justify, as if Sarah's life depended on his arrival. He looked at his watch several times as he approached her room, but the code on its face did not register. Looking at his watch was a reflex, a meaningless act, like a heart beating after death, without purpose or reason, a heart beating on death's door. He had to see her before … he wouldn't think it. What would he do if it was too late?

Yet he barely knew her and realized, even in his agitated state, that he was being irrational.

The door was closed, but he continued the charade and knocked lightly and then opened it. She looked like a huge sack piled on the bed. He closed the door behind him and stared at her trying to see if she was still breathing. A slight movement calmed him and he bent over her for a close look. Her head was bandaged down to her mouth except for her eyes, which were dark blue slits. Her mouth was swollen. Part of her chin was bandaged and her neck as well. As he looked down at the sad lump of a girl, his vision blurred and he sat in the chair beside the bed, not knowing what he would do now that he had found her.

A nurse walked in scowling.

"Are you a family member?"

"No, I'm Doctor Margin."

"You a consultant?"

Realizing he could not keep up the charade, he said, "No, I'm her chemistry professor. Her mother told me she was here. I wanted to see how she was."

"She's doing well considering. We're taking good care of her. Now you have to go."

"Please ... what little family she has can't come. May I stay? I won't bother anyone. I just want to be sure she's all right."

He sounded so sad and emitted such compassion that she said, "Only family are allowed in her room ... well, a few minutes won't hurt. She's having another series of tests in a few minutes. You can stay till then." At the door she turned. "There's a waiting room down the hall. You can wait there. I'll keep you posted."

"Has her brother been here?"

She shook her head on her way out. "Only a policeman wanting to question her. Said he'd come back."

When she returned a few minutes later to wheel Sarah out, the nurse smiled at Edgar. "There's coffee in the waiting room. Go on now. I'll let you know when she's back."

"Thanks."

For Edgar the next hour stood frozen in vast, white, clinical time. He could not believe his watch each time he looked at it. Each time he feared the second hand had stopped moving. He drank two cups of coffee, expecting to see Sarah's brother at any minute. But no one his age came in. Seeing a young man walk down the hall, Edgar thought it might be he. In a moment the young man saw an old man wheeling himself across the hall and brought him into the waiting room to talk.

Finally the nurse appeared. "She's back in her room and she's awake. Why don't you go in? She could use some cheering up."

"What happened?"

"Mugged by a monster too vicious to imagine. Poor thing: three broken bones and a concussion. Even lost a tooth. The police will be here soon."

Edgar thought he would be sick and sat down again. "My God!"

"Are you all right? Would you like something to calm you?"

"No, thanks. Sure it's all right to go in?"

"Sure, but take it easy."

Edgar tapped at Sarah's door and heard a weak, "Come in."

"How are you feeling?"

"Dr. Margin. What are you doing here?"

"You made the newspaper."

"What did it say?"

"Not much. Somebody beat you up."

"Did they say who?"

"Nobody could describe him, except that he was a white male. Did you get a look at him?"

She turned toward the window.

"What is it, Sarah?"

"Nothing. I thought maybe somebody saw him."

"None of the witnesses could describe him. It must have been pretty dark."

"It was."

"Did you know him?"

"Please, Dr. Margin. I really don't want to talk about it."

"That's fine, Sarah. Rest. I'll stay a while. Maybe your brother will come."

Her eyes opened wide as she stared at Edgar. The terror in her bandaged face frightened him. "What is it, Sarah?"

"Nothing. I'm pretty tired ... please ..."

"Do you want me to go?"

"No, no. Please stay ... I mean ... if you can."

"I have all the time you need, Sarah." Then remembering he had a class that morning, he looked at his watch. *Well, too late now.*

"What about your class?"

"All taken care of."

"You're very nice. But you don't ..."

"Just be quiet and rest." He picked up a magazine and began to flip the pages. The next time he looked at her she was still staring at him. "What is it, Sarah?"

"Did you talk with Mom?"

"Yes. I came from there."

She turned away again and asked, "You went to our place?"

"I wanted to know where you were; your mother has no phone listing."

"What did she say?"

"That you were here."

"That all?"

"She was very upset."

"Was my brother there?"

"I don't know. I didn't go in."

When she again turned to look at Edgar her eyes were overflowing into her bandage and she was breathing heavily. "Did she say anything about him?"

"No. I didn't ask."

"Oh, Dr. Margin, what am I going to do?"

"You'll be all right, Sarah. Are you in pain?"

"Some."

"Hold tight. You're going to be fine."

"I have nobody to talk to."

"Try me."

"After a long moment she said, "If my brother comes, don't let him in, please."

"Why?" At that moment all became clear. "Your brother?"

She turned toward the window again and did not answer. In a barely audible voice she said, "I have to tell somebody. I can't tell Mom. Who knows what she'd do."

Edgar wanted to tell her about the voices he heard in the trailer, but dared not. "We've got to tell the police."

She tried to raise her head. "No, no, no."

"But he beat you up. He shouldn't get away with it."

"Really, Dr. Margin, it's not your business. I don't mean to be rude, but don't make things worse."

"I don't see how they could be."

Please stop yelling. It's nothing to be so mad about. I don't get it. Mom looks down at her plate when he gets that mad. I'm too scared to eat. I'm going to be sick. "Please, John, don't." He hit her ... and hit her, with both fists ... she's on the floor and can't get up. I hit him in the back as hard as I can with my fist. Everything goes white with pain ... I'm on the floor ... he's standing over me. He reaches down and yanks me by the arm and slaps me and punches my stomach again. Mom's mouth is bleeding and one eye is shut; she's crying, "Don't hit him again," she says. Daddy looks at her and at me. Is he going to hit me again or her? I can't let him hit her again, but I can't move ... can't get my breath. He's yelling louder, "You're no good for anything; you're no wife." I pick myself up when he isn't looking and run to my room and lock the door. He pounds on the door. It shakes and vibrates with each pound. I'm shaking. Mom is crying. He stops banging. Is he going to hit her again? She's not crying now ...silence. I've got to stop him. I open the door ... front door slams ... Mom still on the floor gasping, "I'll be all right," she says. "He's gone; now go to bed ... school in the morning." I almost can't lift her ... she helps. "Sure you're all right?" "Fine, Eddy. Just fine. Please go to bed. I'll be all right." I go to my room. Next morning is bright, very bright. It's 11:06 on the clock radio. I'm three hours late for school. Why didn't she wake me? God! Is she all right? She's still and quiet in her bed ... still has her shoes on ... face blue and swollen ... pillow's bloody. Mom, Mom ... so still ... I shake her ... she doesn't move ... Mom, Mom ... no movement. I run to the phone ... dial 911 ... the ambulance ... men in white uniforms ... stethoscope ... touch her face ... lay a towel over her face ... cart her out. One of the men says, "Still warm; must have just died." The other man says, "Shut up—the kid," and tilts his head toward me.

Edgar passed out for a moment and suddenly awoke on the floor dumbfounded, his lower lip hanging like that of an idiot. That memory had erupted like a volcano and submerged him in a lava of unbearable fear, anger, and hatred. As real as it appeared, he understood none of it. Sarah tried to move to find him, but couldn't.

"What is it, Dr. Margin?" She was yelling.

He shook his head and immediately recalled that memory, and the fear and anger erupted again, as he tried to understand how he could have buried that memory so deep. *Had I forgotten it? Did it really happen?* But the new memory was there, a knife piercing him from the darkness. Why hadn't he remembered? Perspiration rolled down his back, his heart pounded, he could not move.

After a few minutes the nurse came in and helped him up. "What happened?"

"I called her, Dr. Margin. You fell down. He looked at the nurse and then at Sarah wondering who was this girl. His only desire at this moment was to peel off her bandages and see if she could be ...

"Mom?"

"What is it, Dr. Margin?" the nurse asked.

His shoulders heaved with each breath. "What am I doing here? Where have I been?" He felt himself toppling. He wanted the volcano to stop, but it would not.

"Want me to call a doctor?" the nurse asked.

"Huh?"

She tried to sit him down. "You OK?"

"I don't know. I'll be back in a minute."

"Where are you going? You should wait and let the doctor see you."

Struggling, he stood and walked down the hall to the water fountain and took a sip. Down in the lobby he walked out into a lush garden of green grass, palms, and flowers and sat at a marble bench. The autumn sun felt good. When he again recalled the memory he stood and tried to forget it, but it would not leave. He was still whirling in the vortex; the confusion would not stop. He put his head in his hands.

Is he beating her? He's gone ... she looks awful ... got to sleep ... she'll be OK. Why, Dad, why? ... She looks so peaceful ... just a few minutes ... how could I ... Oh, God ...why was he so mad? Why didn't I help her ... how could I sleep so late ... dead just a few minutes.

He tried to remember how he could have exhumed this truth, now clear and unvarnished as if a scale had been ripped off. *I helped kill her. Sure Daddy was big; I couldn't have stopped him, but I should have tried, done something, anything to protect her ... anything. So I made up the lie. I let her die and said it was a heart attack, and that Daddy just left.*

Edgar felt like vomiting, but in a few minutes the urge passed. He sat on the patio bench. *Like waiting for Daddy when he was with his secretary. What other memories have I buried? Oh, God! Don't let me bury this again.*

Back in Sarah's room he sat by her bed.

"You OK, Dr. Margin?"

"I'm not sure."

"What happened?"

"I don't know. I just uncovered a fragment of memory that I didn't know I had. It was like living it for the first time, so clear ..."

She looked at him quizzically.

"Nothing to do with you, Sarah. I'm going to call the police. We have to make sure he doesn't do this again."

"It'll kill Mom."

"When I talked with her this morning I heard another voice, and she wouldn't open the door."

After a moment she said, "Then he was there ... she knows."

"They're both involved, Sarah."

"Mom didn't have anything to do with what he did to me."

"Perhaps, but she knows now, and she's hiding him."

"Will they arrest her?"

"I don't know, but we can't let this go. It happens all the time, and men like that never stop."

"I know. He's hit her before."

Edgar picked up the phone. "Excuse me a moment."

"The police?"

"I have to, Sarah. Otherwise I'll be an accomplice too."

She looked away.

"Hello, I'm Professor Edgar Margin of the State University. I'm with Sarah Lamb, the girl who was mugged last night. Her brother did it. I went by Sarah's house this morning to find out what hospital she was in. I think her brother was there. That was less than an hour ago."

"How do you know he did it?"

"Sarah told me. Now don't waste time. Go get him. I'll stay with her until you arrive." He gave the officer Sarah's mother's address. When he turned to Sarah she was sobbing. He put his hand on hers and, for the first time, saw that it had a splint under the bandage, so he removed his hand and sat down again to wait.

Half an hour later the police arrived. Calling Edgar out into the hall, the officer said, "What's your part in this affair, Dr. Margin?"

"I was her chemistry professor at the university. She's an excellent student, whom I was trying to help. When she told me she had to quit school to help support her family, I got her financial aid, but she quit anyway. I thought that was strange, but there was nothing I could do … until I read about the beating in the newspaper."

"When did you find out her brother was the assailant?"

I went to her mother's house this morning. I wanted to know what hospital she was in."

"Did she tell you?"

"No. She wouldn't open the door, but I heard muffled talking and scuffling inside."

"Was it the girl's brother?"

"I didn't know at the time. When I asked Sarah about him she acted strangely."

"Like how?"

"She as much as admitted it. Then she asked me not to let him in if he came. When I suggested calling you, Sarah said it would kill her mother. I suspected her brother might do the killing. When I told Sarah about her mother not letting me in and about the voices, she realized her brother was with her and that she already knew."

"Have you any idea why he attacked her?"

"I can only guess, Sergeant. I don't know for sure."

"I understand," the sergeant said, waiting.

"Her mother did not want her in the university. Sarah earned all her school money. When I got her the financial aid, her mother phoned me—blew up and told me to mind my own business, among other things."

"Then Sarah quit school?"

"Right."

"Well, why the brother?"

"I can only guess he wanted to make sure she stayed on the job. He was in trouble with the police and needed money."

"I see. Thank you Dr. Margin. Please wait here while I talk with the girl."

Edgar walked to the water fountain and drank deeply, greatly relieved. His heart was no longer pounding. The recollection had shaken him, but for the first time in memory he felt a new calmness.

In a short while the sergeant came out. "The girl confirmed your story, Dr. Margin. You might like to know that her brother was indeed at his mother's house. He was arrested after trying to fight his way out with a switchblade."

"Did he hurt anyone?"

"He cut his mother accidentally when the officer tried to disarm him and she got between them."

"What'll happen to her?"

"She's in custody for questioning."

"Will you charge her?"

"Can't say. Thanks for your help, Professor."

After shaking Edgar's hand he disappeared down the hall. Sarah seemed quiet and calm. "You all right?"

"I think so, Dr. Margin. They arrested him. What'll they do to him?"

"I don't know, but I think he's in serious trouble."

"You were right. He was bound to get into bad trouble. I hope Mom's not in trouble too."

"Didn't say anything about her except they're questioning her."

"You were right about me staying in school, too."

"It may not be too late to recoup this semester."

"I don't know. You know, Mom ..."

Standing he said, "Everything depends on what you do about yourself. I have a feeling your mother will be fine on her own. Now I have a few things to take care of."

She reached up and took his hand, but said nothing.

"Hello. This is Edgar. May I speak with Vivian?"

After muffled words, Vivian's mother said, "She doesn't want to talk. I asked her, but she won't. Maybe later."

"Tell her I'm coming for her."

Again muffled voices.

"I'm not going home with you, Edgar, so don't bother."

"I'm not asking for permission, Vivian. I'm coming. We'll talk. Then if you decide to stay I won't argue."

"Tell me on the phone. Save yourself the trip."

"Don't be so anxious to save my time. I've got plenty."

"That's new."

"A lot has happened."

"Well don't expect me to lap up your sweet talk this time. I've got it memorized."

"I'll be there in four hours."

Vivian gasped when she opened the door. He had not shaved and his clothes were wrinkled and disheveled. "You look awful. What happened?"

"A lot. I've discovered something inside that I've kept bottled up for years."

"Uh-huh." She turned and sat in the sofa.

Standing behind Vivian, her mother said, "Glad you came, Edgar."

"Hello, Mom."

"I've got some things to do. I'll be upstairs."

"Don't leave, Mother."

"You and Edgar should talk, Vivian, and you don't need me." In a few seconds she disappeared upstairs.

Edgar sat in the sofa across from Vivian and wiped his mouth with his handkerchief, thinking how thirsty he felt. During the next few minutes he recited the story of meeting Sarah Lamb and trying to help her when she talked of leaving school and her mother not wanting her in school. "The first time I saw Sarah she reminded me of Mom. I think that's why I felt as I did."

"You're not going to tell me you're in love with her?"

"Don't be silly. I feel sorry for her. She reminded me of Mom."

She sat with her arms crossed over her chest and her ankles crossed; defiance poured from her eyes. "You've never talked about your mother, Edgar, or your father, for that matter, even when I asked. That's when I began to realize you were strange."

"I just couldn't, Vivian. I didn't know why then, but I just couldn't."

"And you're going to talk about them now?"

"Please, Vivian. Just listen." He wiped his mouth again and asked for a glass of water.

"You'll find it in the kitchen. You know where that is."

He stood and walked out. Vivian waited, one leg rocking over the other, arms crossed. "When I read about Sarah being mugged, I called on her mother to find out where they had taken her. I threatened to stay until she told me, and she finally did. It turns out her brother did it. He beat her badly; almost killed her. Poor girl looked horrible all bandaged and swollen. That's when it happened; the night my father left became clear as glass, but nothing like what I had remembered. I'd had it all wrong. In a flash it was happening right then. He beat hell out of Mom. Hurt her so badly she died the next morning."

"You told me it was a heart attack."

"I don't know why I said that." He finished his water and said, "Looking down at Sarah that horrible night exploded into my mind. He beat us both up that night. I got to bed and fell asleep or passed out; I don't know which. The next morning I found her in bed. It was nearly noon, and she was dead. I later learned she had … died … minutes earlier … Vivian, I could have helped her if I hadn't overslept. I'd never slept late." He began to sob violently.

"You didn't oversleep, Edgar. You passed out. He had beat you too."

"I see it now, but a twelve-year-old ..."

"So you invented the heart attack to avoid believing you killed her."

He shrugged and shook his head.

She moved beside him on the sofa. "I'm so sorry, Edgar. I wish I could have known your mother."

"When I saw Sarah ... so battered ... well ... that's when everything ... broke loose. I thought she was Mom."

Vivian put her arm around his shoulder.

"All these years I've hauled this stony secret inside me. It scared hell out of me, but I'm better now."

"You'd buried the truth and now you've found it."

"I've been looking for truth in my work and closing my eyes to the truth inside. Chemistry feels so trivial now. All those research papers—like laying bricks—they get lost in the vast walls of science. But this is my own little truth, Vivian, and it's whole, its own thing. Feels good and warm, like the scent of bread baking."

"Oh, Edgar."

"I don't understand it all, Vivian, but I know I love you."

"I wondered why you never talked about your mother. Must have been too close for comfort."

"Maybe. I didn't think you'd be interested."

"I love you, Eddy; I was interested in everything about you."

He hugged her, "I hope you still do."

"What about the girl, Eddy? Will she be all right?"

"Eddy ... Mom used to call me that ... Oh, Sarah? The nurse thinks she'll be all right. I never talked with the doctor. Her mother shares the blame; Sarah's brother had beat her up before too."

"What a horrible family."

"Is it so different from mine?"

"What about your father?"

"Never heard from him. I have no idea where he went or if he's still alive."

"How do you feel about that?"

"I don't know. Aunt Bea kept me until I finished high school. All these years I thought I didn't care. Now, I don't know."

"You turned out pretty well considering the stress of concealing this from yourself."

"I worry about Sarah. I hate to say it, but they should put her mother away too."

Vivian nodded. "They probably won't, but maybe she'll let her stay in school."

"I doubt it. Strange … I feel like a massive weight has been lifted."

"And you've found a surrogate daughter."

"I may have saved her life, Vivian. I owe her something."

"If only …"

"Do you think we could …? Maybe I'm adult enough now."

She smiled, "Tell me more about your mother."

SEEING IS BELIEVING

Joe Adams

TRANSCRIBER'S FOREWORD

R*are is the event that cannot be explained. It might even be said that all events are explicable and that an inexplicable event is impossible. The episode described in the following manuscript is such a case. Whether it is true or not is beside the point, for clearly the author believed it to be true. Whether he was in his right mind or merely a tormented delusional soul is also irrelevant. The reader alone must plumb these questions to reach his own conclusions.*

Lest you suspect that I concocted this flight of fancy out of my own imagination, please know that what follows is a faithful rendering of the original as I discovered it at a library book sale. I have no idea how it got there, nor do any of the librarians I asked. The spiral-bound, handwritten manuscript was battered, but the pages were quite legible, except for a few pages that had been torn out. I know this because of the page numbers.

I assume I am the first person who read it. I had it typed and reproduced in the present form because it is curious and strangely charming, if bizarre and possibly wacky. Besides, there is an outside chance that it may serve as the only surviving testament of a forgotten event.

*

It was early when I left home, 6:49 AM, to be exact; I recall everything that happened that day. Having refused to obey all my attempts at order, my thick mop of brown hair felt electrified flopping atop my thin frame as I walked across the athletic field. I liked it that way, long and thick; it gave me a professorial, scholarly look. My students say I bounce when I walk, like a wig on a bone. And that's fine. Being eccentric is all part of being a professor. I don't attempt to be eccentric, but if I am, I won't apologize. Anyway, I don't care what people say. I walk fast even when I'm not in a hurry. I enjoy being busy, and motion is the spark of life.

My father was really eccentric, with long hair before it was stylish, and topped off with a beret. I don't think he was aware of being eccentric or being anything else; he just did and thought whatever he wanted. Dad was a happy man, and I tried to be like him, engaged in work and carefree. But I could not handle astronomy. Math and I kept each other at a distance. Organic chemistry felt more hospitable.

The dew was especially heavy that morning, so I wore my overshoes. They slowed me down a bit, so I walked even faster. Soon after my wife and I moved to the house just beyond the edge of campus at the end of my first year here, I measured the walking distance to the chemistry building on my bicycle odometer. It was exactly eight-tenths of a mile across the broad intramural playing fields and then along a row of buildings that provided shade in summer and shelter during a sudden rainstorm.

I barely noticed the sun on my back. Nor was I aware of its warmth, for my mind was racing. Those morning walks provided welcome solitude to think. That morning's internal conversation began with academic politics, but I angrily pushed that aside in favor of my eleven o'clock lecture and the impossibility of covering a whole semester of general chemistry in six hot, summer weeks. Every time I used that phrase, covering the subject, I imagined myself pulling a sheet over a dead subject and folding my hands in prayer. And I often felt that way in class. With luck I'd soon have a research grant that would pay my summer salary, and I would no longer have to teach this ridiculous marathon.

Barely aware of the wet grass and buildings, I found my way to the chemistry building like a horse, bouncing along the path to my stable. Even through the haze of time I remember feeling good, strong and alive.

As I entered the chemistry building I looked down at my wristwatch: 7:03 (I remember that too). I had made good time. My skin tingled from the exertion, moist spots had formed under my arms, and I felt good. I met no one as I walked down the narrow hall to the stairs and up the two flights to my laboratory. After all these years I have difficulty recalling details of my work that day, but not the day itself. It will be forever imprinted on my brain.

After less than a year I had made a good start on my conducting polymer research. No one had yet succeeded in making plastic electrical conductors, and the possibility dangled like a carrot just beyond my reach. According to theory, all that was needed were long molecules with lots of freely moving electrons, but that was easier to say than to accomplish. Pulling off my overshoes in the dark, I flipped the light switch and brought the dark, windowless laboratory to life. Everything was as I had left it—glassware out on the lab bench ready to assemble for the morning's reaction, lab notebook open to the quantities I would have to weigh out. I moved around the lab, assembling apparatus, weighing chemicals, completely consumed by the passion that had burned since childhood. Inside my laboratory I had no way of knowing if it was sunny or storming outside, for windowless walls and a sharp focus on scientific questions insulated me from the world. I refused a telephone. Of course there was one in my office next door, but I could not hear it from the lab.

I prepared to distill a new compound as if I were a stone-age savage stalking a wildebeest. Only the prize, the joy of the hunt, the eventual adulation of my scientific villagers could have kept me isolated in that dungeon of a lab all those months. But in that space I controlled that tiny part of the world from which would emanate wondrous discoveries that would reach far beyond its walls.

After starting the distillation I glanced at my wristwatch. It showed 7:33. It had taken slightly less than half an hour to set up the apparatus. I paid no further attention to the time.

The distillation was complete in about an hour. I turned off the heater and looked at my watch. It still showed 7:33. I tried to wind it, but it was fully wound. I walked next door to my office to look at the wall clock. It also showed 7:33. It seemed odd that an electric clock would have stopped at the same time. Then I returned to the lab, removed the distilled sample from the receiving flask and poured it into a clean sample bottle and wrote out a label and stuck it on the bottle. I smiled with satisfaction at the beautiful, clear, colorless liquid—hunt completed; prey in its cage. After putting the sample aside I disassembled the still, washed it, and hung it to dry on the rack above the sink. Though I was not sure of the exact time, I always had a good instinct for time and estimated it was approaching the hour for my lecture, so I washed my hands and stopped at my office to pick up lecture notes, colored chalk, molecular models and books. The wall clock still read 7:33.

The moist, cool air embraced me on the fifty-yard covered walk to the lecture hall. Again I had begun to grumble at the stupidity of covering a subject like gas laws and kinetic molecular theory in a two-hour lecture. Fifteen weeks crammed into six weeks is inhumane; no, immoral. As if you could cram a big blob of time into a tiny vial. How can anyone learn such a complex subject in six weeks? And how could I allow myself to become an accessory to such a travesty?

Several students ran past me, but their movements failed to register. Something about the way they ran added to the feeling that something had changed. It seemed early. Later, when I tried to recall exactly how I felt at that moment, I could not. I decided the memory had been lost in the tumble and confusion of what followed. As I walked into the vacant lecture hall, a spider of doubt lurked on the edge of my consciousness. The rows of seats lining the funnel-like amphitheater were all empty. The clock above the chalkboard read 7:33. Puzzled, I walked back out and looked across the quadrangle. As I stepped onto the sidewalk, a bicyclist swerved around me; another young man lay under a tree, smoking. I called out to the young man under the tree and asked for the time. No answer. Across the quadrangle, a group clustered around a two-car wreck. The random movements of people and bicycles struck me as chaotic, as if entropy were somehow reaching an explosive point.

I walked back to the chemistry department office, where I found Mrs. Singleton standing in the middle of the departmental office shaking and with her hands over her ears. Her long, limp, amber hair, normally draped over her shoulders like a silk shawl, now looked stringy and tangled. Through her sobbing she managed to blurt out something about people coming in, asking the time, and shouting.

Several desk drawers were open; papers were strewn over the floor; strange for the meticulous Mrs. Singleton. "What time is it, Mrs. Singleton?"

"Not you too, Dr. Adams!" she said through sudden sobbing. "All the clocks stopped at 7:33."

"Calm down, Mrs. Singleton. What happened?"

"Look at the sky," she said. "The sun…"

I sat her down and turned on her small desk radio. A meteorologist was saying that there should be tremendous wind and tides. Finally he summarized, saying that the sun had not moved since 7:33 A.M., E.D.S.T. and that all clocks seem to have stopped at exactly that moment.

"Now we take you to Cambridge, Massachusetts, where our correspondent Matthew Hardy is talking with Professor John Needlehouse at the Harvard Observatory:"

"Dr. Needlehouse, we're hoping you can tell us exactly what has happened?"

"Something very strange indeed. Not only have all the clocks stopped functioning at exactly 7:33 this morning, but also the motion of the sun across the sky stopped at the same precise time, 12:33 Greenwich Meridian Time, 7:33 A.M. local time."

"But isn't it true, sir; that the sun doesn't really move around the earth; it's the earth that rotates around its axis?"

"Yes, that is true, young man," the professor said curtly. "Thank you for correcting me."

"Then does this mean that the earth has stopped rotating?"

"That would be the obvious hypothesis, young man, but such a sudden stop is inconceivable. Nothing I know of could stop the earth's rotation. But if it did, the abrupt change in momentum would result in wind turbulence and monstrous tides that would unleash forces of dreadful destruction. It's equivalent to stopping a speeding car instantaneously without slowing down and, instead of flying through the windshield, feeling no change in velocity. That is absurd; it defies all laws of physics. It's as far-fetched as saying that hot water in the Pacific Ocean could cause floods and snow in New England."

"What about the clocks, professor?"

"We have no explanation for that either, though the two events do appear to be connected."

"With all the clocks out of order and the sun immobile, how will we know the time, professor?"

"For my own satisfaction I have set up an hourglass and instructed an assistant to turn it as it empties and to keep track of the number of times he turns it. That'll give us a rough estimate."

"What next, professor?"

"The President has called an emergency meeting of members of the NAS in Washington at 5:00 this afternoon. I am leaving shortly for that meeting. He has asked us to make recommendations to the National Security Council as soon as possible."

"NAS is the National Academy of Sciences, right, sir?"

"Of course."

Seeing Mrs. Singleton sitting and seeming more relaxed I asked, "Where is Dr. Buchner?"

"The dean called him for a chairs' meeting."

I went up to the third floor and ran into Charlie Hollowell. "What's happened, Charlie?"

"You know all I know."

As I recounted the radio interview with the astronomer, Charlie Hollowell shook his head. "Beats me."

Charlie's perennial smile had disappeared leaving a blank, red face. For a moment I thought he was going to cry. "Take it easy, Charlie. It can't be what it appears. Everything looks normal. We'll have to wait."

Charlie said, "Think there's a connection between the sun and the clocks?"

"If I were a religious man I'd say we're witnessing a miracle."

"I just called my wife and she's pretty upset," Charlie said. "I'm going home."

I ran into my office and picked up the phone. Ruth's voice sounded shaky. "The radio is reporting strange things about the sun. What's going on, Joe?"

"Don't worry. I'll call Dad to see if he knows anything; then I'll be right home."

The phone rang five times at Dad's office, so I hung up and dialed my mother at home.

"Hello, Mom? I'm trying to get hold of Dad."

"So am I. His secretary said he was at a departmental meeting."

"How are things in Gainesville?"

"Same as everywhere else. You're calling about the sun, right?"

"Yes."

"I don't know anything. When I hear from Dad, I'll call you. Better go; I'm waiting for his call."

I hung up, left my books on the desk and ran down the stairs and out the door and across campus until I ran out of breath and then walked the rest of the way. Though I was distracted by the thoughts racing through my head, I noticed the ground was still wet with dew. It must be near noon, I thought, and it's still cool and wet. Another impossibility.

My clothes were drenched in perspiration when I stumbled into the kitchen and found Ruth rolling out piecrust. She was wearing an apron over a flowered pink dress and a kerchief over her short black hair. She stopped when I walked in and, with a broad smile, said, "I'm covered with flour; you'll get your welcome-home kiss in a minute."

"An apple pie? That's pretty cavalier."

"Apple's your favorite."

"But why aren't you panicking like everybody on campus?"

"Pangloss said to tend your garden just in case the world doesn't end." Then, with her blue eyes wide, she said, "Really, dear, what's going on?"

"All we know about nature tells us it can't happen. It's definitely unnatural."

150

She continued to roll out the dough, laid it in the pie pan, and ladled the cut apples over the crust, poured sugar over it, laid the top crust on that, crimped the edges, and slid the pan into the oven. She looked at me and said, "What do you think?"

"How can I think about it? If the earth stopped rotating, there'd be chaos. Look outside; it's a beautiful day."

"What did your father say?"

"He was tied up. Mom said she'd call when she heard. I'll bet the whole astronomy department is going nuts."

"Could it be an optical illusion?"

"Impossible! This is real. The confusing thing's the time."

"OK; you relax while I fix dinner."

"Relax? How?"

She took off the apron, washed her hands and then walked to me and put her arms around me and kissed me. "Welcome home, dear."

I went into the living room and turned on the television. All channels showed the same: rehashing earlier reports, scenes around the world, and national leaders trying to calm the masses. One of the most engaging scenes showed the half-submerged, luminous sun floating in the Indian Ocean. On one channel a TV evangelist screamed: "Repent, the end is at hand!"

I turned it off and returned to the kitchen.

"Why are religious fanatics so thrilled by the end of the world?"

"How about a glass of champagne?"

"Great. We'll tuck the truth into the bubbles." I sat at the table.

"Take it easy, Joe."

"Just look at that sky. Even you have to admit something's wrong."

"Couldn't ask for a prettier day."

"Suppose it stays like this?"

"Then we'll have a beautiful forever."

"That's silly, Ruth."

"I only know that we're together, it's a beautiful day, and I have a beautiful meal planned. The supermarket had live Maine lobsters, and I've got an apple pie in the oven."

"What am I going to do with you?"

"Want a hint?"

"This could be the end," I said, overly dramatically. I couldn't stand her optimism in the face of such possible doom.

"If it is, we'll end it nicely."

Then she sat across the table, took my hands and said, "Are you going to open the wine or do you plan to grump all evening?"

"Evening?"

"Let's pretend."

I worked on that bottle several minutes before I could pop the cork. She held out two long stem glasses. I filled them.

"To a wonderful, long day," she said, holding up her glass.

"And tomorrow, if it comes."

After sipping the wine she said, "I have candles for this evening.

An hour later we were still talking and enjoying the wine on the back terrace under a large live oak tree. Ruth had managed to calm me. I still wanted to talk about the day, but there was nothing new to say or think. The sun was still glued to the same spot in the sky, clocks still didn't work, and the dew had not yet evaporated.

"Maybe tomorrow," she said.

"Tomorrow as a concept is now in serious question. We may not be able to depend on anything anymore. Everything's up in the air."

Lifting her glass she said, "Right."

"You always joke when I get serious."

"One of us has to face reality."

"Reality is a joke to you?"

"Tell me, Joe. How will your worry help?"

"It's a serious problem."

"What problem?"

"First of all, if we're in trouble, how do we fix it? If it clears up somehow and there's no trouble, we at least have to try to understand it."

"Suppose it doesn't happen again?"

"We'll still want to know what caused it. You can bet Dad's thinking about it. We're scientists, Ruth. Understanding nature's our business."

"Living a happy life is mine, Joe."

"I want to be happy too, for Heaven sake."

"Then let's open another bottle. What do you say?"

"Think we should?"

"Why not? They were on sale. I bought four."

At that I finally smiled. "You're all right, Ruth."

After drowning my worries in champagne, we went inside, where Ruth closed the shades and said, "See? The sun has set." Then she lit candles, and we toasted each other again and sat down to a beautiful meal.

When she mentioned having a baby I reminded her of our plan to wait until my career gelled.

"It's as gelled as it's going to get, and the time is right."

"Really?"

She walked into the bedroom and slipped off her dress.

I said, "How about one more look?"

She caressed me and led me out to see the bright orb still hanging over the trees like a gloating giant reigning over endless morning. The source of life on earth had cast a shadow over the world. All I could think to say was, "Makes me feel like it's time to go to work."

"No way!"

Lifting the telephone I said, "Dad never called. I'll try Mom again before it gets too late."

After three rings Mom answered.

"Any news from Dad?"

"Nothing. The astronomy department met and adjourned, but your father wouldn't leave. He's been in his office since morning. I spoke to him briefly a few hours ago. Said the others had given up, but not him. Said he would call when he found something."

"Thanks, Mom. You OK?"

"Hard to believe anything's wrong."

"I'll keep in touch."

When I hung up I looked over at Ruth. She was under the covers.

I awoke and looked at my clock radio. It still showed 7:33. I turned on the radio at low volume so as not to disturb Ruth's sleep and waited for the hourly news, but nothing newsworthy had occurred. The sun was still stationary and so were the clocks. At the end of the news summary the announcer said a special interview would follow, so I left the radio on.

"We have with us this morning a man who has asked to speak to us about the sun. He has told us very little, and we're all excited to hear it. He is Professor Jonathan Wells. Welcome, Professor Wells. Would you explain your theory on the stationary sun for us?"

"Thank you for inviting me to appear on your program. But first, let me correct your request. The sun is not stationary, and neither is the earth."

"But Professor Wells, everyone can see it hasn't moved in many hours."

"The only way the sun could stand still in the sky is for the earth's rotation to stop, and we all know that is impossible; the reasons have been amply aired."

"Well then, how do you describe what's happened?"

"If you will allow me..."

"Sorry, please go on."

"It's quite simple, actually. A substance has spread across the earth that alters people's perceptions. What we see is an illusion."

"But, Professor Wells..."

"Please, young man, if you will just allow me to continue."

"Of course."

"An alien invasion is in progress. These aliens have managed to spread a gaseous chemical containing a previously unknown, very light chemical element so light that it can penetrate the human brain and cause changes in its response to stimuli. I have not yet determined how they have spread this agent so completely. I'm guessing it was spread from outer space."

"But Professor, no one has seen any aliens. We've heard no reports of..."

"Of course not. We cannot perceive their presence. These aliens are crafty. They have rendered themselves invisible. They are apparently plotting to subdue our planet. That, actually, is why I have volunteered to appear here with you. We must make preparations to repulse them before they completely take over our brains and our civilization."

By this time my heart was pounding. Listening to this lunatic's ranting had completely awakened me. I wondered if it was a terrible joke.

"Professor, how have your colleagues responded to your, uh, rather unorthodox theory?"

After a pause, "As a matter of fact, they have been completely duped by the aliens and have ignored my suggestion."

"Where do you teach, Professor Wells? What university, I mean?"

"I'm not actually in a university. I'm a free-lance scientist."

"I see. And is your doctorate in astronomy?"

"I have not bothered with a doctorate, but my fields of research are astronomy, physics, chemistry and biology. I am qualified in all these fields. My major research for many years has been in unidentified flying objects, UFOs. I have recorded countless sightings of alien spaceships. Perhaps I could appear again to discuss those findings."

"Thank you, Professor Wells. We appreciate very much your taking time out of your busy schedule to enlighten us."

"But I..."

Pop music cut Professor Wells off. I got up as quietly as I could and walked to the living room. I looked up the phone number of the station and dialed it.

"Station WZYX."

"I just heard that crackpot on your station. I'm Doctor Adams at the State University. I'm a member of the chemistry faculty, and I can tell you that man is no scientist. There is no unknown light element. Such an element is inconceivable. The man is an impostor, and you should apologize to your listeners for allowing him on the air."

"Thank you, Professor Adams. As soon as he started with the aliens I began to worry. But he had such a convincing story about his background that we thought it would be a public service to put him on the air. We should have investigated him a little more, I suppose, but...he seemed so cultured and professorial...anyway, I'll clarify the error right away. Thanks for calling."

I went back to bed and continued to listen to the radio, waiting for the apology. After an hour of obnoxious rock music, I got up and again dialed the station number.

"This is Dr. Adams again. I called in a complaint an hour ago, and the person who answered assured me that the station would apologize for airing that crackpot who passed himself off as a scientist. I'm still waiting."

"We've had literally hundreds of calls; yours was the only unfavorable one. They want us to bring him on again, so we're arranging to have him for another interview."

"If that's your audience, then we're doomed. But whatever your ignorant listeners like, you have no right to spread such misinformation and lies. It's trash."

"Thanks for your interest, Dr. Adams."

I stewed the rest of the night, or whatever it was, about Wells and the radio station. Adding to my discomfort were the shafts of sunlight that penetrated the shifting drapes as the non-stop air conditioner blew across them. When I could stand it no longer, I got up and peeked between the curtains. The bright light shocked me, and I drew the curtains shut again.

Ruth slipped out of bed and walked over, put her arms around me, and said, "I had a nice evening, dear."

"Nothing's changed. Look outside."

"I don't care. I'm happy," she said. "How about some eggs?"

"Wait till I tell you about the nut I just heard on the radio."

As I dressed, a radio announcer interrupted the morning news program with a special announcement: "The Naval Observatory in Washington has just announced that the sun resumed its movement at 7:33, and so have clocks everywhere. Whatever it was, it's over, thank God!"

"Did you hear that?" I said walking into the kitchen. I looked at my watch; it showed 7:45. "Look at the wall clock."

"Did he give any explanation?"

"I doubt if anyone can. It's incredible! That moment, 7:33, lasted exactly twenty-four hours, and from all appearances nothing's changed.

I've got to get to the department and see what's going on. I'll just grab some coffee and run."

"Make time for breakfast. I had a wonderful time last night, and I'm not ready for it to end."

I embraced her. "Me too."

A party atmosphere had spread like laughing gas through the chemistry department. When I walked into the departmental office on the first floor Mrs. Singleton smiled and said, "The sun took a day off. I don't know whether to bill it as sick leave or annual leave."

I had never seen her toothy grin so broad.

Charlie Hollowell extended his hand. "Congratulations! The world goes on. Wasn't it biblical? I waited all afternoon for a voice to boom down from the sky."

"I heard a quack on radio last night," I said. "He said it was an invasion from outer space."

"I heard him. What an idiot!"

"I called the station to set them straight."

"No kidding? You called?" Charlie burst into laughter.

"Sure. You should have called too. Do you know they had hundreds of calls asking for more of the guy?"

"Naturally. Our culture is kooky. Anyway, we got a day off, and this may be another one." With curly red hair and a smile that cut through a sea of freckles, he looked like a balloon about to pop.

Harvey Baron, another new member of the faculty, was at work in his lab. I poked my head in and asked why he wasn't celebrating.

"Too busy."

"Haven't you heard? The sun's moved on."

"Fine, fine."

"Come on, Harvey. This is big."

"Got a lot more data to collect for my proposal; deadline's breathing down on me."

"I thought yesterday was the ultimate deadline."

"Please, Joe, I'm busy."

I could not understand such lack of interest. "You really ought to come up for air, Harvey."

Charlie pulled me out and led me to the coffee shop in the basement. With the place full of faculty and students we could barely hear ourselves as we waited in the coffee line.

"I have a question," Charlie said, after they had found a table and sat down. "What day is this?"

"It was July 2nd yesterday when this all started. But you raise a good point, Charlie. Time passed whether the clocks show it or not. I'd say it's the 3rd."

"But hour is determined by star positions. Suppose they didn't move either. It might still be the 2nd."

"Somebody from on high will have to decide."

"The only explanations I've heard are a miracle portending the end of the world and an alien invasion," Charlie said.

"Maybe it is a miracle." He knew I was kidding, but I wasn't as sure.

"Strange word from an agnostic."

"What is a miracle?" I said, assuming a philosophical pose.

"As a matter of fact I looked up the dictionary definition. A miracle is an event in the physical world that deviates from the known laws of nature."

"Right. And isn't that what happened?"

"I think the Devil's hiding in the word 'known'. If someone comes up with an explanation that fits into the known laws of nature, then it wasn't a miracle."

"Right!" I said. "A miracle could be a natural phenomenon that no one can explain—yet. We'll just have to wait and see."

"That's the NAS committee's job," Charlie said. "Wonder what they're up to?"

"Haven't heard. They're pretty smart boys, though. But if they don't find an explanation, it'll be declared a miracle. And that'll really get the nut fringe going."

We finally parted and went to our labs, but I could not concentrate. The ideas darting through my mind knocked out everything else. I walked to the library and checked out several astronomy books and spent the rest of the morning reading.

At about 11:30 Ruth called. She said my mother called to say that my father had had a heart attack and was in the intensive care unit. I called the hospital from my office.

"What is it Mom? Ruth said you called. How's Dad?"

"Not good, Joe. He had just come home after more than twenty-four hours working on his calculations. He walked in the door and collapsed. I called the rescue squad, and they came right away and brought him to the emergency room."

"We'll be there in three hours or less."

"Drive carefully, Joe."

I tried my best, but my foot kept getting heavier and Ruth kept reminding me to slow down. It took two hours and fifteen minutes from the time I picked up Ruth to the minute we drove into the hospital parking lot.

Before I got to the information desk I saw my mother waiting in the lobby. My sister Jean was sitting with her trying to comfort her.

"How is he?"

"It's too late, Joe," Jean said. "He died an hour ago."

Ruth went to Mom, put her arm around her and sat her down. I stood petrified.

"It was so fast," I said. "He was only sixty-two."

Mom was too shaken to talk. She began to sob, and Ruth and Jean sat by her side. Ruth held her as she would a baby.

"Where is he?" I said.

Mom shrugged. Jean pointed to the ICU area.

I found him still on a bed in the ICU. He looked peaceful, but I could not bear to look at him now. His face was chalky-gray, cold, and still. I walked back to the lobby.

"Did he say anything?"

"Yes, but it didn't mean anything."

"What?"

"I knew it would happen…son…stop…son…"

"What did he want me to stop doing?"

"I don't know. I just don't know."

"He always called me Joe. Why would he call me son?"

"Yes, that was strange. I'm sorry. I guess we'll never know."

"Could he have meant s-u-n?"

"I don't know, Joe."

"Did he say what he was working on?"

"Same as always: astrophysics, celestial mechanics, things I don't understand. It was all he thought about."

At that moment I knew I was right. He must have figured out why the sun stopped. "Where are his research notes?"

"In his office on campus, I guess. Wait, a few days ago he brought a stack of notebooks home. I asked him why, and he said he planned to work at home for a while."

"May I have them?"

"I don't see why not."

Ruth and I spent the next few days in Gainesville, helping with funeral arrangements and trying to get Mom back to something approaching normal. Eventually, to ease my worry, Mom agreed to stay with Jean in Gainesville for a while. Better not to be alone, I thought.

That same evening Mom gave me Dad's research notebooks, and I spent several hours fighting through the mathematics and cryptic language with little success. I could find nothing that seemed related to the sun's strange behavior.

The next morning we left Mom at Jean's house, said goodbye, and made Mom promise she would spend some time with us too. I walked to the car cradling Dad's notes in both arms, a treasure to savor later.

Most of the way home I could think and talk of nothing but the long day and the possibility that Dad had discovered something. Ruth indulged me, though I knew she had as little interest as understanding. I loved her for that.

Because no change in the positions of the other heavenly bodies could be detected during the long day, the Director of the U.S. Naval Observatory reluctantly announced that no time had passed during the long day. He tentatively declared that July 2 simply appeared to be abnormally long.

When I read the announcement in the next morning's newspaper, I could not take my eyes off the words, "...<u>simply appeared to be</u>..." With the newspaper under my arm, I went to Charlie's lab. I held it under Charlie's eyes and said, "There it is! The weasel word! It didn't <u>appear</u> to be a long day, damn it; it <u>was</u> long."

"I've seen it, Joe. I've got a class in a few minutes. Let's talk later."

"They've started the cover-up."

"Later, Joe. We'll talk about it calmly and rationally. OK?"

"OK, OK."

By July 7, foreign news stories and sports had crowded the long day off the front pages. The twenty-member commission of the National Academy of Sciences had settled down to preparing a comprehensive report, and the earth continued to spin. As time passed the dire feeling eased, and the long day began to dissolve into the realm of a curiosity. With no explanation, talk of a miracle began to sink roots, as church attendance began to rise. In time the long day crumbled into a brew of murky ideas and omens stirred by charlatans—predicting God's retribution, an alien invasion, or a communist plot—until people, confused by fanciful claims, began to allow the question to cool down into nonsense. Except me, that is. Not only did my interest not wane; it had needled deep to create an exquisite ache in my consciousness. Much of the ache was worry that the event would be ignored, eventually forgotten and, soon, impossible to study. To me the cause of the earth's inexplicable behavior on that July 2nd had become a grail that dangled in space beyond reach, though clearly visible. Even after studying several books on astronomy and cosmology, I still lacked the knowledge necessary to understand my father's notebooks, much less create a hypothesis. The errant sun had left no marks except one: a fracture in man's faith in predictable, understandable nature. And with each passing day, that fracture was generating scar tissue that would eventually preclude examination. The greatest unanswered question in history would remain unanswered, as the question became an obsession, no, an abscess that would not stop throbbing.

After two months I could stand the suspense no longer. Ruth was pregnant, apparently having conceived on that memorable day. As thrilled as I was at becoming a father, a baby could not shove that nagging question out of view.

On the fourth of September I telephoned the Washington office of the National Academy of Sciences. After holding on the line as they shuffled me from one secretary to another, I finally reached someone who was willing to provide a list of commission members. One of the names jumped out as I jotted them down: Rudolf Lazar, my major graduate professor. I telephoned Dr. Lazar's office to get his phone number in Washington, and Dr. Lazar answered.

"What's going on with the commission? I can't stand the silence."

"I read about your father, Joe. My condolences. He was a good man and a good scientist."

"Thanks, Rudy. But what about the Commission?"

"I dropped out last week, Joe."

"Why? What happened?"

"Nothing."

"You didn't quit for nothing."

"Nothing is what we were doing. We weren't accomplishing a damned thing, and my research was languishing."

"But Rudy, this is important."

"That's what I thought, but there have been no effects, no evidence that anything happened. And with no data, no evidence, no facts, we got mired in a hopeless swamp of arcane speculations about ultimate causes and effects. Reminded me of an undergraduate philosophy course I took years ago."

"I don't understand."

"There were no observable disruptions, no scars, so to speak. With no tangible effects, how can you conclude or hypothesize? It's impossible." He sounded tired.

"But Rudy, this is the greatest question nature has ever posed."

"So great that we have no choice but to drop it."

"You mean ignore it?"

"Exactly."

"But the lunatics will steal the day with alien invasions and God's wrath, and people are eating it up."

"Naturally."

"We've got to stop it." I could think of no more persuasive words.

"It'll have to be someone else, Joe. Sorry."

I hung up the phone feeling limp and hollow.

The following week the chairman of the National Academy Commission announced that he had resigned also because his research was suffering. There was no announcement in the press. I discovered it in a brief note in Science Magazine, which said that several members had resigned after Dr. Lazar, and they were replaced. I recognized none of the new names. By the time their work was done, the Commission consisted completely of unknown and undistinguished scientists.

The Commission finally submitted its report on March 29 of the following year, nine months after the long day. I found that date ironic because that was the day my daughter, Esther, was born. None of the original Commission members signed the final report. The report attracted little attention. Most newspapers ignored it. A brief article in The New York Times explained that the commission failed to find an explanation because the long day produced no physical effects. "In fact," the article said, "strange as it might seem, the commission found no conclusive evidence that there was actually a long day or if there was, how long it lasted." Furious, I threw the newspaper into the waste bin and then retrieved it, cut out the article, and filed it. I immediately telephoned the Washington office of the National Academy of Sciences.

"I just read the New York Times article on your report of the long day. I find it ludicrous that competent scientists have reached that conclusion. I'd like a copy of the full report."

"Of course, Dr. Adams. I'll put it in the mail right away."

Two weeks later the letter came from the National Academy of Sciences with the seventy-five-page report. I ripped open the package, sat at my desk and read it from beginning to end. When I had turned the last page I knew the New York Times article had been accurate. The Commission had crafted the painfully long, excruciatingly detailed report to satisfy every political, religious and scientific persuasion. After a few minutes I walked down the hall to Charlie's lab.

"You won't believe this."

"Huh?"

"I've just read the report on the long day. They claim nothing happened."

Tapping a manometer without looking at me, he said, "Yeah, I saw the New York Times article. I don't get it."

"Lack of evidence."

"But the whole world saw it."

"Like the eye witness account of Moses parting the Red Sea?"

"I give up. What evidence did they want?"

"Scars, like the bombed-out buildings and cemeteries of World War II."

"And there aren't any."

"Right. Nothing adds up, the expected weather, nothing, not even astronomical evidence that time passed. That's why they denied it happened. Hard as it is to swallow, they figured their conclusion would go down easier than declaring it a miracle and stirring up the loonies. Unless there's a repetition, people will forget it anyhow."

"OK. Except for getting you a baby daughter, it hasn't made any difference that I can see."

"Come on, Charlie. You know it happened! We can't let them sweep it under the rug. Can't you see what this means?"

"I see that I need research results to get tenure, and so do you."

"How can you ignore this fantastic research opportunity, Charlie?"

For the first time since I walked in, Charlie turned to me. "What do you have in mind?"

"I don't know yet."

Returning to his experiment he said, "You'll be working out of your expertise, Joe. Watch out. Also, you'll be taking on the whole scientific establishment."

"We'll see."

That afternoon I went home a little before four o'clock.

"I'm glad you're home early," Ruth said. "Esther wants to see you."

With my mind still racing, her words made no impression.

"Don't you want to see your daughter?"

"Oh, sure. It's just that I got that NAS report today. The newspaper was right."

"How could they?"

"To please everybody."

Ruth had picked up Esther from the bassinet. "Take your daughter, Daddy."

I took the baby and smiled at her momentarily, then abruptly said, "I can't take this lying down."

"You just got home, Joe. Let it rest. You'll do better tomorrow after you've slept on it."

"Got to do it now, Ruth. It's driving me crazy."

"Joe, this wonderful little baby needs her father even more than I do."

"I'm sorry, Ruth, but I've just got to. I can't think about anything else. I'll be back as soon as I can."

"Try to get back by suppertime. I'm getting tired of eating alone."

"I'm sorry, Ruth…"

Ruth turned and took the baby back to her room. She so rarely got angry at me that I almost stayed, but something I couldn't resist urged me on.

After throwing away three drafts of a letter, I sat back and reread the toned-down fourth draft:

"Thank you for sending me the report of the Special Commission. I must express my dismay over their conclusion that nothing occurred on July 2 of last year. I respectfully request that I be allowed to appear before the commission to testify to what I observed and what I have learned. If that is not possible, then I demand the right to append a statement to the report."

For the next five weeks I heard nothing. On Friday of the fifth week I resolved that if Monday's mail brought nothing I'd phone them again. In the mailroom on the following Monday morning I found a letter from the NAS:

"Dear Professor Adams:

"The commission disbanded on the day it submitted its report. While the NAS sympathizes with your feelings, we bear the burden of facing public reaction. We feel that the commission's conclusion, though scientifically unsatisfying, is scientifically sound, intellectually honest, and expedient. It will enhance public order and calm.

"The issue is closed. We thank you for your interest."

I immediately sat down and wrote another letter. It wasn't easy to remain calm; I was approaching my boiling point. My letter read:

"I just received your letter denying me permission to address the commission about the long day. By precluding further investigation you have assured that the most important question that nature has ever posed will remain unanswered. I cannot accept your or the commission's judgment, and I insist on testifying or at least adding my own statement to the report."

Until I dropped the letter in the mail slot, I had not thought about the testimony I would give. With no theory or tentative hypothesis to explain the long day I could think of nothing constructive except its vital importance, but it didn't matter. I would not allow this question to drown in the murky prose of political posturing. I even imagined myself testifying in a Senate committee room like those I had seen on television, sitting alone with long, hostile faces staring down at me. I'd face them down. Yes, I'd testify, and I'd have time to prepare.

Two months passed before I convinced myself that there would be no answer. By that time I had decided on another approach. I would write articles and letters to all the scientific journals and newsmagazines I could think of warning that if such an event went unexamined, it would remain a mystery, and the world would never know if and when it would happen again. But most importantly, we would miss a chance to understand something deeply significant about nature. Few people responded, mainly those who saw that day as a sign of doom. I began to feel I was hanging on a cliff of loose gravel wondering whether nature could suspend its laws: Would water boil the next time I heated it?

Would a baseball return to earth at the next home run? A cavern of chaos and unpredictability had opened its door into deep darkness.

After a few months journals and even newspapers began to reject my letters and articles. I now began a different approach, one that could help me professionally as well as satisfying my curiosity. I looked up the new astronomer on the faculty and dialed his number.

"Hello, Stanley Starr?"

"Yes."

"I'm Joe Adams from chemistry. I'd like to discuss something with you."

"I have a class at ten. How's eleven?"

"I have one at eleven. How about one-thirty this afternoon?"

"I'll be here."

At 1:25 I knocked on Dr. Starr's door.

After introducing myself, I sat down. "I have a research idea I'd like to talk over. It deals with the day the sun didn't move. I think it's terrible the way the scientific world has ignored this phenomenon, and I want to do something about it. What do you think about working together on it?"

"First of all, call me Stan. That was quite a day!"

"Got any ideas?"

"Wish I did. Apparently nothing in the heavens moved, not even the stars. But the most interesting part was that clocks stopped too, as if time itself stopped."

"Has the astronomical community shown any interest in it?"

"At first, but no more."

"Astronomers should be jumping in with both feet."

"I know."

"Well, how about it?"

"How about what?"

"Working on it. I'd like to submit a joint proposal, you and I, to NSF. Maybe we could dig up something. First thing would be a complete literature search."

"You'd have to start with the Bible. That's the only known reference."

I wasn't sure whether he was laughing at me or not, so I didn't comment.

"I wouldn't know where to begin, Joe."

"Good enough. I'll get something together and then we'll talk. In the meantime, these are my father's notebooks. My mother gave them to me when he died."

"J. P. Adams was your father? I didn't make the connection."

"Yes. His last words were pretty cryptic. He might have known it in advance. I can't follow his notes. Would you mind looking them over?"

"Wow! I'd be honored. He did nice work in astrophysics."

"Thanks. See you soon."

I submitted an inquiry to the National Science Foundation. In it I explored the possibility of funding for a search of scientists who would want to study the long day. It would be, at first, a meeting of people who could think creatively about it and perhaps outline a method of attack. The project would involve faculty and graduate students from all over the country and overseas too. The objective was to tackle this problem from every possible scientific point of view.

Within a week I received the answer. Apparently they took me for a troublemaker, for the NSF offered no hope of funding and didn't even ask for a formal proposal. When other governmental agencies followed suit, I took the responses to Stan Starr's office and sat down. I must have looked dejected because he could barely look me in the face.

"As bad as all that?"

"Here they are: all rejections. Any ideas?"

"For a while I thought I had something."

"What?"

"It doesn't hold water, but it was nice for a while."

"Tell me."

"If we accept the expanding universe, there are two opinions of what will happen eventually: If the total mass of the universe is great enough, then there will eventually come a point where the force of gravitation will overcome the centrifugal force of the big bang and the universe will begin to shrink. If the total mass of the universe is not great enough, then the expansion will continue forever."

"And?"

Stan smiled sheepishly. "What if the universe reached its outer limit of expansion and started to contract. At that crucial moment everything would begin to run in reverse. But for an instant, which could be pretty long in universe time, time and everything in the universe would stand still as it stopped expanding and started to shrink. I have no way to test that idea or even to know if it makes sense. Nobody knows what would happen at that point."

I sat amazed at the simplicity.

"But after thinking about it, I realized it doesn't make sense. To account for the observed immobility of the sun, we'd have to show that the earth's rotation stopped. Nothing about the idea would account for that."

I could not hear his objections, but only the possibility. I was frozen to my chair. Finally, I said, "Do you realize, Stan, that's the first sensible idea I've heard from anybody. And that would explain how my father could have predicted it."

"Actually, that's where I got the idea. His notes contain calculations of the expanding universe. He didn't relate it to the sun's motion, though."

I stood to leave and said, "I've got to think about this."

"We'd better forget it, Joe. I discussed your plan with my department chair. Without blinking an eye he said to drop it."

"Another ineffectual academic with no imagination."

"I wouldn't say that. Smith is a respected astronomer."

"Uh-huh."

"Your father was doing some interesting work, but it wasn't related. I'll be blunt, Joe. My chair has heard of your interest in this problem."

"And?"

"He thinks I should stay as far as I can from it and you."

"You agree?"

"I don't know. He's pretty sharp, and he is the chairman."

"You mean he's got you by your tenure."

He grimaced and nodded.

Standing, I said, "Thanks for nothing."

"Wait, Joe. Don't take it personally. Only the real scientists ask the tough questions, and I respect you for that. Most people take on sure-fire projects that yield lots of papers even if nobody ever reads them. I mean it, Joe. But the thing is, well, frankly nobody I know has any ideas on how to tackle this one. Working alone as a chemist you'd have no chance. I wish I could help, honest. If I had any idea at all I would, irrespective of my chair. But I don't. And neither has anybody else."

I stood through Stan's speech and when he finished I opened the door and turned. "Thanks anyway, Stan. Maybe we can have lunch together sometime."

"I'd like that, Joe. Anytime."

The phone was ringing as I opened my office door.

"Dr. Adams? My name is Professor Jonathan Wells. I understand you're interested in pursuing the long day phenomenon."

"Are you the person who was on the radio that night claiming it was an alien invasion?"

"That's right, Dr. Adams. It was the station that gave me your name. I want to have a televised seminar on the long day. The station has agreed to host it. I'm inviting several scientists and others to discuss that highly provocative phenomenon, and, well, with your interest and credentials, I thought you would be a good person to have."

"Not interested."

"Sorry to hear that, Dr. Adams. It would be good to have representation from an academic scientist like you."

"Who else is participating?"

"I'm hoping to get men and women of excellent credentials from industry, science, the clergy, and a philosopher."

"I'm not interested in associating with charlatans."

"Oh, no, Dr. Adams. These are all respected people, community leaders who are vitally interested. It would be a good opportunity to promote your ideas."

"What's the format?"

"Each person will make a ten-minute presentation, followed by a thirty-minute discussion period, and then we'll take telephone calls from listeners. One hour total."

In spite of my doubts and suspicions I agreed to appear. It could be an opportunity to convince people about the urgency of a serious study. After all, the scientific establishment had chosen to ignore it. Perhaps common people could do what intellectuals could not.

Ruth was excited when I told her. She said she would get all her friends to listen.

The program started at eight o'clock PM the following week. Professor Wells was pleasant enough and looked distinguished with well-groomed, gray hair and moustache. I could see why he had impressed the radio people. He was tall, handsome and athletic. The others were ordinary looking, and I neither knew nor recognized any of them. One, an evangelical preacher, also tall and husky, had eyes that could bore a hole through you. He said little, apparently awaiting his turn.

The moderator, a pleasant young woman from the radio station, started the program by introducing all the members of the panel in a voice that smiled. I was the only scientist. A short, chubby man, a math teacher in a parochial school, seemed meek and frightened. An elderly woman who taught science in a public high school asked to speak first. The moderator politely told her that Professor Wells had organized the forum and would present the issue first. "You can speak right after him," she said. The woman looked anxious as she fidgeted with her purse and finally laid it on the floor beside her.

When the clock hit eight o'clock, Wells began, "I have appeared on the radio several times over the past months, and many of you already know my hypothesis. However, for those of you who do not know, I will repeat it. I believe the phenomenon we call the long day was an illusion produced by aliens who somehow spread a light, hitherto unknown chemical element that has penetrated our brains to produce the illusion. The sun did not stand still; the earth did not stop rotating; time did not stop. All was illusion. These aliens are taking over the planet unobserved. To those of you who wonder where these aliens are, the answer is simple: the light element has rendered us unable to see them. It's part of the illusion."

The fidgety woman did not wait for an introduction: "I'm Mildred Garcia, and I teach high school science. I have never seen or read of any reliable evidence for aliens or unidentified flying objects, although some people seem to love the idea. Of course, the thought that we are not alone in the universe is seductive, but where is the evidence? Why have the government and the science establishment ignored them? The only answer is these things don't exist. But in answer to Professor Wells' theory that the apparent long day was an illusion: how could everybody on earth have had the same illusion? Those aliens, Professor Wells, must be plenty smart and thorough. Your theory is nonsense, Sir. I believe that long day was simply a quirk of nature. The universe is a beautifully complex machine, and its mechanism failed temporarily, as all machines do occasionally. I have no idea what the failure was, but it apparently corrected itself. I think that's all there is to it."

"Professor Adams," the moderator said. "What do you think?"

As much as I wanted to describe Stan Starr's idea of the contracting universe, I knew it was half-baked and no better than Wells'.

"First of all, neither of these explanations is a scientific theory or even a hypothesis. A scientific theory must be testable. That means we should be able to use it to predict something observable. If the theory fails to do that, you must find another. Mr. Wells' idea cannot be tested because the aliens have rendered all humans incapable of perceiving them or the motion of the sun. So his so-called theory precludes any testing or verification. Besides that, Mr. Wells, there cannot be an unknown, light element. Hydrogen is the lightest element in the periodic table. There is no way, within atomic theory, to account for an element lighter than hydrogen. If any such element were found the entire atomic theory would have to be scrapped. At any rate, because this element is imperceptible, it has no observable properties, so we can never hope to isolate or study it. So his hypothesis precludes the possibility of finding either the element or the aliens. As for the aliens, I know of no credible scientists or other professionals who have seen them. Only amateurs and crackpots have reported seeing them.

"Mrs. Garcia's suggestion that the universe merely had a temporary failure suffers from the same fault: it is not testable or verifiable. Her idea is not a theory either. It is merely a story that offers a false feeling of understanding."

"What do you propose, Dr. Adams?" the moderator said.

"I have not been able to devise a testable hypothesis. And that's what makes this event so frightful and fascinating. When someone offers a real theory, we will be on the road to understanding that day."

"Doctor Adams," Wells said, "I would appreciate it if you would refer to me as Professor Wells."

"In your radio interview you said you did not hold a university faculty position. You also said you do not have a doctorate."

"That is insulting!"

"The truth feels that way sometimes. Call me Mr. Adams or Joe if you like. I don't mind."

"I expected to come here for an intellectual discussion, not a personal attack."

"So did I. When do you plan to start? What I said about your ideas is rational and scientifically correct."

"Reverend Watkins, you have something to say?" the moderator said. "Go ahead, Reverend."

"It's clear to me that you are all looking in the wrong places. It is not difficult to see the cause of that day if we have eyes to see. Only God could produce such an event. In his universal benevolence, God has performed a miracle for the entire world to behold." He looked upward and paused a moment before continuing. "What is there to understand? What more do we need to know? His warning is clear. The Lord has stopped the sun for a reason. What reason can He have but to warn us? We have become a complacent and Godless society. Just look around at the disasters our cities have become: havens of divorce, abortion, drugs, crime and countless other sins. And what has science done but lead us out of the path that God prepared for us. Science claims to explain everything, but in truth, it explains nothing, for science is the Devil's work: carefully crafted fabrications pasted together with slimy lies.

"Our scientist friend here wants a theory. What theory can explain God's will? This is not the first time God has intervened in the workings of the natural order. In the midst of battle Joshua said, '...Sun, stand thou still upon Gibeon; and thou, Moon, in the valley of Ajalon. And the sun stood still…in the midst of heaven, and hasted not to go down about a whole day. And there was no day like that before it or after it.' Yes, God works miracles and always with a purpose. We may not yet know God's purpose in this case, but that He has one cannot be denied."

Mr. Devon, would you care to comment?

I felt sorry for the poor meek man. He looked so nervous and out of place straightening his tie. Finally he began in a slow, raspy whisper: "We are the wrong people to be discussing this phenomenon," Mr. Devon said. "None of us can claim expertise in astrophysics. Dr. Adams is right about theories, and I wish he had one. Everything he said is correct, in contrast to the other panel members, but we seem to be stuck with whimsical, bizarre explanations that can be neither verified nor falsified. I am not an astrophysicist either, so I have little to offer, except this: No one has brought up the question of evidence. What actually happened that day? Mr. Wells says nothing happened and that we've been duped by aliens. I think the first item of business is to determine precisely what happened. And the only way we can do that is to measure the effects of that day. Trouble is, there were no effects. None whatever! Not the disruptions in weather or changes in motion and inertia. With no effects to observe, it is very difficult to say that anything happened. The NAS Commission members were forced to conclude that nothing happened. Logically their conclusion is valid.

Mr. Devon's statement made me feel hollow. "Mr. Devon," I said. "I appreciate what you said. And I understand that without effects we have nothing to grasp except superstition, religion and quackery. But I'm not ready to give up the way the NAS Commission did."

"You see, even the NAS Commission agrees with my theory in part," Wells said. "I mean that it was an illusion."

"I read their report," I said, "and they never mentioned either aliens or perfuming the planet with light elements."

"OK, so my theory is weak, but a weak theory is better than nothing. Two centuries ago chemists believed that when something burns it releases a gas they called phlogiston, a material whose mass could be positive, zero or negative. That theory was replaced by Lavoisier's theory of combustion and the discovery of oxygen, but only after phlogiston had held sway over chemist's work for centuries. I maintain that my hypothesis is valid until a better one comes along. What do you say to that, Dr. Adams?"

"Phlogiston was shown to be wrong, but it was a valid theory because it contained within its statement the means for chemists to confirm or deny it. Can one substance, phlogiston, have a mass that changes with circumstances? Scientists of the time thought so; today we know better. However the theory proposed such a substance, so chemists worked for years trying to isolate it so they could measure its properties. They never did, of course, but the search led to the discovery of hydrogen, oxygen, carbon dioxide, and other gases and with them, a useful theory of combustion. Can you explain how your theory of aliens leads us to facts of any kind?"

"Just a moment," Mrs. Garcia said, "If the universe were to break down again, what could you do to fix it? Nobody, no nation in the world, controls the universe."

"That's what we're trying to understand, Mrs. Garcia," Mr. Devon said. "Your suggestion is a nice idea, but it doesn't help. The only answer to your question is that only God can fix the universe when it breaks down."

Mr. Wells said, "I see this panel is not as open-minded and unbiased as I had hoped. We'll get nowhere as long as we bicker about falsification and verification. I'd like to hear somebody react to my theory of an alien invasion.

"Since you proposed it, you should explain how it will help us understand," I said.

Feeling overwhelmed, the moderator broke in. "I think we've heard the panel's views. Let's take some phone calls. Our lines have been busy since we started. Hello, welcome to our panel on the long day."

"Hello. Am I on?"

"Yes, go on, please."

"Well I'm sick and tired of these high falutin' scientists talking about things nobody understands and then telling us what to think. The reverend is right. God can do anything He wants, and what right do we have to dispute Him? And furthermore, like the reverend says,

God has a purpose. He's telling us to mend our ways or be damned! That's what I believe and that's all I have to say."

"Thank you," the moderator said. "I don't think that call requires a response. Our next caller is a young man. How old are you?"

"Seventeen."

"Go ahead please."

"I'm in Mrs. Garcia's general science class, and I want to tell you she's great. She explains science for us real good. I really like her, and I think you all should listen to her."

"Do you have any opinion on the long day?" the moderator asked.

"No, Ma'am. We got a day off from school, though. It was pretty nice."

Before she dismissed him I interrupted: "Young man, from your age I guess you must be a senior."

"Yes, sir."

"I also assume that you didn't take chemistry, since you're in general science."

"No way! Chemistry ain't for me. Mrs. Garcia gave us two weeks of it, and it was awful. I don't think anybody understood it."

"Yet you like Mrs. Garcia as a teacher?"

"Sure. She gives us stuff we understand. You know, like ecology and stuff like that. You know, how we're all part of the ecosystem of animals and plants, and how we all live off each other."

Reverend Watkins could not hold back: "Young man, God made the animals and plants for man's use. Man is special and should not be grouped with animals, let alone plants."

"I beg your pardon, reverend," Mrs. Garcia said. "Ecology is an important body of knowledge, and we better pay attention to it if we are going to survive on this planet."

"Oh ye of little faith!" the reverend said. "God provides for our needs."

"God helps him who helps himself," Mrs. Garcia said.

As Mr. Devon sat shaking his head and looking down at the table, I understood why Dr. Lazar resigned from the NAS Commission. The phone calls lasted half an hour longer. Most callers either subscribed to the notion that nothing had happened, or that it was a miracle that could never be understood. But the most astounding thing was how many of them talked to me as if I were the Devil himself.

When the hour ended the moderator summed up: "It is always interesting to hear people's opinions. I'd like to take this opportunity to thank you all for a very informative and entertaining discussion. And for our listeners, please stay tuned for more in our new series of enlightening and provocative discussions on timely topics. Again, thank you all."

When the broadcast ended I moved toward Mr. Devon to speak with him, but he was leaving. I left without comment or conversation. I had had enough of popular opinion.

"You were wonderful, Joe," Ruth said. "At least four friends called to say you were the star of the evening. You looked so handsome on the screen."

"Maybe, but it's hard to beat dedicated ignorance. If you win, what have you won? If you lose, you lost to ignorance and stupidity. Either way it doesn't matter."

Having failed at every turn and with nowhere else to go, I presented a modest proposal to the chemistry department. In it I proposed only to set up a seminar on the subject of the long day and invite scientists and students from all relevant departments.

At a faculty meeting called to discuss my proposal, I gave an oral presentation. Harvey Baron was the first to speak, and from his comment the verdict was clear.

"Have you applied for external funding?"

"I've tried NSF, Department of Energy, the Army, the Navy, and the Environmental Protection Agency."

"Does your request for departmental support mean they turned you down?" he said.

"That's correct, but no one condemned it as unworthy of study; only that they had all their funds committed. They suggested I approach it locally, which is why I'm here."

"Odd," Harvey Baron said. "The way you described it suggests that the problem is world-wide. Why should it be a local problem?"

"What do you mean the way I described it? It was worldwide and everybody on earth saw it, including you."

"We really don't need to get into that. I'd like to keep the discussion on a rational and professional level."

"So do I. And I don't appreciate the suggestion that I'm not rational or professional."

Harvey Baron raised his eyebrows in mock surprise and looked around at our colleagues. "No offense, Joe. I simply meant that this is not a real proposal. You haven't presented an experimental plan. Without direction this would have little chance of success and will only drain our meager budget."

"The point of this proposal is to bring people together to work out a hypothesis. If one arises, then we can begin to tackle the problem."

"Why don't you pursue the public media? You made a start on TV the other night."

"That was awful."

"I agree," Harvey said. "Sounded like the lunatic fringe."

Before I could respond, George Buchner spoke with a hint of impatience: "Joe, you're asking us to devote departmental funds to pursue a project that only you find important. Have any colleagues shown any interest?"

"I think some would if we had some support."

"But to divert our attention to a questionable project isn't fair to the rest of us, is it? A bird in the hand is worth two in the bush."

I looked around the room at my colleagues' faces. They looked like students afraid to be called on, their eyes down on their hands. "I think I have the department's answer. I withdraw my proposal, but I think we're making a mistake we'll regret some day."

I did not wait for the chair to adjourn the meeting, but rose and walked out. Charlie Hollowell followed me. "Come on, Joe. I'll buy the coffee."

When we sat down at an isolated table near a large window of the basement coffee shop he said, "I heard one of your students say you were going to schedule your final exam the next time the sun stands still, so they'd have plenty of time."

"To hell with them. They're stupid too. Don't you understand, Charlie?"

"Not really, unless you're trying to squash your chance at tenure."

"Damn it, Charlie, you remember that day as well as I do."

"Sure. Classes were canceled. We all had a day off and threw a party. Let it go, Joe. No one else cares."

"The most important event in human history, and all it meant was a day off and a party."

"It wasn't that much of an event, and no one else thinks it's important." Charlie saw that I was teetering between anger and confusion. "OK, it happened—once." He put his hand on my shoulder. "Is it worth your job? Think about your family. You've got to put tenure and family first, Joe. Harvey and his ass-kissers say you've abandoned science for mysticism. They're trying to make you out a weirdo."

I felt dumb and powerless. A great injustice was being committed in plain view, my best friend didn't care, and there was nothing I could do. Without comment, I left Charlie sitting there, walked back to my office, turned off the light, and walked home.

As I crossed the playing field at the edge of campus I saw a bird soaring high above. My first impression was a circling vulture. The bird certainly remembered nothing of that day. How carefree to fly through life worrying only about the day, staying alive, and caring nothing for the beautiful, the strange, the inexplicable. Just fly and feed and live until your days run out. Sure, Charlie's right.

When I walked through the house to the back porch Ruth looked surprised. "What happened? It's only eleven-thirty."

I sat in a recliner beside her and remained silent for a moment. "Nothing...no, that's not true. My colleagues think I'm nuts. And so do my students."

"Nobody thinks that, Joe. It's just..."

"I know. I worry too much about wrong things. How can they, Ruth?"

"Well, dear, everyone sees the world through different eyes. Other people don't or can't see what you see. Your mind's eye peers into the unknown, and drives you to distraction. What do you see, Joe? I mean besides that day and the beautiful sun rigid in the sky like a gold medal? Is it a sign of something? Sometimes I feel you see too deeply. Not like the others. They don't have your faith in the order of nature."

"Faith, is it?"

"Probably. Think of the spectacle of an immobile sun and the horror it conjured, Joe. I can see why people might pretend it never happened. To emphasize it is discomforting."

"What could Dad have meant, Ruth?"

"You'll never know. Does it matter?"

"It does to me." Anger was beginning to swell. "He meant something. It was s-u-n, not s-o-n. I'm sure of it. If only I'd been there. I'm always away at the wrong times."

"Like when?"

"The big award he got in New York for his work in astrophysics. I could have gone, but I was too busy. It would have meant a lot to him."

"You can't do everything, Joe. He understood."

"You know, Ruth, we had a big competition going between astronomy and chemistry, all through my undergraduate and graduate days. I thought it was fun competing with my dad until I realized it wasn't fun to him. He was a member of a group of a few hundred astronomers. There are hundreds of thousands of chemists. His field was tiny compared to mine. He was well known in his field, but I had the impression he felt sheepish about it."

"Why would he?"

"Big frog in a small pond, maybe. I was swimming in an ocean of scientific sharks. When I finally realized it I stopped enjoying the competition. I always respected his work, though, even when I didn't understand it."

"It would be nice to link his name to this greatest of all astrophysical events, wouldn't it?"

"That's not the reason, but...sure. I suppose so."

Ruth always surprised me. Here she had spotted a kernel in a bushel. She had cracked the outer shell of a buried feeling I was not even aware of. When I took her hand and said, "You're always right," she reached over and kissed me.

"You've been running yourself into the ground, Joe. That's what worries me. You have so much talent and energy, it's a shame to waste it on a fruitless fight when you have so much good work to do in chemistry. Not to mention our beautiful daughter."

After a few silent minutes I stood. "I'm going outside. The hedges need trimming."

"Good! I'll fix something nice for lunch."

The next morning I arrived at my lab not remembering anything between the time I left home and that moment. It was as if I had walked out of a dream into the bright light of day. My desk lay like a corpse under a pile of books, papers, and magazines, seemingly dropped there entropically from the sky. At that moment I realized how much time and energy I had devoted to the long day at the expense of my legitimate research. That pile of papers, journals and books represented the chaos I had to dig out of. I knew then that people were right: I had spent enough time embroiled in things I did not understand at the expense of those things I had worked toward all those years. Hardly knowing where to start, I dug through the pile, separating out journals I had not read into a stack and returning books to the bookshelves. When I had introduced a little order into the chaos, I lifted the top journal off the stack and looked at it as if it were a foreign object. I laid it down on the small piece of clear desktop and turned pages, scanning titles, until I came to one that sent a cold shiver through me. The article described a new, highly conducting organic polymer made from a semiconducting one. The authors claimed that it conducted almost as well as copper. I devoured the pages, rereading to make sure I had understood. A Japanese and an American, working together, had, for the first time, polymerized acetylene gas to make a semiconducting film. Others had tried and succeeded only in making dry powders. Polyacetylene film was exciting enough, for it was a good semiconductor. I read on to learn that the authors exposed the semiconducting film to iodine vapor and converted it into a silvery, lustrous film that behaved essentially like a metal, except that it was plastic, light and flexible. They theorized that the iodine removed negative charge in the form of electrons from the otherwise rigid polymer molecules, creating positively charged "holes" for other electrons to move into. Electrons from a current source could then move through the film by jumping into holes leaving new holes behind them for more electrons to move into. The explanation was simple, clear, and beautiful!

When I finished the article I looked through my chemical agents for iodine crystals and a sample of one of my polymers that conducted slightly. I found them both and put the polymer sample in a wide-mouth jar beside a few iodine crystals and covered the jar with a glass plate. Within minutes purple iodine vapor filled the jar, and the sample began to turn reddish and lustrous, like copper. I took out the sample and tested its conductivity. It conducted like mad! But as it stood on the lab bench the sample reverted to its original, nondescript cream color and its conductivity dropped off. I repeated the experiment inside a large dry box that I kept free of moisture and atmospheric oxygen. This time the sample's conductivity was even higher, and did not diminish nor did its color change as long as it stayed in the dry box. I spent the entire afternoon exposing samples of all my polymers to iodine vapor and measuring their conductivity in the air and in the dry box. Some showed improved conductivity and some didn't, but the results were thrilling. I couldn't stop. As five o'clock approached I called Ruth to say I'd be late for supper.

"What's wrong?"

"Big breakthrough. Tell you later. Gotta go."

When I got home two hours later, I ran in and picked her up. I could barely get the words out: "Right under my nose, Ruth. What a breakthrough!"

"That's wonderful. It was time for a break."

"Tomorrow I'll try some other agents beside iodine. There are countless oxidizing agents, you know."

"This calls for a celebration. And I have a bottle of the same champagne we drank on the long day. Remember?"

"What are we waiting for?"

Over the next few weeks I experimented with other oxidizing agents besides iodine and found several that worked even better. Working late every day I managed to submit four papers to the journal before the end of the academic year. As they began to appear, requests for reprints began to pour in. One was a phone call from a French electrochemist named Marcel Moré in Paris. He told me he wanted to apply for a travel grant to visit my lab and asked if I would support his application

"Of course, Dr. Moré. I've read all your papers."

"Good. I would like to spend a month working with you to learn about conducting polymers. I believe we could make them electrochemically."

We talked for a long time about the possibilities and agreed that Marcel Moré would travel as soon as he could get approval from his department and the French government.

Two months later I picked him up at the airport and drove him to the university, where I had reserved an apartment for him on campus. Marcel brought several boxes of electrical equipment with him. "I thought you might not have access to these, and I did not want to waste time ordering them."

After dropping off his bags at the apartment, I drove him to the chemistry building and showed Marcel my equipment and some of my polymers and how we measured conductivity. Then I helped him set up the electrical equipment he had brought.

He set up his delicate electrolysis apparatus and explained how he planned to prepare my films. I called two of my graduate students to watch. First Marcel dissolved my starting compound in a solvent that would conduct an electric current. He then poured the solution into a special glass tube fitted with two platinum electrodes. Controlling the voltage carefully, he turned on the electric current so it passed through the solution between the electrodes. As the current flowed, a coating began to form on the positive electrode.

We watched with fascination at the color change of the electrode, as Marcel explained what was happening: "The monomer molecules drift to the positive electrode, where the electrode rips off an electron and bonds the molecule to the electrode. When another molecule approaches, it takes the electron from the attached molecule and thereby becomes bonded to that molecule. The process continues until we have a long string of conducting molecules connected to each other—the polymer."

"Beautiful," I said, as we watched the electrode change to shiny black.

"And this polymer should be a good conductor already because it has been conducting electrons from the individual molecules into the electrode," Marcel said.

He then disconnected the cell without exposing its electrodes and solution to the air and moved it to the dry box, where he opened the cell, peeled the film off the electrode, washed it with a non-conducting solvent and dried it by blowing dry nitrogen gas over it. I then measured its conductivity.

"Slightly better than the same polymer we made using iodine vapor," I said. My students could not stop staring at the product and asking questions. Finally Marcel reached into his briefcase and handed each of them copies of his latest papers on the process. "Read these, and then we will talk."

After we had made several more samples using Marcel's apparatus, I called Ruth to say I wanted to invite Marcel to dinner.

"Of course, Joe. I'm fixing a roast."

When Marcel and I showed up, I kissed Ruth and introduced Marcel."

Ruth put out her hand to shake his, and he took her hand, leaned forward and kissed it. Ruth blushed and tried not to appear shocked. "Come in. We'll have cocktails first. What would you like?"

"In America, martinis, always."

"Come, Marcel. It's my turn to teach you my technique."

Ruth moved out of my way and put the roast in the oven. "How do you like your beef?" she asked.

"Done to perfection."

"Me too," I said.

"You two aren't much help," she said, as I added vermouth and gin to ice in the shaker.

"You won't believe what we did today, Ruth. What took us a week, Marcel accomplished in minutes. Pure films that conduct like metal. Amazing. We'll set the field of conducting polymers on its ear."

"It is new for me also. I have never worked with conducting polymers."

"How do you like Florida?" Ruth said.

Beautiful, warm and green. It is quite chilly yet in Paris."

"And your wife? Will she be joining you?"

"I am afraid not. We have two children in school. Next time, perhaps."

"Too bad. I'd like to meet her."

"You and Joe must visit us in Paris. We will show you the City of Lights."

"I hear it's beautiful."

"Incomparable. The most beautiful city in the world. Of course, I have a slight prejudice."

"And rightly so," she said. "Have you seen New York?"

"A mighty city."

"It may not be as pretty as Paris, but it is wonderful too," she said.

"I like the wilds of Florida," I said. "It's primitive, but it's my birthplace."

"You speak English very well," Ruth said.

"I spent three years as a post-doctoral fellow at Columbia University."

By the time we had finished two martinis, Ruth had the roast out of the oven and we sat down to dinner.

The month of Marcel's visit could not have been more profitable for both of us with six joint research papers. His method allowed the graduate students to expand their research projects to the point where they submitted their dissertations the following year.

I had not mentioned my interest in the long day to Marcel, but on the drive to the airport I could not resist bringing it up. His eyes lit up when I started.

"It was truly astounding," he said. "I shall never forget it."

"You don't know what that means to me, Marcel. People here have ignored it completely. Did you read the NAS's report?"

"It was shameful, Joe."

"How about looking into it?"

Marcel's brows wrinkled. "I read some of your articles and letters about it, Joe. I wanted to write to you then, but it did not seem appropriate."

"Why not?"

"Two of my friends in astronomy wanted to work on it, but the pressure was quite powerful against it, so they did nothing."

"Politics?"

"I do not know for certain, but I think the government was afraid of exciting the religious extremists. Europe has always had problems with troublesome religious groups that gladly cast doubts on science to gain support for their fanatical views. People high in the government did not want to stir them up."

"I never suspected our government was involved. I blamed it on weak-willed scientists who saw only the low odds of success."

"There was that, too, of course. If only someone had produced a viable theory. Anything that could explain it."

"We have the lunatic fringe here too, Marcel. One guy blamed aliens who spread something in the air to alter people's perceptions."

"That's not a bad thought."

"Come now, Marcel. You don't believe in aliens?"

"Of course not. I mean the alteration of perception. The part of the phenomenon that intrigued me most was that the clocks stood still. Time did not stop, of course. We continued with our lives during that day, but all clocks stopped. We do not know how much time actually passed."

"What are you saying?"

"Let us assume that nothing happened on that day; that it was a day like any other. Then at some time later, an artificial memory of the event was spread over the world so that people had a memory of something that never occurred? Would that not explain it?"

"But there's still the means of introducing such a memory over the entire world's population. I can't imagine it."

"Nor can I. That is why I never pursued it and why I did not contact you at the time. I could not imagine how such a thing could happen so completely and so perfectly."

"I've never heard that explanation, Marcel. It's intriguing."

"Leave it alone, Joe. It will bring trouble."

"I can't tell you how much this problem has bothered me, Marcel. No one else seems to care, but I can't leave it alone. I had put it aside, but…"

"We have mapped out a new research path that will profit us more than that most intriguing long day."

"I know you're right, Marcel, but…"

I managed to set the long day aside, and by the end of the next year Marcel and I had applied for half a dozen patents on our process and on several useful materials we had prepared. My career was back on track. When I came up for tenure my resume was so good that even Harvey Baron didn't argue against it.

In one of my letters to Marcel Moré I wrote of the irony of my work: "The scientific community so readily accepts our work on molecules, electron holes, and other hypotheses that no one can ever hope to see, but they will not accept that day that everyone saw."

When he received my letter Marcel telephoned. After the usual pleasantries he said, "Joe, I have thought about the long day quite a bit since we spoke in Tampa. As enticing as it is, I urge you to put it aside. Consider this: if the cause became known, what difference would it make? We shall never duplicate the phenomenon. It has been years now and no ill effects have followed. Abandon it, Joe, and continue with the work for which we have been trained and for which you have an amazing talent."

"Marcel, I didn't tell you before, but my father died the day after that long day. Before he died he said something that still haunts me. His last words were: "I knew it would happen … sun … stop … sun …"

"Could he have meant you, his son, rather than the sun?"

"That's what my mother thought at first, but he never called me son."

"It is very sad to be left with a fragment of a thought, but what does it have to do with this?"

"He was an astrophysicist, Marcel. I think he knew something."

"That is certainly different…but I still advise you to leave it. Our work is more important now."

"That's what everybody says, Marcel."

"Let us keep in touch, Joe. I have a new paper on my desk. I will send you a copy for your comments before I submit it."

"*Merci, mon ami.*"

*

In this section of Joe Adams's notebook several pages have been ripped out. I am not able to determine why they were removed, but I assume they contained personal items that were unrelated to the issue at hand. In this chapter, I have indicated the gaps.

*

I heeded Marcel's advice, and my academic life proceeded with success that some might call astronomical, though I call it routine. But it led to invitations to give seminars around the country as well as to give a plenary lecture at a national meeting. I easily attained the rank of full professor with the concurrence of Harvey Baron, which surprised me. I was on top of my scientific world, but still I felt hollow.

After our daughter Esther earned her Ph.D. in chemistry at Cornell University, she came to work in my research group. As a physical chemist she added a much needed expertise. She also stood to gain valuable experience in a burgeoning field.

During her first semester with me she met Frank Wright, a young electrical engineer who had just joined the engineering faculty. They were married the following summer, and she continued to work with me until the birth of her first child, a boy they named William. As normal she took a few months off to take care of Billy.

(Three pages missing)

Before she was due to return to work she told me she was thinking of quitting, saying she and Frank wanted another child soon. Of course

I was not happy with her decision. I told her how promising her career was, and it would be a shame to abandon it. I even offered her a year or two off, hoping she would be ready to come back by then.

Her response was typically feminine: "As much as I love chemistry, Daddy; I can't imagine walking out on that baby for any job."

Ruth later told me that Esther told Frank about my objection, and he became furious saying, "They raised their child; we'll raise ours."

(Eight pages missing)

Ruth and I dropped in to see Billy his first day home. Ruth went straight to the baby's room and found him awake and brought him to the living room saying, "Such a cute little bear."

Esther stood beside her and looked down at the child. His eyes were still sticky, and his arms flailed at random. He was cute. I poked at him a little and then went out with Frank.

Ruth later told me she approved of Esther's decision to stay home with the baby. Esther told her that I didn't. To which Ruth said, "He'll get used to it. It'll be good for Billy."

Frank was showing me some citrus plants he had put into the ground. "Wish I had planted some," I said. "How long before they bear fruit?"

"Three or four years."

Unaware of Frank's strong feelings, I said, "Esther should be back to work by then."

"Hire somebody else, Joe. She's staying home."

"That should be her decision, Frank."

"Right, and she's made it."

"It's a shame to throw away her career."

"Not for Billy."

Noting Frank's tone, I dropped the subject and asked how his work was going. After a few seconds he said, "Took the entire year to get funded and equipment set up, but it's finally going. I'll be cranking out papers before long."

"Good. Stay with it. I wish I knew more about electrical engineering."

"Microelectronics is hot stuff right now."

"I know. I'm on another end of that field."

From that day on I never again broached the subject of Esther's career.

The blow came ten years later. In fact it was my thirty-fifth year at the university. My weekly graduate student research meeting was ending, and the department secretary stuck her head in the door to announce that Harvey Baron wanted to see me. I never understood how that humorless autocrat had managed to get faculty backing for the Chairman's job.

His office was next door to the conference room, so I went in. "Hi, Harvey. What's up?"

Skipping his usual, cool courtesies, Harvey Baron stood behind his large desk, passed his hand over his slicked down, sparse, dark-dyed hair, and looked over his glasses: "I called you in to talk about retirement. I understand you had your sixty-second birthday recently."

"I have no plans to retire, Harvey."

Ignoring my response he continued: "If you accept retirement this year, I am authorized to sweeten the pot with a $10,000 salary raise retroactive to the beginning of this academic year. That will boost your retirement income significantly."

"Not interested."

"My offer is good only through this week. If you don't accept it by Friday, it will be withdrawn. I have the approval of both the dean and the provost on the offer and the conditions."

I was stunned. The well-oiled, political bastard was making no effort to sugar-coat the pill. He'd made up his mind to push me out and had the support he needed. Our differences started over the long day, and though we rarely spoke outside of faculty meetings we were usually on opposite sides. The mutual antagonism grew when he became Chairman, so I didn't expect sympathy, but I didn't expect such cold brutality either. I hit him with all the logic I could muster: my research was going well and bringing credit to the department, I was still actively publishing and had enough ideas and funding to continue for several years more, students consistently ranked my teaching above average,

I still had much to offer. Harvey's answer left his feelings completely bare: "With your salary, we can hire two young assistant professors with fresh ideas and lots of energy, people who won't keep the department stirred up. Whether you retire or not, we'll need half your research space this semester for the two new faculty members we just hired."

Harvey's eyes unveiled the core of his hatred. Realizing that logic could never prevail over such feelings, I walked out and went to my office. Someone spoke in the hall as I passed; I didn't hear or see who it was. Memories of years of battling swirled me into a vortex of confused anger. All my years at the university focused like a laser on that blinding moment in Baron's office. I felt like the worn exhaust of a massive institutional machine with my arch-enemy finally in command. I considered refusing, perhaps suing the university. But win or lose, I knew I would end up the loser. I grabbed a blank sheet of paper, scribbled a cryptic memo accepting his offer, and walked it back to Baron's secretary. Then I started packing, as anger and frustration continued to build. My brain swirled as I filled trash cans and boxes with papers, notebooks, and records. In an eruption of aboriginal anger and frustration I threw out everything that reminded me of thirty-one years of anger. I opened the file drawer containing my documents related to the long day and threw them out too. After souring my years in the university, that terrible day would mock me no longer. "If there is a God, why in hell would He do such a senseless thing?" I said to myself.

The sun was setting when I threw the last of my files into the Dumpster behind the chemistry building and dragged myself home. I told Ruth what had happened and what I had done, expecting her to be angry at me for being so destructive.

"That's wonderful, dear. I've been hoping you'd retire soon so we could enjoy each other more." I should have expected her response, but Ruth always managed to surprise me with her abiding generosity.

For the rest of the semester I worked out of my home and came to the department only to meet classes. I soon realized how much I would regret throwing out my files that destructive afternoon. That history would now live only in my memory like the stories of long-dead grandparents who still speak through our memories of them, though we can no longer touch or talk to them.

At first, retirement was not bad. I didn't miss the classroom or even my research much and the politics and committees not at all. Ruth was wonderful. With Esther married and in charge of her own life, we took the European vacation we had long planned. Eventually, I began to collect my thoughts for a book about the long day. But everything stopped the day Ruth came home from the doctor's office with news of a devastating cancer. The next year and a half was a nightmare of surgery, radiation, chemotherapy, traveling to medical research centers, but mostly tortured waiting.

Finally it came. The world faded, and a gaping hole opened. Only the dull, gray, dissonance of the passing days reminded me that I still lived. Survival seemed impossible, worthless, and futile. I barely remember those days now, staring vacantly at the TV, hearing and seeing only the reverberations in my own mind. Charlie Hollowell called me for lunch a couple of times, but strangely, we had little to talk about. He was still working and talked about problems that no longer mattered to me.

Five years later my daughter prevailed on me to move in with her and her family. She was afraid to leave me alone after I had two minor fender-benders in the same week. The day she talked about moving, I had left a stove burner on that caused a minor fire and burned a hole in a Tupperware bowl. I hated the idea of moving, but Esther was sincerely worried, and I didn't want to cause her grief. At least I would be near my grandchildren. It had become easier to talk with them than with adults.

While Frank and I were moving my things in, Esther called me aside for a cup of coffee. Standing at the coffee maker, she said, "Daddy, we don't think you should drive any more."

"Why not? It wasn't my fault either time."

"We don't want you to hurt yourself or anyone else, Daddy. You don't go out that often anyhow. We'll drive you wherever you want to go. It'll be like having a chauffeur." She handed me the coffee with a smile.

"I'd be stranded."

"Don't worry, Daddy. We'll take good care of you."

I was already regretting the move.

"Also, please, Daddy, don't mention that long day anymore."

"Why, for heaven's sake?"

"Just don't, please."

"It's important. Your mother understood. She never bought the popular denial; not her. She saw through the smoke screen."

"See, Daddy? You start ranting when you get on that subject. Frank and I think it will confuse the children and make them feel insecure."

"Esther, you were born nine months after that July day. You probably wouldn't be here if it had been an ordinary day."

"I know, Daddy."

"You heard about it when you were a kid. Did you feel insecure?"

"No, Daddy, but Frank was too young to remember."

"What's the harm in talking?"

"Please, Daddy. All right?"

I didn't answer.

It took a week to arrange my things. Happily, my room was big enough for my desk. I kept up with a few chemical journals and didn't go out much. Once or twice a week I'd wander through campus, but never the chemistry building. Sometimes I would spend the whole afternoon browsing in the library.

Returning from a walk this afternoon, I overheard Frank in the kitchen. "He's getting crazier and refuses to let it go. We'll have to put him in a nursing home eventually; I say now's the time. Hell, he's seventy-five."

Before Esther could reply, I burst in. "I lived it. It's part of me. Why is it crazy to talk about something I lived through?"

"Because you seem to be the only person who lived through it," Frank said. "You're supposed to be a scientist, but you sound like a religious fanatic."

I stopped a moment to calm down. "Listen to reason, Frank."

"For Christ sake, even your generation doesn't remember it."

"Some people say the Nazi Holocaust never happened. How do you think the survivors feel about that?"

"How do I know there was a Holocaust? I wasn't there, and I don't know any survivors. As for your miracle day, maybe the day *seemed* longer; it was a hot July; maybe everything just slowed down. All I know is your long day is bullshit." Frank glanced at Esther with his lips curled around an angry smile and stalked out to the kitchen.

"Daddy, why do you rile him like that?"

I said nothing, and she went out to calm her husband. When she was gone, I said aloud, "I won't give up even if I'm the only one left who believes it. Oh, Ruth. How could you abandon me like this?"

That evening, feeling I had little to lose, I sat my grandchildren beside me on the sofa and began to recount the details of the day that stood at the focus of my life. As I began, Frank said, "That does it. He's outa here." Then he walked out the back door and let it slam.

My voice quivered; Esther's face showed resignation and perhaps a trace of relief. Soon the telling began to calm me. I found myself basking in the sun's true light. Ten-year-old Billy and eight-year-old Ginny listened passively.

After I had told them about that day and the days that followed, I continued: "The blue silence had spoken, not in sounds, but in beautiful stillness. Through the years I have begun to sense its meaning—that you can know some things without knowing all things. Uncertainty and confusion spawn anger and hatred. Love demands certainty and simplicity, but, like the sun's presence, we can enjoy its beauty without understanding it."

Ginny had fallen asleep on my lap.

"That was a neat story, Grandpa. Tell another one."

Smiling through her tears, Esther embraced me and then went out to her husband.

In summary, I can only say that the above is as true as anything can be in this world.

Quietly, I turned off my desk lamp, put on my robe and slippers, and went out to the back porch. Night was beginning to bleed into morning. I sat in the oak rocker with my notebook looking at the lake through the Spanish moss. The brightest stars were dissolving into the hushed celestial solvent. Out of the chaos, my thoughts fell upon

Stonehenge, its tumbled monoliths a testament of the human desire to understand things beyond our reach. Certain that humanity sprang from this yearning, I fell into a stilled rapture at the silent prelude, the almost imperceptible crescendo of new light. Then, in the immense climax that vaporizes the brooding web of fears, the sun burst over the world as it did on that July morning with a glory that never fades. I now see that the time between sunrise and sunset can vary. It can be a moment or a lifetime.

Joe Adams

*

The following postscript was handwritten by Joe Adams's daughter, Esther. Reading it, I assume it was the first time she had seen it.

*

I found Daddy still on his rocker. I had just put on the coffee and walked out to take in the beautiful morning and found him slumped over. I knew from the peaceful expression on his face that he was gone. He looked so serene that I did not disturb him. I sat beside him and took his hand and held it. The notebook into which he had been writing fell to the floor with his ball point pen. I picked up the notebook and read it through tears.

Using his pen I added these lines to complete what he considered his life's most important work. Out of love and respect for my father, I shall not attempt to publish it, for the time is not right; I do not want him to receive further ridicule. Perhaps some day the world will remember the wonderful day they have pushed out of their memories. On that day Professor Joe Adams will finally be vindicated.

Esther Adams Wright.

THE CONFESSION

Harold Pitt

Father Otis had been sitting in the confessional for almost an hour with his shoes off and the door open. He consoled himself with the thought that St. Olaf's was the coolest place in town. Fanning himself with a missal, he studied the stained glass windows and mumbled, "Twenty, one for each year of my priesthood." Unlike the classic churches he grew up with, St. Olaf's abstract images evoked only chaos.

Shafts of light stood like luminous planks against the walls, sliding upright as the sun climbed into the sky. Always fascinating, the dancing dust that livens the slanted light pillars never settle—suspended in the vastness—like his soul. Morning confessions offered repose and a time to finish waking. He thought of it as meditation, but in truth it was more an attempt to erase thought, to make his mind empty, like the vast space of St. Olaf's. That great dark angular interior was to Father Otis another expression of God's mystery—enveloping and hard, protecting and inscrutable. Only the gilded altar's gleaming arabesques and holy icons reflected the leaning light beams. Like a golden moon in a deep sky, the altar shone brilliant in the otherwise bleak vault broadcasting Jesus' message to a deaf, stony world. The Church's riches might wake the poor to God's glory, but it could not ease their hunger.

During confessions Father Otis filled his emptiness with the emptiness of others. His life of repetitious rituals and deadening routine was far from the expectations of his youth. Hearing others' problems seemed to lighten his own. The welcome relief was only temporary, however, like a dunk in a cool spring on a hot afternoon, for the heat would still be there after drying off. As pastor of St. Olaf's he kept busy, but parish administrative work—raising money, overseeing the parish school, courting politicians—and the masses, baptisms, funerals, and weddings left him mentally numb and tired to the bone without the pleasant fatigue of physical exertion.

"Bless me Father, for I have sinned. It's been almost a year since my last confession."

"Yes, my son."

As Father Otis prepared to listen he leaned back against the back of the confessional, smoothed back his thinning black hair with one hand and continued fanning himself with the other.

"I cursed my wife."

"Why, my son?"

"She nags all the time. Can't stand me around the house."

"Love the good in her, my son. Concentrate on what attracted you to her when you were young. And you might try to get out more; see friends. It'll give you something to talk about."

"Yes, Father."

"Is there something else, my son?"

"I guess not, Father."

"Say five Hail Marys and one Our Father, and try to replace your anger with love for her as a human being. You are absolved of your sins. Now go and sin no more."

As the man left mumbling to himself, Father Otis mused on the poor man's predicament, "Retired: a life sentence with a hostile cell mate."

Engrossed in mental rambling he didn't notice the man who had entered the confessional and remained standing for a moment before sitting. He seemed out of breath.

"I'm sorry. I didn't hear you come in." Hearing nothing, he said, "Well?"

"Father, I've done something...unspeakable."

"How long has it been since your last confession, my son?"

"I'm not..."

"That's all right, my son. Go on."

The man began to sob violently, bent over with his face in his hands. Father Otis sat up and saw that he was African-American.

"Come now, tell me and you'll feel better."

In a whisper the man said, "I've murdered my wife and daughter."

"My God!" With pounding heart and labored breath, he felt as if someone had poured ice water over his shoulders. Fighting to control himself he repeated, "My God!"

Silence nearly suffocated them as Father Otis tried to collect himself. The resignation and agony in the man's voice assured the priest he was telling the truth.

Looking down, he said, "How could you…I can't…it's inhuman. And you ask for forgiveness?" He was nearly shouting. He turned to look at the man, but he was gone.

"Wait. Come back."

By the time Father Otis could put on his shoes and walk around the confessional, he saw the church door slowly swinging closed. Hoping to get a better look at him, he jogged to the front of the church, pushed open the massive front door that had almost closed, and saw the man running down the street. Though he hadn't seen his face clearly, Father Otis thought he might have seen him at a recent mass. *Must be crazy; probably didn't do a thing. Some people make up stories like that as outlets for their guilt.* He let the door shut out the morning heat.

The rest of the day dragged by as Father Otis tried to think of what he should do. *If he really did it, who knows what he'll do next? I'll call the police. I'll ask if any deaths were reported today, but they'd want to know how I…If only he hadn't stormed out I might have talked him into turning himself in.* His duty to his church and to society crossed like bloody swords.

By late-afternoon, Father Otis had calmed down. Listening to a Public Radio music program as he read through his mail, he froze at the hourly news: "Harold Pitt, his wife, and their six-year-old daughter were found dead in their home, victims of an apparent murder-suicide. Pitt is a chemistry professor at the state university. Mrs. Pitt is a former member of the City Council."

My God! He went home and committed suicide. Compounded the sin…maybe it's better that way. At least he won't do any more harm." Father Otis tried vainly to imagine a more sinful act, shuddering that he had sat in the shadow of such evil. How can such an act ever be forgiven?

When the housekeeper came into his study, Father Otis was standing before a mirror fastening his collar with his jacket draped over his arm.

"Mrs. Olivera is here to see you, Father."

"Tell her to come back later, Agnes."

"She says she wants to talk about her will."

"Not now. Be polite, and tell her I have to go to the police station right away." Thrusting one arm through his jacket sleeve he said, "I might have been the last person to see Pitt alive."

"Who?"

"Pitt, the man who killed his wife and children."

"How awful!"

"They may blame the wife, and, if so, I'll be able to clear her."

The slow traffic afforded him time to meditate. But the sun blazing down like a giant, spectral demon prevented any serious thought. At one stop light the glare off the car ahead nearly blinded him. Stopping, starting, turning and twisting through the business district, he finally reached the police station. The sun's raging breath blasted down like retribution. Shading his eyes from the sun's anger, he longed for the cool darkness of St. Olaf's. Only the rare exhilaration of such an important act—a murder, no less—could have drawn him out that hot afternoon.

The air conditioned building offered a welcome reprieve.

"I'm Father Thomas Otis of St. Olaf's. I'd like to speak with someone about Professor Pitt, the man who died this morning."

"One moment, please." The sergeant walked into one of the offices and, in a moment, returned with a stocky man in his early forties. He was adjusting his tie as he approached Father Otis.

"Thanks for coming in, Father. I'm Lieutenant Garcia. We were about to pay you a visit. I understand you saw Professor Pitt this morning."

"How did you know?"

"Please, just tell us what you know, Father."

"It was my morning to hear confessions. I had heard one earlier, just before an African-American man came in panting. I couldn't get a good look, but he was very excited."

"A parishioner?"

"No. I have few Black parishioners, and I know them all."

"How did you know it was Pitt?"

"Figured it out when I heard the four o'clock news on the radio."

"And?"

"I knew right away he wasn't Catholic; he didn't know the ritual."

"But what did he say?"

"That he'd murdered his wife and daughter. When I tried to talk to him, he ran away."

"What did you tell him?"

"I was flabbergasted. How could anybody do such a ghastly thing?"

"You told him that?"

"Not in those words exactly, but I was terribly shocked."

"Thanks for coming in. You've been very helpful." The police lieutenant politely escorted Father Otis to the door.

On the way out Father Otis said, "It was terrible. Very disturbing. Horrible, horrible. What a monster."

"Thanks again, Father."

"Can you tell me if he has family in town?"

"A cousin named Petula Pitt. It'll all be in tomorrow's paper."

Opening the door Father Otis felt the wall of hot air lean against him.

"Did he leave a suicide note?"

"We can't discuss details until we complete our investigation."

"Of course. Well, if I can be of any further help, please call."

"Thanks again."

Father Otis would not be so easily pacified. He drove to St. Olaf's and went directly into the rectory office to search the computer file. Always intimidated by computers, he searched, moving, clicking the mouse, mumbling: Dumb, insensitive, inhuman machine. So damned efficient if only I could figure it out. In the membership file he found no Harold Pitt. Sally Anne Pitt appeared as a member of St. Olaf's Parish; parents, Sam and Anna Iglesias, Catholic; husband, Harold, non-Catholic; daughter, Pearl, Catholic. Just as I thought, but unusual for Protestants to come to confession. Then he looked up Sam Iglesias' address in the telephone directory.

"Father Otis, supper is ready."

"Not now, Agnes. I'm going out again."

Petula Pitt's house was nearby, so Father Otis walked. By now his curiosity was soaring. This rare excitement in his otherwise dull life had generated a surge of energy.

Parked cars filled the neighborhood. The front door opened to reveal a slim, young African-American woman. Behind her, the living room was filled with people.

"Ms. Petula Pitt?"

"Yes."

"I'm Father Otis, pastor of St. Olaf's Catholic Church. I hope I'm not intruding. I've come to offer condolences."

She broke into tears, and a rather long-haired, white man in a poorly fitting black suit took her arm and escorted her to a chair and sat her down. The man returned to Father Otis, pushed his hair back, and said, "Come in, Father. It's been a terrible shock for the family; for all of us. We didn't realize how bad it had gotten."

Father Otis sat on an overstuffed chair across a coffee table from Dr. Quinone, who said, "I was one of Harold's colleagues. We're all pretty shaken."

A large white Bible lay on the table between them. A young black woman was passing through the crowd offering coffee. Near the far end of the room sat an older black couple. The woman was weeping; her husband trying to comfort her.

"I saw Dr. Pitt this morning. He was beside himself. What a ghastly thing."

Donald Quinone's lip trembled slightly, but he regained his composure and said, "Did you know his wife was terminally ill?"

"No. They weren't regulars at St Olaf's. Perhaps I could have helped."

Donald Quinone looked into Father Otis's eyes with a vacant expression that made Otis cringe. After a long pause, Donald Quinone said, "I doubt it." He opened the Bible on the coffee table and extracted some folded sheets. "Harold left this. It's a photocopy. The police kept the original."

"Are you sure it's all right? The police said …"

Quinone nodded. As Father Otis began to read, Donald Quinone rose to speak with a group of other mourners, who turned to look at the priest sitting, reading.

Dear Petty, Sam, Anna, and my parents,

I hope you can all forgive what I have done and what I am about to do. Sally Anne's pain had become unbearable. The thought of spending her last days in agony terrified her more than death itself. Eventually she resigned herself to the awful reality and began talking about ending her life. Imagine that girl who loved life so much. She couldn't do it herself and asked me to do it, but how could I? She would smile through the excruciating pain and softly whisper, "Please, if you love me…but not yet…when the time comes." I saw her decline day by day into the gray world between life and death. One night she said her life would end before her body died, and she wanted to erase that last interval. She knew the doctors wouldn't. When the abyss of death had become more a promise than a condemnation, God help me, I agreed. That quieted her, and in a way she looked more beautiful than she ever had. She asked only that I not tell her when I was going to do it.

Last evening I brought ten grams of sodium cyanide home from the lab. It's quick and painless. I didn't sleep thinking about what I was about to do and wasn't sure I could. This morning I dissolved the cyanide in some orange juice. I planned to leave one glass with Sally Anne at her bedside as I always did for her to drink later in the morning, and then take Pearl to school before she could know what had happened. I knew I wouldn't be able to watch Sally Anne drink it. I would return home to write this note to you explaining everything and attaching it to the will Sally Anne and I prepared weeks ago. Then I would drink the second glass of juice because

I didn't want to live with her death on my conscience. Without thinking I left my glass of juice on the kitchen counter and went into our bedroom. I put Sally Anne's juice on the night table and kissed her. I told her I would give Pearl her breakfast and take her to school and go to the University for a while. When I walked into Pearl's room to call her to breakfast as I always did, she wasn't there. At that instant, horrified, I ran to the kitchen and found my poor child on the floor. She had drunk some of the juice thinking it was for her. The glass was half full and still on the counter. I tried to revive her, but it was no use. The next thing I remember was lifting my forehead off the floor and trying to get up. When reality again hit me, I ran out of the house not knowing where I was going. Somehow I ended up at the church. Sally Anne loved St. Olaf's. I thought I might find her there or at least find some understanding. I found neither and returned home to write this. When I arrived, Sally Anne was lying by Pearl on the kitchen floor. She must have heard the commotion, come in, figured out what had happened, and drunk the rest of Pearl's juice. I moved them both to their beds and found Sally Anne's untouched glass by her bed. I can't stand another minute of the evil I have done. Forgive me.

Harold

Father Otis dropped the paper on the Bible that still lay open on the coffee table and stood. His awkward rising knocked the paper to the floor. Petula Pitt and Donald Quinone watched him walk to the door, open it, and walk out.

"Poor man," she whispered.

Thomas Otis dragged his legs step by step through air that felt like syrup. A low-lying branch scraped his head; he barely reacted. The temperature had dropped slightly with the setting sun. The brief red sunset's glow was imperceptibly yielding to deep blue night, but Thomas Otis saw none of it. Like a deaf, blind man he walked through the neighborhood, past an area of run-down student housing, then a slum neighborhood, and finally along the deserted street past St. Olaf's.

THE OUTLANDER

Edgar Margin

Vivian Margin drove the long, black Buick into the driveway and screeched to a stop. Edgar was lying face down in the middle of the front yard beside the azalea hedge he had planted the previous week. His jeans and khaki shirt were torn and frazzled. Her heart pounding, she threw open the car door, ran to him, and turned him over. His face and arms were covered with scratches; some still oozed blood through his clothes. She tried to revive him, but could not. Her heart racing, she ran to the door. It was locked. Fumbling the keys she muttered, "Go in, damn you!" Finally it did. She ran to the phone and dialed 911.

The next two minutes oozed like eternity. She tried vainly to revive him by mouth-to-mouth resuscitation. Within minutes the ambulance stopped in the driveway behind her car, lights flashing. Two men dressed in white rushed to Edgar. Vivian moved back. They listened for his heartbeat and then pounded his chest and listened again, but could find no sign of life. Finally one of the men turned to Vivian: "Are you OK?"

"Of course not. How's my husband?"

"Let me check your blood pressure."

"I'm all right."

The attendant led her to the ambulance and placed the sleeve around her arm as she continued to object. "One-seventy over ninety-five. That's pretty high, Mrs. Margin. Is it normally that high?"

"Damn it, don't just leave him there! Do something."

"I'm sorry, Mrs. Margin. He's gone. We'll have to take him."

"What do you mean he's gone?" she said through jerking sobs. "He was fine when I left a few hours ago."

"Looks like a massive heart attack."

"That's impossible. He was very healthy—jogged, dieted, did everything right. It can't be."

As the men rolled the stretcher into the ambulance she noticed the roll of papers in his left hand.

Prying his fingers loose she said, "Wait. What is this?" Noticing the patch of white skin she grabbed his wrist and said, "Where's his watch?"

The attendant shrugged. "Judging by the scratches, it may have been ripped off. Want to ride with us to the hospital?"

"He never made a move without his watch."

The men anchored the stretcher inside the ambulance. She was about to say something when another car arrived. The driver emerged and spoke quietly with the ambulance driver. Vivian watched dazed, the papers clutched in her hand.

"Excuse me, Mrs. Margin." The man, wearing a tee shirt, jeans, and a baseball cap, showed her his open wallet. "Detective Hopper, Tampa Police Department. I know how upset you must be, but would you mind answering a few questions?"

"You don't look like a detective," she said.

"I can't discuss that, Ma'am. Just a few questions if you don't mind." He walked to her car, turned off the ignition, and handed her the keys. "This where you found him?"

"Somebody took his watch. He never went anywhere without it. I think the ambulance people ..."

"We'll look into it, Mrs. Margin. Now try to remember."

"I found him by the azaleas. It was a little past three when I drove up. I almost couldn't get in the house to call 911. Then I tried to revive him. These men say he's..."

"Yes, Mrs. Margin."

"He was clutching these."

Stretching out the ream of papers he said, "Larger than usual…U.S. Government watermark. Is this the paper he normally uses?"

"How the hell do I know? What's the difference?" she said, sobbing. "He's dead."

"I'm sorry, Mrs. Margin. It may not mean anything, but he looked a little battered. These papers might shed light on what happened. May I have them?"

"I don't…I suppose so…wait. Who are they addressed to?"

Finding the first page he said, "To whom it may concern."

"Well it concerns me and I want them."

"OK if I run down and make a copy? It won't take long. A few minutes at most."

She nodded through sobs. The ambulance driver asked again if she wanted to go to the hospital. She waved him on without answering.

Vivian Margin waited on the front porch tapping her foot, her hands shaking. Still pretty at sixty-two, she wore her long hair up in a bun that flattered her slim face and high cheeks. Tall and slender, Vivian refused to relinquish her image of the slim, curvaceous beauty. Her green eyes blazed with anxiety and anticipation. She wondered why she was waiting there in the cold, when she could as easily go inside and sit down. But she remained frozen to the spot, tapping her foot on the brick tile floor. She was not sure she was trembling from the shock or the cold, January day, mouthing to herself, "I'll call Laura when I know what happened. She'll be devastated to lose her father."

Half an hour later Detective Hopper returned with the copy and found her still standing on the porch. He stepped up to the porch with the papers and said, "It's very interesting reading, Mrs. Margin. I think you'll be interested. Here, take a look."

"Now?"

"Just the first page, if you don't mind."

She frowned through teary eyes as she read and soon began shaking her head. "Poor thing…sounds like he was hallucinating."

"Possibly, but is it his writing?"

"Pretty erratic. Edgar was always extremely precise about everything. But yes, it's his."

"It's a strange story, Mrs. Margin, and you'll want to take your time. I'd like to send the original to Washington for an opinion."

"Opinion? About what? Why Washington?"

"It may not be important, Mrs. Margin. But if it's...well, I don't really know, but considering his story, it bears examination. You'll see why when you've read it. The folks in Washington may say there's nothing to it, but I'd prefer to tie up the loose ends."

"I guess so."

"I'll be back as soon as I hear something."

Vivian Margin walked into the house, sat in the living room sofa, and straightened out the pages of Edgar's manuscript. It read as follows:

*

To Whom It May Concern:

My name is Edgar Margin. Until I retired on June 30, 2000, six months ago, I taught chemistry in the University of South Florida. The chemistry building sits eight tenths of a mile due west of my house. I am 63 years and nine months of age and in good health. I am married and have a daughter named Laura. The last time I saw my wife ... no, not yet. Laura is, was, a recent graduate of Harvard University and lives in Cambridge, Massachusetts with her husband, a physicist. I apologize for wandering so.

I have not yet grown accustomed to retirement. Having worked all my life in a profession I love, it is difficult to turn it off like a faucet. I must admit that I succeeded beyond people's expectations and have achieved considerable recognition from my peers in chemistry. I say this to discourage you from reading this testimony as the ranting of an ignoramus or lunatic, even though what follows will sound implausible. As anyone who knows me will attest, I am not given to flights of fancy.

I report the following not because of its devastation, but because it defies scientific reason. Devastation is neither unusual nor uncommon. But unnatural events are extremely unusual. Just days ago, I would have said they are impossible. Please understand: I do not mean miracles. I consider miracles mere flights of overactive imaginations. I am confident that one day science will explain what I have endured, but for now it strains all reason. However, beyond reason lies the indisputable fact too dreadful for words. Though this testament may be futile, I have no other alternative than to hope it will one day find its way into understanding hands.

Beginning makes me feel like a child trying to grasp a swimming fish and feeling it slip past.

I shall include every detail as it occurred so you will see that I have not concocted this unbelievable (absurd is probably the better word) story.

I begin with my first recollection of that morning four days ago: the clock radio went on at 7:27 and pushed a dream out of my mind. As Vivian pulled the covers over her ears, I lay still, my eyes closed, trying to recall the dream while the radio announcer, in a high-pitched, irritating voice, frantically described the weather and the advantages of saving at the First Suburban Bank. I could not recall the dream. Taking my pulse for one minute by the digital clock radio as I often do, it was 126 beats per minute.

"Must I go first?" I said.

"Don't rush me, Edgar."

Vivian grudgingly threw back the cover leaving me partly uncovered. I scrambled to cover myself as she tiptoed on bare feet into the cold, tile brilliance of the bathroom. A few minutes later she pinched my toe through the covers to let me know she had finished and was going downstairs. I rose carefully out of a chronic backache that dissipates soon after I stand and move around.

The only thing I recall about the bathroom was that Vivian had moved my shaving gear, and I spent time looking for it. When finished, I walked down stairs in my bathrobe. Breakfast was nearly ready, so I helped Vivian set the table. We each had an egg over light, toast, coffee, and a small glass of orange juice. The digital kitchen clock showed 7:55 when I sat down.

"Where's your watch, Edgar?"

"I left it in the bathroom. You moved my things again."

She chuckled, "I like to keep you on your toes, Edgar."

I ignored her and mention this only to demonstrate that I am not the neurotic timekeeper some people claim I am. As usual, I read the paper during breakfast.

"There's a University Women's Club meeting today. I'll eat with them and then do some shopping. Will you need the car?"

Flipping the page of the newspaper I said, "I'll be at my desk most of the day. If I need to go on campus I'll take my bike."

"Shall I leave something for lunch?"

Each morning began like this—a series of nonsequiturs to interrupt my reading. "I don't care. Aren't we dining at the Buchners'?"

"Yes."

"Then I'll make a sandwich." Throughout the conversation I did not look out from behind the paper hoping she would leave me alone. Oh, how I wish I could hear her voice now. But I mustn't ramble.

I finished my coffee, folded the newspaper under my arm, and helped Vivian gather the dishes into the dishwasher. She spoke, but I don't recall her words. Something in the newspaper preoccupied me, but it, too, has slipped my mind. I moved into the living room to finish the newspaper. The next time I saw Vivian she was walking down the spiral stairs.

Jerking my bare wrist into view I said, "When will you be home?"

"It's a little past nine; I'll be back around two thirty."

"It's not a little past nine, Vivian; it's 9:33. And now that we're at it, what does 'around' two-thirty mean?"

"Damn it, Dr. Perfect; what the hell's the difference?

"Please, Vivian; you know I detest profanity! How can you possibly plan your day with such imprecision?"

Shaking her head as if she did not want to argue, she bent over, kissed my cheek, and left. Through the window I watched her back down the gentle slope of our driveway and glide down the tree-lined street and around the corner. I poured myself a second cup of lukewarm coffee and walked upstairs to my study to work on my new book.

My desk faces a large window that overlooks the front yard and down the hill to the bend in the road. Our house stands (or stood?) at the highest elevation in the area, 113 feet above sea level. I can see all around and down to the Hillsborough River approximately half a mile east. In our front yard stands, or stood, a massive live oak. It was that tree that sold me on this property. Its eight-foot diameter near the base made it a landmark in our neighborhood. One of my first acts when we moved here was to plant azaleas around the foot of the tree. We designed our house to take advantage of its shade. One large limb stretched past my study window. Often a squirrel would perch on it and watch me work. The oak rose from the pinnacle of our hill and shaded most of our house.

Sitting at my desk staring at the pile of chapters, I tried to think about the book and not the trivia of my daily life. I wanted to devise a thread that could link concepts together into a new, different, rational whole. Yes, I had retired from the university, but not from chemistry. I would write a textbook that would revolutionize chemical education.

All general chemistry textbooks are essentially the same. As I looked at the pile of papers, a new approach gelled spontaneously like a flash of light in my mind. And with it came a strange and serene confidence—a revelation, you might say: Why not present the subject as it developed historically, giving experimental observations first and then explaining how theories evolved from them? It wasn't foolproof; a historical approach would repel some instructors, who, saying they want change, always adopt textbooks that follow the same old approach. But it could work, and it would be more true to the science as well as more interesting. Students would learn from the start how chemists know what they know and not just memorize facts and concepts to be used in subsequent courses. The idea lifted a massive weight from my shoulders. I fished out my tentative table of contents, turned on the computer, and began composing an introduction to lay out my new rationale. I've seen and used many texts in my career, but I've never seen this idea expressed or developed. I imagined this book spreading my name through the chemical world like magic dust and transforming the teaching of freshman chemistry. My research had not chiseled my name into stone for posterity. I had produced chips at most. My work had been solid, but pedantic; journeyman's work, with little brilliance. I had not explained any of the important mysteries of nature. My new textbook would show the world that I am an innovative scientist after all. Time vanishes when I dig into my work; it is like entering a timeless cavity with no awareness of the world outside—a chronological vacuum. I've always enjoyed that state. I don't remember even once lifting my wrist to check the time. I got up once to relieve myself and took a page to proofread and forgot to retrieve my watch; such was my concentration. I don't know how much time I spent fleshing out the rough draft of that introduction, but the words poured out miraculously. At a stopping point I walked downstairs to the kitchen, turned the burner on under the pot of leftover coffee, and looked at the kitchen clock—10:06. I went outside and the cool January day raised goose flesh on my arms. The morning was still gray. A squirrel scurried across the top of the wooden back fence and jumped to the lower limb of a water oak. Trees sold me on this lot. This one dominates the rear of the property but not like the large live oak in front. The shade made summer gardening possible. The squirrel looked at me quizzically, darting his head and tail nervously. I sat on the back steps, and we watched each other.

Remembering the coffee, I stood, and the squirrel scurried away. The pot was still cold, and the digital clock still showed 10:06. Irritated, I jerked my wrist into view, but saw only blanched skin. I flipped the light switches and they were out too, so I went to the breaker box in the utility room, flipped each one off and on, and returned to the kitchen. Still no electricity! I picked up the telephone to dial my neighbor—no dial tone.

Wondering what had happened, I looked out the window. The neighbor's house was not there! Tall grass and scrubby oaks covered the area. With my forehead pressed against the window I saw only virgin forest. I dropped the telephone and ran out the front door, forgot about the large flowerpot, and knocked it over as I turned and ran down the steps. The lawn was intact. It had been trimmed the day before and ended on a precise line where the street had been. But there was no street, no power lines, no streetlights; just forest. The driveway ended at a young pine. I ran to the back of the house, looked, and ran around the other side to the front again. The fence and all the shrubs and the four citrus trees I had planted years ago were still there. My property was a neat rectangle carved out of a dry, brown forest. I felt I had lost my mind, but reasoned that asking the question meant I hadn't. My house and yard were intact. My vision turned yellow-brown. I saw myself falling and could not stop.

I could barely lift my head off the ground. Slowly, trying not to fall again, I walked to the house and leaned against the stucco wall. *Calm down and think*, I told myself. I went inside and sat in the living room sofa. My stomach felt queasy; I began to salivate copiously and tried to hold it as I ran to the bathroom, but it was no use; I vomited all over the floor. The total absence of a rational explanation gripped me by the throat; I was afraid to fall again. It was too much: like a sharp needle in my chest.

Maybe other parts of town still exist, but I can't telephone anyone. I found my wristwatch on the dresser—1:45. Vivian had been gone four hours and twelve minutes! I tried to think calmly about where she might be and how I would find her, but it was no use. I ran out of the house, pulled the bicycle out of the garage, and pedaled as fast as I could, failing to comprehend the new pine tree. I ran into it at the end of the driveway and picked myself up trying to separate the real from the unreal. Luckily only my right arm and face were scratched. What was I thinking? Did I think I could maneuver a bicycle through a forest? Leaving it I ran over crunching grasses and under scraping branches trying to follow where the street had been. *Where is Vivian?* The silent, unfamiliar terrain held no trace of human life—no houses, streets, power lines, no roaring of the nearby interstate highway—only deep, silent wilderness. I wandered through the scrub and over the landscape of my mind for over an hour before I made my way back up the hill. That was when I began to understand that I would not find Vivian. I repeated her name and my daughter's over and over, trying to make them exist.

As I caught sight of my house and the backyard perimeter fence, the university popped into mind. The edge of campus lies only a hundred yards west of my house. I walked through silent woods at least half a mile before I allowed myself to believe that all I had known was gone.

With a pain in my throat I stood where I judged the chemistry building had been and began to cry violently. Finally I gave in to exhaustion and sat with my face in my hands under a large, moss-draped live oak that now dominates the landscape. I may have dozed off; I can't be sure. I hoped the campus would reappear when I opened my eyes. Instead, my watch's nonjudgmental face scowled the time— 5:09. As the sun dropped behind the trees I made my way home, not knowing if it would still be there.

The sun was setting as I arrived. Though I hadn't eaten since breakfast, I was not hungry. I took ham and cheese out of the refrigerator and put together a sandwich, reminding myself not to open the refrigerator door unnecessarily so the food wouldn't spoil. As dusk approached I rounded up all the candles and matches I could find and spent the early part of the evening in the living room watching a candle burn. I thought of the ancient Greek philosopher Heraclitus: *the flame changes but it doesn't change.* Just like me. I imagined the holocaust of activity in that flame—a hurricane at the atomic level. The candle burned calmly, the wax yielded gently, and I derived more rational comfort than physical warmth. I had spent my life looking for order in nature. Where's the order here? I knew there had to be a rational explanation. And I knew I was not crazy! This was real and I had to understand it. In my lifelong search for order, I had ignored the chaos. The sum of disorder may be order after all, like the candle flame.

I struck a match to light a second candle, but decided that watching candles burn would lead only to running out of candles, so I blew it out and sat a while in semidarkness. The moonlight entering the large window lighted my way upstairs. I sat on the edge of the bed. Cool blue light bathed the Singer sewing machine and the picture of our beautiful daughter. I began to weep again, but this time no sobbing, only the ache in my throat. After a while fatigue overcame me and I lay down. Within a few minutes I began to feel calm for the first time. I slept lightly and felt awake much of the time, but I have learned that when I am not sure whether I've been asleep or not, I've slept.

The Second Day:

As the sun lifted past the treetops it was difficult to visualize yesterday's view out this window—roofs of neighbors' houses, driveways, cars, palms Midwesterners had planted to remake the rough, natural beauty into their image of Florida. All I saw was forest—moss-draped scrub oaks and pines shading brown weeds and an occasional wild flower. A squirrel flicked its tail on the great live oak branch near my window.

Surveying the backyard I suddenly realized it wasn't the same! Everything seemed so natural that I'd barely noticed—the backyard fence was gone! Yesterday it limited my property and held back the forest that had spread over the rest of the world. Now the fence was gone, but the grass and fruit trees were still there. My stomach again began to roil. I ran outside and found the shrubs I had planted against the fence had also disappeared: all forty-two of them. The four citrus trees seemed younger, smaller, but they still had fruit. The house, its shrubs and flowers were still intact. I tried not to think about tomorrow, knowing that if this process, whatever it was, continued, my house and I would soon disappear. Not only was the organized world disappearing and leaving only chaos; the chaotic forest was tightening like a noose. Out my study window I saw the great live oak in the front yard. It was smaller! No more than four feet in diameter. It had grown younger. The full disk of the sun clarified the scene, but offered no other clarity. Long shadows of dread spread across the lawn. After gulping down some milk, stale bread, and jam, I stood out back listening to the birds and squirrels chatter. My book manuscript flashed across my mind. Total nonsense now! I went inside with a stride of determination, though I had no clear idea, no plan.

Out loud I said, "I'm a scientist. I study natural phenomena. That's it!" I found my 100-foot, metal tape measure in the utility room, ran up to my study, picked up a clip board, a pen, and a magic marker and ran to the back yard. First I noted down the positions of the citrus trees—two navel oranges, a Duncan grapefruit, and a Meyers lemon: all were there. Then I numbered each fruit on each tree with the magic marker and jotted down how many each tree held. In the next hour I measured the entire yard: back, sides, and front. The forest was indeed closing in. The width of my yard had contracted from 100 to 89 feet. The depth from 150 to 127.5 feet, approximately (there were no straight lines any more). I then measured the circumference of the great oak in front: thirteen feet, which equals a diameter of 4.138 feet. I had spent my scientific life measuring rates of chemical reactions to learn how molecules interact with one another. Perhaps the rate of disappearance of my yard would shed some light on whatever was happening. The width had shrunk eleven feet and the depth 12.5 feet. I'd have to wait until tomorrow to determine whether the rate of shrinkage was accelerating or constant.

Immersed in these measurements and calculations, thoughts of my family receded. Having measured everything, I sat on the back porch. Suddenly my mind drifted to Vivian and our daughter. The horror of having lost them to some unknown process was unbearable. I tried to think of something else—anything—but I couldn't. I spent the rest of what may have been the longest day of my life on the porch trying visibly to observe the forest move in. I couldn't.

The Third Day:

Looking out the window at the sooty cavern of morning, I began to feel a loneliness I had never known before. Alone in prison or stranded on a deserted island, you can at least take comfort in the knowledge that you are separated by walls or vast oceans. My situation was nothing like that. For all I knew the entire human race had disappeared leaving me stranded on a deserted planet. It was too much. I had to shake loose from these thoughts of isolation and try to comprehend what nature was telling me. Reading nature is the work of science. I would resume my measurements. But the thought of encountering a wild animal stopped me.

A candle lighted my way to the kitchen, where I ate two oranges. As I stood at the back door, violet-red had begun to stretch its fingers into the sky, and I became aware of the scent of wet grass. Persistent insomnia had offered many sunrises in recent years, but this one was to be different. As the red disk silently pierced the sky, I was able finally to see that my citrus trees had vanished! Near where the water oak had stood, a young pine rose. My suspicion was right: the change was definitely accelerating. Further measurements were unnecessary.

Though I had steeled myself for the inevitable, a surge of panic nearly overcame me. Except for electrical and water failure, the house was still intact as far as I could tell. At this rate the house would soon be gone. As to what would happen to me, I could not imagine nor did I wish to. I could disappear along with everything else. Perhaps that wouldn't be so bad if it happened quickly. I might not even perceive it. As the world closed in on me I felt at its center or at least at the center of a tightening circle of being. But I ran through the forest that first day, so I knew I could exist outside. Also the mirror verified that the change did not include me. I had not changed.

The change had been strange in another way: it had left no uprooted plants or fence boards, only pristine land with no evidence of previous civilization. But whatever was happening, I would soon have to find another shelter, for our house would not stand much longer. That word, *our*, struck a sharp chord in my chest. Where are they? I had to force myself not to think about them, for doing so would certainly inhibit my ability to carry on, as I knew I must.

The Fourth Day:

That night I slept downstairs, reasoning that if the house disappeared, it would do so as the yard had: at its extremities. I awoke wet and trembling on the living room sofa beneath a starry sky. The second floor walls were still up, but the second floor and roof were gone. Not knocked down or battered, the house looked as if it had been abandoned in mid-construction. Was it being carefully disassembled? Watching the sun light up the eastern sky, I knew time was still moving forward and at approximately the same rate. The moisture I thought was perspiration turned out to be dew; I was trembling from the cold. The kitchen was gone too, along with my meager food supply. The archway leading to the kitchen now dropped off to the dense forest that had now devoured the entire yard. My house looked like an interrupted construction. A pine branch reached into the living room. At that moment I knew that would be my last day there.

It took less than half an hour to gather what I needed—knife, pliers, fish hooks, fishing line, extra set of underwear, two oranges, candles, matches, first-aid kit, compass, sweater, raincoat, and a water-repellent hat. Before leaving I saw my old Boy Scout hatchet in its carrying case on a shelf and strapped it on. I have never been a religious man, but I slipped Vivian's small bible into my coat pocket. I felt ready to face the irrational world and the irrational in myself. Finally, I stopped at the live oak in my front yard. I did not measure it, but it was no more than a foot in diameter. Assuming it would grow to the great tree I knew, I hacked my initials, EM, big and deep into it using the hatchet with a vengeance I neither recognized nor understood. Then I looked around guiltily to see if anyone had seen me. Stupid! I calmed down and stood back to survey my crude handiwork, so unlike my research papers on which I had slaved to insure clarity and precision. Those initials did not represent me. Stiffening my back and throwing my head back, I carefully carved away the rough places with the knife to make the letters clear and presentable. This mark, after all, may be the last tangible trace of my presence in this world. My wristwatch showed 8:52 AM.

Having decided that the river would offer my best chance for survival, I headed east. I had seen it daily from my second floor study, but not from ground level where trees obscured it. At least the river would provide fish and water. I walked about a hundred yards and turned for a last look at my house. The walls were gone, and a thin pine rose where the living room had stood. Nothing I had known remained. I felt an urge to go back, took a few steps, and stopped. Confusion, remorse, and fear filled my brain. Bracing myself, I looked around to get my geographical bearing, took out my compass, and continued east to the river.

Though the day was cool, the sun pounded mercilessly, and I soon felt my scalp burning. I put on the hat I had rolled up in my pocket. By that time I was approaching a swampy area I recognized as the edge of the north campus. The university kept that large area as a wild life preserve. Where I stood, four lanes of Fletcher Avenue had bordered the swamp just three days ago. I always detested the roar of traffic; how I wanted to hear it again! With no evidence of civilization, the breeze filtering through trees broke the eerie silence. I wondered if the earth itself was alive. It was, of course: tall cypresses with their bulging bottoms, sparse leaves and "knees" popping out of the water, and grasses and all kinds of smaller plants. I had never noticed how many different kinds of plants there were. A frog croaked. I recalled hearing that alligators make a croaking sound. I sped my pace east around the swamp along the high ground that had been Fletcher Avenue until I spotted the river through a thick stand of cypress trees. Speckling sunlight through a canopy of branches seemed inviting. Increasing my pace I reached the water's edge at 9:16 AM. The trek had taken only twenty-four minutes. Though I knew where it was, I was surprised to find it. Nothing these days made sense. Perhaps I could control, or at least understand, some things. For all I knew the terrain and the path of the river could also have changed. My hands were bloody from scraping branches. I wiped my face with my handkerchief and it was bloody too. Walking through this dense forest I felt engulfed in the earth. I had always felt I walked on it, but now I was in it. Enveloped in green and brown I recalled the movie, "Snow White" and how the trees in the forest grabbed at the frightened girl with gnarled, knotty fingers. The earth is a silent force greater than the roaring of any wild animal. Across the river an otter sauntered lazily. To my left under a tree a cotton mouth moccasin lay with its blazing white mouth open wide waiting for someone or something curious enough to inquire.

The river, quite broad at that point and curving sharply, had been the University Park. Oak limbs hung over to shade large patches of water, whose movement was imperceptible. A fish jumped; a fat alligator lay calmly on the opposite shore. After making sure there were none nearby, I looked for a place to dig worms. I had not done that since childhood in Alabama. They were not hard to find, and in a few minutes I was sitting under an oak, my line rippling the water, and, for the first time in days, I felt calm.

A guttural moan shook me out of my reverie with a lightning bolt through my chest. Horrified, I turned toward the sound. On the bank leaning on a tree stood a man holding a rifle in his left hand. His right sleeve was wet with blood, his stance unsteady. As I stood he whipped his rifle in my direction using only his left hand. I raised my hands, oscillating between fear and joy at finding a fellow human being. The man's faded gray trousers had a pale stripe down each side and looked vaguely familiar. His large-brimmed, crumpled, gray hat shaded a deeply grooved face. Black whiskers grew high up his cheeks. The holes in his hat could have been bullet holes. With his apparent weakness his rifle quivered.

I asked if he was all right. His right arm hanging, he pointed his rifle at my chest and said, "Reb or Yankee?"

"What?"

"Sir, I asked you a question. Kindly answer."

Sensing he was deranged, I forced a smile and tried to humor him: "Please put down the rifle. I'm not armed. Let me treat your wound."

"I won't repeat it."

Slowly, with clear, deliberate movements, I slipped my first aid kit out of my backpack and sat him down, which was not difficult considering his weakness. I lifted his arm; he winced, and his rifle butt hit the dirt. I carefully rolled up his sleeve. The source of the bleeding was a gash just above his elbow. He probably needed stitches, but I could not provide them, so I reached for the alcohol. Realizing I wanted to help, he did not resist, but gripped his rifle. Before applying the alcohol I said, "This will hurt, but the wound has to be cleaned."

He gritted his teeth as I cleaned around the gash with an alcohol-soaked cotton swab and spread antibacterial ointment over the cut. Then I laid a piece of gauze over the wound, and bandaged it tightly to close it as best I could. All the while I distracted him with chit-chat about my experience of the past four days.

"I used to live about half a mile west of here, but…"

"You talk like a Southerner."

When I finished he said, "Stand over there, against that tree."

"How did you get such a nasty cut?"

"Indians."

"There are no Indians here."

"Maybe you'd like to go upriver and tell them."

This man did not sound crazy. When I asked what day it was he stared at me dumbly. I repeated the question and he said, "Mid-January. I don't know exactly. I've lost track."

"And the year?"

"1866."

"At that moment I was convinced he was indeed crazy and wondered if a crazy man with a gun would finally end my chaos. His musket looked new, but old-fashioned. My grandfather kept one like it hanging over his mantle in Alabama.

"Where did you get the rifle?"

"Thomasville, Georgia…when I joined up."

"Joined?"

"Enough questions! You going to answer me or not?"

"You're not making sense."

"And you are not being forthright," he said, squinting and leveling the muzzle at my chest. "What are you concealing?"

"Nothing! I'm from Alabama, but I've lived in Connecticut and Michigan."

"So, a Reb by birth and a Yankee by sentiment?"

Looking deep into the barrel I said, "Hear me out, and please believe me. The Civil War ended a hundred and thirty-six years ago. The year is 2001."

"I don't know what you're up to, stranger, but I don't have time to put up with a crazy man, so I'll explain it once: Lee surrendered April last, and I've been shot at by half a dozen murderous Yankees since then. That's why I'm in this mosquito-infested country. Maybe you ought to tell those damned Yankees the war has ended."

"It's not 1866; it's 2001."

He stood and dug his feet into the ground to steady himself.

"It really is 2001," I repeated, lifting the antibiotic tube from the first aid kit and pointing to the label. "See: December 2000."

"12/23/00? Those are just numbers."

"That's shorthand for December 23, 2000. And look here: University pharmacy, Tampa, Florida."

Seeing him staring at my wristwatch I held up my wrist for him to see.

"What is that?"

"A wrist watch."

He held my arm and studied it. "It has no hands. Just numbers flashing. How does it do that?"

I slipped it off and handed it to him saying, "It's a digital watch. It gives the time in hours, minutes, seconds."

He looked at it closely and held it to his ear. "It doesn't tick."

"Believe me," I said. "You're wrong about the date."

"What are you doing out here without a weapon?"

"I'm a chemistry professor in the university just a mile west of here."

"They ain't nothing but scrub and swamp in these parts. Down river there's a town of white folks. That's where I'm headed. The war may have ended, but that hasn't kept rabble and carpetbaggers from taking shots at me."

"You're a Confederate soldier?"

"Look at what's left of my uniform. Of course! I'm Sergeant Rudolph Alexander, Georgia Seventeenth Patriots."

"Please, let's sit and talk. My back is killing me." Apparently he needed rest, so we sat beneath the oak facing each other.

Unless one of us is crazy, I reasoned, I've moved back in time. I could easily prove the year by showing him my house and the university, but they're both gone.

I tried to explain: "If you really are a Confederate soldier, then I've somehow moved into the past—back in time! I've always considered time travel to be wishful thinking. On the other hand, I read recently that one could move out of the flow of time by tunneling through the boundary of the space-time continuum. Problem is that I don't understand what that means.

"Now, to analyze this logically I propose two hypotheses: First, one of us is insane. I think we can rule that out. Back in Alabama as a child, I knew an old man who thought he was still fighting the Civil War. Of course, no one took him seriously. That's why I questioned you, Sergeant. Second, moving back in time explains the disappearance of my house and family and the university and the city and everything. All signs of 2001 have disappeared, and where I lived looks as it might have looked in 1866! This second hypothesis is also consistent with the gradual disappearance of my home and yard without leaving debris, as if time was moving in reverse. This second hypothesis is also consistent with finding you, a Civil War soldier, who has fought Indians and carries an antique rifle. What it doesn't explain is why I didn't grow younger and disappear along with everything else and why the sun didn't move in the reverse direction. That last question will have to wait; I have no ideas about it."

Sergeant Alexander was looking at me strangely, as if I were raving. I suppose I couldn't blame him. The story was indeed bizarre.

Squinting suspiciously as if not to rile me, he said in a patronizing manner, "I'm grateful for your help, mister. I've never heard of going back in time, but who can say? Strange things do happen. The Lord stopped the sun." Then he stood. "I'm feeling fine now; I'd best be going if I'm to reach the village ere nightfall. Thanks for the bandage. It feels much better."

"Wait; I know it sounds crazy, but...listen, my name is Edgar Margin. I'm sixty-three and three-quarters years old. I retired from my university position six months ago." I held up my wrist watch and said, "Anyway, it's only 10:07 AM. You've got plenty of time, and I'd like to walk with you. But let's rest a little longer. Tell me about yourself. Please try to understand: if I have indeed moved back in time, it could be the most scientifically significant event in history!"

The look on his face told me he didn't believe me. Perhaps he felt sorry for me because he sat again saying, "I estimate eight to ten miles to the town. I don't want to get there after dark, but I am obliged to you for bandaging my arm...all right: I was born in Thomasville, Georgia. My family has lived in Thomasville since before the Revolution. I remember Granddaddy talking about fighting Indians not far from our farm."

"Amazing! I've read about the Indian Wars, of course, but to hear about it from you, well..."

"We Alexanders have always owned our land. Not big farms, but we grew lots of cotton before the war. Mother taught me to read after supper when the day's work was done. We read the Bible. It was the only book we had. Poppa owned a hundred and twenty acres two miles south of Thomasville. Five years ago he came down with bad rheumatism. I was the elder son, so he asked me to take over the farm. My younger brother Alvin stayed on to help. He was fifteen and wasn't married. My sisters, Ruth and Virginia, stayed too. We owned fourteen slaves when the war started. And we cultivated over sixty acres of cotton. As soon as South Carolina seceded, almost every young man in Thomasville joined the Georgia Seventeenth Patriots. We fought in South Carolina, Tennessee, even Mississippi. But the worst was Chickamauga. Half our boys died, but we won. Then we lost Chattanooga just days later. Anyway, when word came down that Lee surrendered, well, I walked home. On the way I stopped at a cousin's farm north of town. They were packing to leave. Said they'd been ransacked; they were three years behind in their taxes, and some Yankees bought them out. Carpetbaggers took my farm too, after killing my wife, my parents, and my sister, Virginia."

At this point his voice began to crack.

"Alvin and Ruth ran off and waited for me at a cousin's house near Tallahassee."

"So you didn't return to the farm?"

"No, Sir; not right away. Alvin and I went there by night to look around. From the barn we could see them in the house, moving around, eating, like it was theirs. Everything my cousins said was true. I wanted to break down the door and kill the damned, thieving carpetbaggers, but Alvin wouldn't let me. Said the authorities would get me sure. He was right, of course. Nothing's sacred any longer.

"Alvin said there weren't many folks living south of Lake City, and I ought to be able to find land there. He was sharecropping for another carpetbagger and said he'd join me later. Alvin's a good boy. Knowing what I would do if I met any of them, he got me out of Thomasville. Kept saying, 'Georgia ain't ours no more.'

"I walked south till I found a spot south of Tallahassee. Good soil, a river, lots of water, and nobody around—I thought. But it had already been claimed. A stranger I met a little ways south of there told me about a town at the mouth of the Hillsborough River called Tampa. That's where I was headed when I ran into the Indians and then you."

I had begun to feel comfortable with this man, so obviously rough-hewn, but intelligent, honest, and forthright. I recounted my background: raised in a little town near Birmingham, then studied at Yale and the University of Michigan, then my first job at the university nearby. He listened politely, nodding occasionally.

"What do chemists do?"

"With your background you wouldn't understand."

His face hardened. After a few seconds he stood and said, "Thanks for the help, Professor, but I'd best be going."

"Wait. I wasn't expecting to find another human out here. I'm really glad we met."

"I may not be educated, Professor, but I'm not stupid. I was taught that education is important, but respect, honor, and duty are more important. Good day, Professor."

I picked up my pack and followed until I caught up with him. "I apologize, Sergeant Alexander. That was rude of me. May I walk along?"

He nodded.

I told him about my university work, the academic battles over what I now consider trivial matters—scrounging for research money, fighting to reduce my teaching load.

He smiled throughout. When I paused he said, "I guess the difference between us is your problems are complicated; I've got only one, and it's simple—staying alive."

He was right. For the first time in my life I saw how difficult staying alive could be. We kept within sight of the river. As a result, we walked farther than necessary. Tired as I was, I enjoyed talking with this man. When I ran out of topics I told him about the disappearance of my home and family. "I'll admit: it doesn't seem real."

He nodded.

The walking and talking seemed to calm him. Finally he said, "You an inventor?"

I thought long before answering, not wanting to insult his intelligence again. "We scientists strive to understand nature, hoping that one day some smart inventor will use what we discovered in the service of mankind. We never know if our work will be useful. But I'll say this: when Michael Faraday discovered the laws of electricity and applied for a patent they asked how it would be used. He said he didn't know, but he was sure the government would one day tax it."

He smiled and said, "Somebody must think your work is important, or they wouldn't pay you to do it."

"In the long run research pays off. It's brought us air travel, radio, television, automobiles, telephones, computers, x-rays, cat scans, MRI, and lots of other advances, and, of course, nuclear energy."

He shook his head. "I never heard of none of those things."

I spent the next hour explaining twentieth century innovations. I enjoyed the lecture more than any I ever gave at the university, for he was interested; unlettered, but intelligent; and he drank in my words with a thirst I rarely saw in the classroom.

We reached a large open area where I asked to sit a few minutes and rest my back. Treating me as if I were an old man, he helped me down and sat beside me. He stared when I opened my backpack zipper. "Is that one of your new inventions?"

"No. I don't know how old it is."

"Sure is nice—better than buttons."

"Have an orange; from my trees."

"I haven't seen an orange in years."

After eating the orange he stood, reached down, and helped me up. I thanked him and we walked on.

"I don't understand all this business about moving in time, Professor, but it is interesting. And it sounds true the way you tell it."

"I'm not sure what's true anymore."

"Tell me more about the year 2001."

"Last week this area was a city park. They had picnic tables all around where people could come out on weekends. There was—I should say, will be—a dam across the river to control the water flow. Tampa will be a city of three-hundred-thousand people. The bay area will have over a million. You must see the beautiful beaches twenty miles west of Tampa. People from all over the United States take their vacations there. That is, they will."

"Hard to believe. What about the Yankees? Will they get out of the South?"

"People from all over the country will move to Florida. Native Floridians are a minority in 2001."

"What about the Darkies?"

"They're citizens like you and me."

"I reckon I'm not a citizen anymore."

"You will be."

"What about slavery?"

"It's gone, but race still bothers some people."

"I reckon."

We passed an area where tall oaks hung over the river. It was too beautiful to pass up.

"What's wrong?"

"Look at that, Rudolph. We seem to be floating in air. The water is so calm you almost can't see it. It reflects the trees above it to make it look like a cavern. I'd love to be out there on a boat. It would be like flying."

"It certainly would, Professor. I don't know when I've seen a more enthralling sight. Would you like to stop a while?"

"If you don't mind."

We sat at the edge of the river to look at the vision of weightless water. We were both speechless. The silence was absolute with not a bird or insect stirring. All I could hear was my breathing. After a few minutes our reverie was broken by a strange rattling sound. After looking around carefully, Rudolph slowly rose and reached for my hand to help me up. "Don't make any sudden moves, Professor. It's a rattler. He's beyond striking distance, but we'd best not rile him. Do you see him? Up ahead, there."

I nodded.

"Just back up slowly and we'll be fine. If we don't threaten him he won't strike."

In less than a minute we had evacuated our blissful spot and were again walking downriver.

"It seems you are never safe out here," I said. "But it was beautiful."

"That water back there reminded me of our battles," Rudolph said. "Sometimes we would spend an hour waiting for the command. During those times it was so quiet you could hear a leaf fall to the ground. I remember one battle in particular, when the silence was finally broken. It was Armageddon with all the yelling and shooting and cannons ripping the air. I led my men, rifle in hand, not knowing where we were going, for we could not see the enemy. They exploded in our faces when they started firing. The forest was blazing. It's a time in your life you can never forget, but while it's happening, you have no idea what you're thinking. It's as if an invisible will drives you. When it ends you try to think about it, what you did and why, but it's all a blur."

I was breathing fast listening to Rudolph's recital. "What battle was that, Rudolph?"

"They were all pretty much like that; the one I was thinking of was Chickamauga. For a time I thought we had gone to hell. We could barely see the enemy with all the trees, the thickest forest we ever fought in. We lost a host of good Georgia boys there. I remember my closest friend, Corporal Matthew Gay. We signed up together in Thomasville. A Yankee bullet entered his chest, and he slumped over. I couldn't do anything during the fighting or even help him until it calmed down. How much later I don't know. Time seemed to stand still. He lived ten days in terrible pain, delirious much of the time, before he finally died. We won that battle. I suppose that means we kept the position and the Yankees retreated. Matthew lost the battle, though, along with hundreds of others.

"Trouble was, not long after that, we engaged them again at Chattanooga, and they whipped us. I sometimes wonder why so many good, honorable men had to die. What did it accomplish?"

"Rudolph, all I know about your war is what I've read in history books, but the Union survived. Most people thought the war was fought over slavery, but the real result was that the United States remained one nation."

"So you're glad we lost?"

"I wouldn't put it that way, Rudolph. I wish you hadn't had to fight the war in the first place. But if you insist on an answer, I'd have to say I'm glad the United States remained intact. In the next century we would become the most powerful nation in the world."

"Being from the next century, Professor, you see our war more calmly than I can. I've been up to my ankles in the blood of boyhood friends; it's not easy to be calm about that."

We walked along a few minutes before either of us spoke. "But you may be right, Professor. If we had won, the South would be a separate country. But I'm not sure why that would be bad. What's wrong with having two nations instead of one?"

"I've never really thought about it, Rudolph. We could not be as strong, but I frankly don't know."

"You seem to be an intelligent and kind man, Professor. The war's over. We've got to move on. There's nothing else we can do."

"Moving on is impossible for me, Rudolph. How can I go on? My life is in another century. Am I to become part of this time, this world? What of my wife and daughter?"

"I have no answer, Professor."

Not expecting an answer, I hesitated. Something had changed. Afraid time might continue changing, I looked up to see great, black clouds rolling over us. "Those clouds look ominous, Rudolph."

"Never fear. They're not the Lord's wrath; only water."

"We'd better hurry."

"Rain is nothing new to me, Professor. I have lived in the rain for days at a time. I reckon we'll manage."

Our journey took on a different hue as the sky darkened. It was only 3:16 PM, but it seemed like dusk. Without consulting Rudolph, I hurried my pace. He smiled and kept up. Intensifying the darkness was the forest that swallowed us. Tall, arching oaks and cypresses at the water's edge seemed to be closing in on us. It is strange how menacing nature can be. I had rarely noticed that before, probably because I had never been so deeply embraced by it. I felt as if I were treading on new ground, earth that had never before known the feet of humans. Of course, Indians had lived in the vicinity for centuries, but somehow, that was different. I was treading virgin earth much as our earliest ancestors had done. How could they have survived to create, in just thirty or forty centuries, such a vast, complex world as mine in the year 2001? It truly was a miracle. I detest that word. I have already said what I think of miracles, but truly it is difficult to imagine such advancement. Now, here, in this dense, primeval forest, I can feel the gap between that early ancestor and me. Was it genius, or did something else push him along? I suppose that kind of question drove early man to create gods: to answer questions he could not answer. I suppose even early man had questions. And they needed answers too. Today, we seek answers in experiment and observation; early man had not yet conceived science. They merely observed and created answers that seemed reasonable. We know today that the reasonable is not necessarily true, though it might be quite satisfying.

It grew so dark I was sure we would perish in a celestial deluge. The great rain god seemed to be waiting for the right moment to drop us to our knees. We raced, as Rudolph smiled at my fear of rain. Within a very short time—ten minutes at most—the sky had cleared away useless fears. I felt strangely happy and relieved. Then I realized that weather comes and goes, but my situation, whether under clouds or clear skies, had not changed.

Spotting a man in the distance, Rudolph said, "Look over there at that fellow plowing a field. We must be getting close."

We walked to the man, who stopped his mule and stood waiting. The look on his face was not welcoming, but neither was it threatening. As we approached, Rudolph said, "Good afternoon, sir. We're headed for Tampa. How much farther is it?"

The man looked us over before he spoke. "Two or three miles along the river. But if you take the path over there, it's a little shorter, and the going's a little easier. A little ways down you'll find a foot bridge. Take it or you'll end up across the river from town."

"I don't see a path, sir," Rudolph said.

"It starts just past my house over there. In fact, it's my path...I see you're a soldier."

"Yes, sir. Georgia Seventeenth Patriots."

"I fought with Sherman in Georgia."

Seeing the two men staring menacingly at each other, I said, "My name is Edgar Margin. I'm from a little north of here. Gentlemen, the war is over. Do we need more hostilities?"

"You're right, Professor," Rudolph said, and turned to the man, "Thanks for your help, sir. Maybe we'll see each other before long. I plan to settle here. Know of any farm land available?"

The man's face uncurled, and a smile broke out. "There's plenty if you're willing to work. Find the land office in town. It's on Ashley Street along the river. They'll help you."

Rudolph thanked him graciously.

"By the way, my name's Clarence Knapp. I was born in upstate New York, but I lived most of my life in Michigan. I got my fill of war and decided to settle down here. The weather's too good to pass up. Good luck."

Rudolph put out his hand and said, "Good meeting you, Clarence. Reckon we'll be seeing each other again."

As we walked away, Rudolph said, "Another carpetbagger."

"Perhaps not. Land must be plentiful if all you have to do is claim it."

"I reckon."

As we joined Knapp's path, two wagon ruts in the grassy land, I felt we were traveling finally on a paved road. The storm clouds had completely disappeared, and the path to our destination looked inviting and clear. Soon we found the bridge and crossed it."

We reached Tampa at 6:26 PM. The sun was setting. We walked west into town on an unpaved, dirt street marked Whiting Street. Whiting seemed to end at the river several blocks farther west. To our left stood a high wall with an entrance marked "Fort Brooke, U.S. Army." At Morgan Street we passed a gate to the installation. The gate was set back fifty feet or so from the outside wall. I suppose it was designed to stop intruders before they could get inside the fort. Inside, we could see wagons and lots of horses. We walked past a sergeant who looked at us, smiled sardonically, and tipped his hat. Rudolph kept his gaze straight ahead and picked up the pace to Ashley Street five blocks ahead. Beyond Ashley flowed the river.

Tampa is little more than a scattering of houses radiating out from the eastern edge of the river at Whiting and Ashley Streets. Ashley Street is lined with frame houses and a few businesses, including a post office, a barbershop and dentist's office, a doctor's office, a general store, and a blacksmith's forge. At the point nearest the mouth of the river a fish market sells the catch of the day. Rudolph wanted to stop at the Land Office to inquire about farm land and found that it was part of the general store, so I browsed as Rudolph talked with the clerk. Judging by the goods for sale, the major occupations seemed to be farming and fishing.

"Lockwood's the name," the clerk said, extending his hand. After shaking our hands he turned to Rudolph: "All you got to do is find a parcel to your liking and let us know where it is. We'll register your claim right here, then you can start farming. Try up river about half a mile, beyond the last farm, the Collins place. The land's better near the water. When you're ready to buy seed, tools, or anything else, come by. I'm the only supplier around, and I'm here to help my fellow man."

Mr. Lockwood stood tall, lean, and strong. A broad black hat covered a thick head of sandy hair. He was about forty and smiled as he spoke. Rudolph's now familiar squint told me he was not impressed.

"Alexander's my name. Where can I put up for the night?"

"Right here," Lockwood said, pointing up. "A clean room upstairs with a bed you gentlemen can share."

I didn't like the thought of sharing a bed with a man and asked for a private room.

"Sure, if you're willing to pay."

I hadn't thought about money. It wouldn't have mattered; my money would be as alien as I am. "I'll find a place outside somewhere."

"I'll stake you, Professor," Rudolph said.

I was inclined to refuse politely, until I imagined sleeping outdoors. I followed Lockwood and Rudolph upstairs. The bed barely fit in the tiny room with a small table with pitcher and pan, a ladder-back chair on either side of a window that opened to the unpaved main street. Between the chairs stood a spittoon. Beyond the street and across the river a forest of sable palms rippled in the breeze and, beneath them and hugging the water, mangrove. The elegant Hyde Park neighborhood would one day dominate that area past the mangroves. Nothing is familiar; I'm sure none of these buildings will remain standing in 2001. I had spent my entire working life in the university. Seeing the pristine river pour languidly into the bay, I wished I had spent more time enjoying the beautiful Florida landscape. But that was the price of a career.

After sharing Rudolph's provisions, I went to bed. We faced opposite directions, but I still felt uneasy about the arrangement. After a while I quietly got up.

"What's the matter, Professor?"

"Can't sleep. Hope you find good land tomorrow."

"And I wish you well too."

I sat in one of the ladder-back chairs by the window. I could not bear any more thinking. "I'm afraid my future's evaporated, Rudolph."

"It's been hard on all of us, Professor, but we have to have faith in better times ahead."

"Time…I've dribbled out my life in minutes and seconds, and now I'm one-hundred-and-thirty-six years from home with no way back."

"God will lead us."

"You don't understand, Rudolph: I've been yanked out of my life. I don't belong here. My family exists somewhere several lifetimes away. Sure, you've lived through a war, but that's nothing compared to what I face. You still have family who know you and need you. I have no one. I'm an alien."

For several seconds Rudolph said nothing. Then, "We each have our crosses to bear, Professor. You might think of the string of your forefathers that stretches all the way back to the first day. You must have family in Alabama. Why don't you look for them? You're not an alien; this is not a foreign land. It's your past. You might not get back to your time, but you're here now and you're alive, and you have the chance to see where you came from."

I was weeping when he paused. "I can't. I just can't. It's unreasonable. I can't reason my way out. I can't."

He raised himself on one elbow. "Stop whining! Of course you've trouble; that's what it means to be alive. I've watched men die, their legs and arms and eyes blown away. That's trouble. You're so used to your petty, sheltered life you think every setback is a disaster. Lay aside reason! Reason won't help; what you need is courage. Face the day like a man. If you can't do that you're not worth saving. Now go to sleep. I've got to get up in a few hours."

No one had ever talked that way to me, and it shook me. After a while I said, "You're right, Rudolph. You're a very wise man, maybe the wisest man I've ever known."

"It's not my wisdom, Professor. It's the Bible's. Read Ecclesiastes sometime."

As he lay back on the pillow, I lifted Vivian's Bible out of my coat pocket and looked through the table of contents. "Here it is— Ecclesiastes." I turned to the page and read. When I came to the end I looked at Rudolph. His eyes were still open. My wristwatch showed 9:55. I wondered if he had ever heard of daylight saving time. I stared at the face of the mute timepiece waiting for the minute to drop into the next minute, as I had done countless times. *I've spent my life tracking time!* With determination I slipped off the watch, held it a few moments, and then handed it to him.

"What...?"

"I saw how you admired it this morning. I want you to have it."

"I can't accept this, Professor."

"Please, Rudolph. By the way, you can't wind it. The battery will one day run out and then it will be useless. As of today it's useless to me. Rudolph, you staked me and fed me common sense. You've been very generous. As Ecclesiastes said, *"To everything there is a season, and a time to every purpose under the heaven."* I have been given two seasons. When you've lost more than a century, minutes and hours lose their importance. For the first time in my life I can truthfully say that time has unraveled and no longer has meaning to me."

He accepted the watch graciously and thanked me. I read a while longer and finally got into bed. I must have fallen asleep within minutes because I don't remember anything after that.

I expected to sleep poorly, but I don't think I moved until the sun lit the room. Rudolph was gone. On the chair I found a note:

> *I am gone to seek land.*
> *Let us talk again this afternoon.*
> *Keep faith.*
>
> Rudolph.

I washed my face, put on my shoes, and went downstairs.

"Reckon your friend headed up river; seemed anxious to get going."

When I told him he was a Confederate soldier, Lockwood smiled. "Can't miss him in that uniform. But that don't bother me. War's over, and I hold no grudges. Every man's got to find his way through these awful times. I came down from Ohio; had enough of no work and hard winters. Where you from, Mr. Margin?"

A strange feeling overcame me. As a courtesy I was about to explain my predicament, but I couldn't bring myself to repeat it. Rudolph was fulfilling his future, and I was facing my past. I may never understand what happened, but Rudolph was right: what would it matter if I understood? I could head for Alabama to look for ancestors. It might be worth a try. I don't know.

Instinctively I jerked my wrist into view and saw the blanched skin that had tried for years to breathe under the ever-present digital watch.

I looked up to see Lockwood staring at me. "Something wrong, Mr. Margin?"

"Oh...no. I'm from Alabama. Say, where can I get some writing paper?

"Seeing as how you don't have any money, I don't know. Maybe the post office next door. Sam's a nice fellow. Want me to ask him?"

"I'd appreciate it."

He went out the door and in a minute called me out. "Meet Sam Stephens; Sam, Mr. Margin."

Shaking my hand and handing me a stack of writing paper, Sam Stephens said, "You're welcome to this, Mr. Margin, compliments of the Union Government. Got anything to write with?"

"No, sir."

"Well, there's a bottle of Union ink and a Union pen on that table. Sit down and help yourself; stay as long as you like. I don't watch the clock. Writing home?"

"Yes."

"Where you from?"

"Alabama."

"Well, good luck to you, sir."

The post office is nothing more than a small store with a counter half way back, a desk and a safe behind the counter, and a simple table in front of the counter by the window. I'm sitting at the table with a bottle of ink at the upper right corner, a pen in an indentation beside it. Outside the window a woman is tending flowers in her front yard.

Jerking my wrist into view and seeing pale skin, I wondered when I would stop repeating that useless act.

One thing has never left my mind: returning home. It's irrational, I know; irrationality seems to be infectious, but I want to; no, I *must*. That lonely forest is the only home I have.

Nature wins! Rationality loses! And I don't mind! The more I think about that piece of land, the heavier irrationality presses on me—not a pain exactly, but a pressure, a drive to move, to do something.

It is mid-morning as I write these last lines. The sun is high above the horizon. I don't know the time, and it doesn't matter. I will return as we came: along Knapp's path and then the river.

Edgar Margin

*

The following week Detective Hopper knocked on Vivian's door.

"Hello, Lieutenant. Won't you come in?"

"Just for a moment."

"Care for some coffee?"

"No thanks; I have to be across town in a few minutes. I saw you at the funeral, but I didn't want to intrude."

"You've been very kind, Lieutenant. But I still can't believe he's gone."

Hesitating, he said, "About the stationery he used: it could've corroborated his story, but the FBI said it's quite ordinary. I still wonder about the pen and ink, but they didn't seem interested in that either; just said I should drop it."

"Edgar was meticulous; you might even say picky, but frankly he had little imagination. I don't think he could make up a tale like that; yet, the watch bothers me. He lived by it. He wouldn't have lost it. Giving it to that man, Rudolph Alexander, makes sense."

"I guess we'll never know for sure. Anyway, I didn't mean to stir you up."

"Not at all, Lieutenant. Oddly, his story has helped me through the ordeal. It makes a strange kind of sense. Anyway, I appreciate your interest and your help. Sure you won't have some coffee?"

Extending his hand he said, "Thanks, but I really can't."

"By the way, what about the original document?"

"They kept it and returned a photocopy."

"But it's mine. I want it back."

"I don't understand why they'd keep it if it's nothing, so I called Washington. All they'd say was it was routine to keep original evidence.'"

"Evidence of what? I thought they didn't believe his story."

"They say they don't, but they won't budge. I'll have to let it drop, Mrs. Margin. Sorry."

As Vivian walked him to the driveway she said, "It's mine and I'm going to get it.

He shook her hand again and wished her luck. Her eyes followed his car until it turned the corner. Halfway back to the front door she stopped, turned, and went to the great oak in the front yard. She moved around it passing her hands over the bark. She saw no semblance of carved initials until she stood back and looked again. "My God!" she said aloud. It's not possible." Broad, gentle undulations in the bark could be E.M. "It can't be."

Printed in the United States
139289LV00004B/7/P

9 781438 928999